Dear Reader,

Thank you so much for joining me on another trip to Marble Cove! I love these four friends as if they were my own, and I wish I could book a trip to their hometown to eat at Captain Calhoun's Crab and Lobster House and go for a walk to the Orlean Point lighthouse.

While I love to cook, I am not a very good baker—something always ends up burned, either me or the food! So it was a fun challenge to write about Shelley, baker extraordinaire, and her yummy baked goodies. I had to keep reminding myself that Shelley would never have flattened pound cakes or dry muffins! But inspired by Shelley's story in *Pressing On*, I decided to try an easy brownie recipe and my husband said in response to his first bite, "Not bad. At least they're not burned this time." I laughed because he really has had to suffer through a lot of burned baked goods in the years he's been married to me.

I love hearing from readers. You can write to me at Camy Tang, PO Box 23143, San Jose, California 95153, and you can visit me on the Web at www.camytang.com.

In Christ,
Camy Tang

MIRACLES *of*
MARBLE COVE

PRESSING ON

CAMY TANG

Guideposts

New York

Miracles of Marble Cove is a trademark of Guideposts.

Published by Guideposts Books & Inspirational Media
110 William Street
New York, NY 10038
Guideposts.org

Acknowledgments

Every attempt has been made to credit the sources of copyrighted material used in this book. If any such acknowledgment has been inadvertently omitted or miscredited, receipt of such information would be appreciated.

"From the Guideposts Archive" originally appeared as "Mysterious Ways" by Carolinda Jankel in *Guideposts* magazine. Copyright ©2009 by Guideposts. All rights reserved.

Cover and interior design by Müllerhaus
Cover photo by Dara Burge
Typeset by Aptara, Inc.

Printed and bound in the United States of America
10 9 8 7 6 5 4 3

CHAPTER ONE

Diane Spencer breathed in the tangy scent of the sea air. This was a perfect end to her day.

She headed down the beach, her dog Rocky racing ahead of her along the sands. The June day was still bright despite the waning afternoon.

Rocky chased some seagulls, his golden coat almost gleaming in the sunlight. It wasn't until the second ring that Diane realized the shrill sounds she'd been hearing weren't from the gulls, but from her cell phone. She saw her daughter's name in the caller ID and answered quickly. "Hello, sweetheart. How are you doing?"

"Hi, Mom. I'm fine. Things in the firm have finally started slowing down..."

Jessica talked about some of the stresses she had with a case she'd been working on, but it was obvious from the lilt in her voice that she still loved her job as an associate at her prestigious law firm in Boston.

"But, Mom, now that the case is over, I can take a few days off," Jessica said. "How about I visit you for a few days?"

"I would love that." Diane had a lot of writing to do over the next few weeks, but no way would she pass up a chance to spend time with her daughter. She'd just have to work hard to get it all done before Jessica arrived.

"And, Mom..." Jessica now sounded unsure. "Would it be okay if Martin came with me?"

"He would be more than welcome. He can sleep on the foldout couch." Diane couldn't help being intrigued by this chance to finally meet her daughter's boyfriend. Jessica had been so busy for the past six months that she had barely had any time to spend with Martin, let alone bring him to meet her mother. But Diane thought it was high time they met, especially since Jessica had been to see Martin's family at Thanksgiving. "When will you both arrive?"

"Not for another week or so. I'm still waiting to clear my days off. I'll e-mail you to let you know the exact dates, okay?"

"That's fine." The more time before Jessica arrived, the longer Diane had to try to plow through all her work.

"Great. I'll talk to you later, Mom."

"Bye, sweetheart."

Diane disconnected the call and whistled to Rocky. Her daughter was coming to visit. How wonderful! And she'd be able to meet Jessica's boyfriend too.

Still, she couldn't help feeling apprehension about him. Would any man be good enough for her daughter?

Well, she thought, *here's my chance to find out.*

"Diane!"

The voice behind her made her turn.

Beverly ran toward her, waving a piece of paper. "I went to your house first, but when you weren't there, I thought you might be on the beach. I have something for you."

"*Ooh*, a present? I love presents." Diane grinned.

Beverly caught up with her and gave her the paper. "Something like that." She brushed a windswept lock into place. "Maybe a treasure."

It was a printout. Recently they'd found an encoded message on the back page of an old prayer book, and it looked like Beverly had copied it—not an easy feat since it had been a dense paragraph of capital letters in seemingly random order.

"This is typed out. Did you actually input it into a computer?" Diane asked in amazement.

"In a sense. I traced it out by hand, then scanned it into my computer. I had software that translated my handwriting into typed text. Then I double-checked it to make sure it was accurate and printed out copies for everyone. I wanted to have a copy of the message on my computer in case I found a software program that would decode the message."

"Do you really think it would be that easy?"

"I'd love to think so, but..." Beverly shrugged. "How has your day been?"

"Busy." Diane sighed. "I really needed to get out of the house and go for a walk in the fresh air."

"Have you been at your computer all day too?"

"I really don't like to complain, because I've been busy promoting my book, and it's a dream come true. But I recently got a lot of requests for blog interviews and guest blog posts—the publicity manager at my publisher set up a blog tour for me."

"A blog tour?"

"Basically, I write a guest piece for an established blogger to help promote my book. Usually the host asks questions and I answer them. So I have lots of little pieces to write for different bloggers."

"Isn't your second book due soon?"

"No! Just the first three chapters." She laughed. "Don't give me a heart attack like that." But Diane had to admit the thought of the three chapters *and* all the interview questions to answer *and* the guest blog posts to write did seem overwhelming if she really thought about it. *Just work on one thing at a time,* she told herself.

"Will you be able to do the chapters with all this extra stuff you have to write?" Beverly's face was concerned.

"I'm pretty sure I will. I used to be a reporter, you know, so I'm used to writing short pieces very fast." Diane knew she sounded more confident than she actually felt. If she gave in to her worry, it would only paralyze her and she wouldn't get anything done. "Besides, my research for my second book involves reading up on ciphers, which is perfect for this puzzle." She held up her copy of the message. "The only problem is that my research has come up with dozens of different types of ciphers it could be. How would we know which one this is?"

"Well, we know it's about the same age as the prayer book, which would put the cipher at late eighteenth century."

"So we can limit our search to ciphers created before then. That'll help a lot because there are a ton of really complicated ciphers created in the twentieth century, especially for wartime."

"This one looks difficult enough," Beverly said.

"I wonder why the owner used this cipher," Diane said, thoughtfully. "If this did belong to Jeremiah Thorpe, I'm guessing it's in code because it relates to the treasure mentioned in the letters. But did Jeremiah receive this coded message from someone, or did he write it, intending to give it to someone? Was there someone in particular he was trying to hide it from?"

"If other people knew he had a treasure, they'd all want to get their hands on it. I'm guessing there wasn't any one person he had in mind."

"But I think there was one particular person he had in mind when he—or whoever it was—wrote this coded message. He meant for at least one person to find this message and know how to decode it."

"Or maybe this was a message *for* Jeremiah," Beverly said. "It might not have anything to do with the treasure, but have some other reason for secrecy."

"Wet blanket." Diane winked at Beverly. "That takes all the fun out of it."

Beverly laughed, then glanced at her watch. "I'd better go. I need to go start dinner for my father, and I'll let you get back to your walk. Bye!"

Diane waved good-bye and continued down the beach. The sea breeze ruffled her hair and seemed to clear her mind of stress. She lifted her face to the light and breathed deep of the fresh, salty smell, grateful to God for blessing her with her home here in Marble Cove, her friends, and her career as a published novelist.

And thank You for the exciting scavenger hunt we've been on, looking for Jeremiah Thorpe's treasure. I pray You'll help us to find it so that we can save Old First.

CHAPTER TWO

On Monday morning, Margaret's hand froze as she turned the key in the lock of her gallery's front door.

The door was already unlocked. Had she forgotten to lock it last night?

Or had someone broken in?

Her insides twisted. Surely if someone had broken in, the door would be more mangled, right? Not that Margaret had a lot of experience with locks that had been picked. Weren't they supposed to have scrapes on the lock like she'd seen on those crime television shows? Her lock was pristine.

She happened to glance at the front window... and a gasp caught in her throat.

The painting she had just sold at the art fair last week, the one she was displaying in her front window until the customer could come retrieve it, was gone.

What was even stranger was that one of her other paintings, a typical lighthouse scene, was propped in the window instead. What kind of thief would take a painting and replace it with another one? Maybe the thief thought she wouldn't notice the switch?

With her heart hammering and her breath coming in gasps, Margaret fumbled with the doorknob and hurried into the gallery.

The familiar smells rushed at her—the scent of freshly worked wood from Allan's furniture, the tang of oil paints, the slight metallic edge of the new metal sculptures displayed on tables. Everything was in its place, just from a quick glance. Nothing toppled over, nothing missing from the three fabric-hung walls or the one brick wall of the gallery. The track lighting on the haint blue ceiling reflected brightly in the polished wooden floor.

Quiet. Completely quiet. Except for Margaret's ragged breaths.

What had happened to that painting?

She'd been so proud of it. Not just because it had won an award last week at the art fair, but because it had been different from her usual style, something unique that had made her feel wild and creative as she painted it. She'd titled it *Sea Breeze* because it had been an abstract mesh of colors and shapes, a hint of a starfish, a glimpse of a seashell, a suggestion of waves. As if an ocean breeze had taken a photograph of the seashore and swirled it together into a gentle, soothing mix of colors and forms.

And it was gone.

She knew she hadn't moved it from the front window. She hadn't intended to change the front window until the customer who bought the painting came to pick it up. She'd been contemplating what to place there but hadn't yet decided.

She went to the window again, as if maybe the painting would miraculously reappear. But the same lighthouse painting was there. *Sea Breeze* was not. At the bottom of the window lay the tiny paper with the name of the picture and the yellow SOLD sticker, next to the two ribbons it had won.

Margaret turned back to the gallery. She wasn't dreaming. Her painting had been stolen!

She scanned the walls and caught sight of the small blank space where the lighthouse painting had rested before the thief had placed it in the window. She always had plenty of open space on her walls between pictures so she hadn't noticed it at first.

Her hands shook as she dialed Allan. "Allan, the-the...the painting..." She couldn't get the words to form.

"What is it? What's wrong?" Allan's voice had a sharp edge of panic.

"I'm...gallery..." She let loose one strangled sob, then took a deep breath, trying to control herself. "The door was unlocked. There's a painting missing."

"Call the police, Margaret. I'll be right there."

Somehow calling the police was rather frightening. She dialed 911.

"What's your emergency?"

"I'm M-Margaret Hoskins at the Shearwater Gallery. I've had a break-in, and one of my paintings was stolen."

"I'll have an officer there in a few minutes, Ms. Hoskins," said the dispatcher.

Detective Fred Little arrived quickly, before Margaret had a chance to pull herself together. He had a grim expression on his face as he entered the gallery. "Margaret? Tell me what happened."

"I went to unlock the front door and found it already unlocked." She pointed to the door he'd just walked in through and belatedly realized it now had both her and his fingerprints on it.

He must have realized that too, because he grimaced slightly. "Go on."

"There was a painting in the front window that won an award at the art fair last week, but it's gone. Whoever took it replaced it with that lighthouse painting."

Fred went to look at the painting. "Is there a chance that someone else who worked in the gallery switched it without telling you?"

"I haven't had anyone else working here recently. I was going to keep the painting there until the customer who bought it picked it up in a few weeks."

His graying eyebrows rose toward his buzz cut hairline. "It was sold already?"

"Now do you understand why I'm so upset? What do I tell my customer?"

"When does the buyer come back?"

"In about three weeks."

"Let's hope we find it by then."

"Margaret," Allan said as he hurried into the gallery, Adelaide in tow. "Are you all right?"

The sight of her husband and daughter was like a dam bursting, and she suddenly began to cry.

"I'm going to get someone to examine the door before more people get their prints on it," Detective Little muttered, and pulled out his cell phone as he headed toward the front door.

"It's all right." Allan put his arm around her.

Adelaide put her arms around her, also, her face etched with concern. "Mom, what's wrong?"

Margaret wiped at her tears. "I'm much better now that you two are here with me."

"Was it *Sea Breeze* that was stolen?" Allan pitched his voice low.

Margaret nodded.

"Did you put the new painting in the window?"

"No. That's what's odd about all this. I'm wondering if the thief put the lighthouse painting in the window hoping I wouldn't notice?"

"Maybe."

"I just finished that painting yesterday." Margaret glanced at the blank space on the wall where it had hung only a few hours ago.

"Margaret, I don't think anyone picked your lock." Detective Little approached their tight family group. "It doesn't look like the lock was tampered with. Is it possible you forgot to lock up last night?"

Margaret's heart dropped a few inches, and tears welled up in her eyes again. "Yes, it's entirely possible."

"Are you sure the painting was the only thing that was stolen?"

"I think so. Everything else looks untouched." She glanced around the gallery, but every flat surface had an art piece for sale, none of Allan's furniture pieces were missing, and aside from the space where the new painting had hung, there were no other blank spots on the walls.

"Do you have a photo of the missing painting?" Fred asked.

"Yes." Margaret disentangled herself from Allan and Adelaide and went to get her digital camera. She'd taken several shots of the painting before heading to the art fair.

She showed the photos to Detective Little. "Can you e-mail them to me?" he asked.

"Sure. I have them on my computer already."

"Do you know why anyone would want to steal that particular painting?"

"Well, it just won an award last week. And I had just sold it to someone."

"Was there anyone who might be jealous of your award?"

"Maybe, but I wouldn't know who. No one said anything to me."

"How about anyone who also wanted to buy the painting? Or maybe showed marked interest in it?"

Margaret thought back. "At the fair, there were three people who were interested in the painting, and then later I sold it to John Wilson."

"Do you have any names or descriptions?"

"I don't remember names, but I can tell you what they looked like."

Margaret gave the information to the detective, closing her eyes to picture the three people who had expressed the most interest in the painting. She'd been so flattered at the attention. Had one of them come here, seen it was already sold, and then been so disgruntled that they'd stolen the painting?

"We'll go ahead and dust for prints on the doorknob and the lighthouse painting," the detective said.

Margaret perked up. "The lighthouse painting frame should only have my prints on it, and the person who moved it. I just put the painting up late yesterday."

"That's good. Don't worry, Margaret, we'll get this person."

He meant to sound encouraging, but Margaret wondered if it was just what he said to every victim of a theft to make them feel better. She felt absolutely horrible. She felt violated and also anxious about the buyer of *Sea Breeze*.

"I think you should go home," Allan said.

"No, I have to stay to watch over the gallery—"

"I'll stay. You take Adelaide home, and I'll join you when the police are done. We'll just close the gallery for today."

"Allan, we can't do that."

"Would you really be able to work today after all this?"

He had a point.

"I'd rather you were home with me and Adelaide. At least, until the time for her to go to the community center today." He ran a gentle hand down the back of his daughter's head.

"I... I guess."

"I think that's the best thing for you today. You can come back to work tomorrow. And in the meantime, I'll call the insurance company and see what we need to do."

Margaret nodded. She knew he was right—she wouldn't be able to get any work done, whether it was painting or working on the gallery paperwork. She'd just be here seeing the blank space on the wall and fretting about who stole *Sea Breeze*.

She drove Adelaide home, but then her daughter saw Aiden playing in his front yard with Prize. Shelley sat on the front stoop, watching Emma tottering around trying to keep up with them.

"Mom, can I go play with Aiden and Prize?"

The sight of her neighbor and friend was exactly what Margaret needed.

Chapter Three

Beverly ended the phone call with her Realtor, feeling very odd. She went downstairs to her father's library, where he sat reading the newspaper in his comfy leather chair. He looked up as she entered the room.

"I just got an offer on my house," she told her father, "but it's lower than I had hoped."

His pale gray eyes studied her through his thick glasses. "How low?"

She told him the offer and also her listing price. "It's only been on the market for a couple of weeks, you know."

He frowned. "This is the first offer, right?"

She nodded. "It's a large house. There aren't many people who can afford to bid on it."

He *hmphed*. "Seems to me that anyone who can bid even that much can bid the full price."

She thought so too, but the bidders probably just wanted a good deal. "The housing market right now is depressed."

He chortled. "Maybe it needs to take some antidepressants."

Beverly rolled her eyes at his humor.

"Why don't you ask Jeff and your friends what they think?" he asked. "They probably know something about the housing market. Might have some good advice."

Having her father suggest it suddenly made Beverly wonder why she hadn't thought of that. Jeff had a solid head on his shoulders and she would both value and respect his opinion. She had come to rely on him more and more, and looked forward to hearing his voice on the phone or seeing his face when she heard the doorbell ring.

She also had three women who really cared about her and wanted to help her. They were like the sisters she never had, and she had slowly been growing closer to them. "That's a good idea," she said. "I'll call Jeff first. He's in California right now on a photo shoot, and they're three hours behind, so I might catch him before he starts his day."

She had left her cell phone in her office, so she went upstairs to call him. She also smiled to herself as she admitted that she felt a little uncomfortable talking to him in front of her father, in case their conversation turned to something other than her house.

She dialed and his voice, when he answered, was deep and a little sleepy, but she heard his smile as he said, "Hi, Beverly."

"You sound tired."

"I was just getting up. It's going to be a long day, so I wanted to get as much sleep as possible."

"Is the trip going well?"

"Fantastic." He yawned. "How are you doing?"

"I have something I need your advice on. My Realtor called with an offer on the Augusta house, but it's lower than I had hoped." She told him what it was.

"*Hmm.*" Jeff thought a moment. "It's low, but not insultingly so."

"I'm not sure if I want to sell for lower than my asking price."

"Do you need the money?"

Beverly bit her lip. "Since I decided to turn down that job in Chicago and develop my consulting business, I do need some money in the bank until I can pick up more clients. I'm not sure how long that's going to take."

"How much is it going to cost you if you reject the offer and keep the house?"

"What do you mean?"

"Mortgage, taxes, utilities, that sort of thing."

"No mortgage, but I do have to pay property tax in a few months. The house's value makes for a rather steep tax bill."

"I can imagine," Jeff said thoughtfully. "You may want to sell it now, even though it's low. You haven't had any other offers and you may not get another one for several months more."

"Father said the housing market needs antidepressants," she said.

Jeff chuckled, and the low timbre of his voice sent a warm thrill through her.

Then he asked in a quiet voice, "Are you all right with selling the house?"

He didn't need to say it, but she knew what he meant— Was she all right with selling Will's house?

"I...I think so. I'm not sure." She took a deep breath. "I probably won't really know until I start actually packing up the house."

"Beverly, don't ever be afraid to be honest with me and with yourself."

The concern in his voice made her smile. "I know. I appreciate that."

As she chatted with him, the house phone rang downstairs, and she hesitated, but then heard her father answering it. Soon his step sounded on the stairs and he knocked on the office door. "Beverly, it's for you."

"Thanks, Father."

His steps headed back downstairs.

"I'm sorry, Jeff—"

"No problem. I'll talk to you soon."

"I...I miss you," she said shyly.

She again heard the smile in his voice as he said softly, "I miss you too."

After she hung up, she took a moment to collect her thoughts. Her relationship with Jeff seemed to be on the brink of something...different, but in a good way. She hoped that selling Will's house would be a step in the right direction for her.

She answered the extension of the house phone in her office. "Hello?"

"Margaret's gallery had a break-in," Diane said breathlessly.

"What? Is she okay?"

"She's fine. We're at Shelley's house right now. Can you come over?"

"Sure." She hung up, headed downstairs, and told her father, "I'll be at Shelley's for a little while."

He had already returned to his newspaper. "Don't worry about me."

Beverly greeted Adelaide, who was with Aiden and Prize on the front lawn, then headed inside Shelley's house. The women were gathered in the kitchen, with Emma playing with some toys on the floor.

As soon as Beverly saw Margaret, without even thinking about it, she walked over and gave her a hug.

Margaret wiped away a tear as Beverly released her. "I'm so glad to have all of you here."

"Where else would we be?" Shelley was making some tea and had already set out a plate of oatmeal cookies. Beverly supposed that a soothing herbal tea was probably better for Margaret's nerves than coffee.

Margaret explained about the unlocked door and the missing painting.

"I don't quite understand why someone would switch the other painting." Shelley kept half an eye on Emma, still playing on the floor. "It seems pretty obvious that Margaret would notice that right away. I mean, it was her painting and it's her gallery too."

"Maybe the thief didn't know it was her gallery?" Diane suggested.

"I passed out Shearwater Gallery business cards at the art fair," Margaret said. "If someone wanted to steal the painting, they would have to know it was my gallery if they looked at the business card."

"It could be that the thief wasn't at the art fair," Beverly said. "They might have seen the painting and taken it. They switched it because they didn't think the gallery owner would notice for a while, not realizing the artist owned the gallery."

Margaret's shoulders sagged. "That makes even more people who might have stolen the painting, aside from the three at the art fair."

"What three?" Shelley asked.

"Three people were interested in the painting and asked about it. I gave their descriptions to Fred Little."

"Could it be that a jealous artist stole the painting?" Diane asked. "Someone who didn't like the fact that you won the award last week?"

"I don't know if that really makes sense," Shelley said. "If I were insanely jealous—emphasis on insane—I'd destroy the painting, not steal it."

"I also have no clue who might have been jealous," Margaret said. "I didn't notice anyone looking disgruntled at the fair. Certainly no one said anything to me."

They were all silent for a few moments, then Margaret said, "I think the worst part is that my faith in the people of Marble Cove has been shaken."

"I can't think it's someone from Marble Cove," Shelley said.

"Maybe it's someone who just moved here," Beverly said. "Or maybe it's a vacationer here for the summer."

Margaret sipped her tea. "I feel so vulnerable now. It's a terrible feeling."

Shelley put her arm around her.

"Margaret," Beverly said slowly, as the thought formulated in her mind, "you mentioned people at the art fair who were interested in the painting. But was anyone interested in the painting before the fair?"

"Before...?" Margaret's eyes glazed over as she thought back. "Actually, right when I finished the painting, a very short woman came into the gallery and tried to buy it."

"Who was it?"

"She didn't give her name. She was very short, less than five feet tall. Short, straight brown hair, and round glasses. She had a rather deep voice and a sort of...schoolteacher air."

"You didn't want to sell it to her?" Diane asked.

"She wanted me to sell it for an incredibly low price. I really try hard to accommodate customers, but this was too low. Plus I needed to take it to the art fair, and she wanted it right then. I couldn't do that."

"How did she react?" Shelley asked.

"She got this prim set to her mouth, but then Mayor Waters came in to buy a vase. The woman left a few minutes later."

"Did you tell Detective Little?" Beverly asked.

"I hadn't thought about it until now. I'll call him later."

"What are you going to do about the guy who bought the painting?" Diane asked with a wince.

Margaret gave a deep sigh. "If the police don't find the painting, I'll have to refund his money. But I had been so happy to have that sale because funds are tight right now. Several of the artists who usually send me pieces to consign have sold out and don't have anything new for me, so stock is a little low for the first part of this month."

They circled around and around the topic for a few minutes more, then Margaret said, "I appreciate you all being here. I can't begin to tell you how much it means to me."

"Of course we'd be here for you," Shelley said.

"Let's stop talking about my problems." Margaret straightened in her chair and took a deep breath. "How are all of you doing? Oh, Diane, I took you from your work this morning. And you too, Beverly. Shelley, you don't have more baking to do today, do you?"

"Nope. Now that I have my kitchen, I do most of my baking early in the morning and Dan helps me make deliveries before he goes in to work."

It was the barest of flickers, but something like a shadow passed over Shelley's face. Beverly wasn't entirely sure she'd seen it correctly—maybe it was just a trick of the light.

"I needed a break," Diane said. "I was in the middle of a twenty-five question interview for a blog. But I have to admit the questions are interesting. I think the next question was something like, 'If you were a crayon, what color would you be and why?'"

They all laughed at that, even Margaret.

"Really? They ask stuff like that?" Shelley asked.

"This particular blogger did. Most of the time, the questions are things like 'What inspired you to write this book?' or 'What do you want the readers to take away from this book?' or 'How did your background in journalism help you in writing your novel?' Stuff like that."

There was a pause in the conversation and Beverly snagged a second cookie off the plate. "I have some news. I got an offer on my house in Augusta today."

"That's great!" Margaret said, but then she saw Beverly's pensive face. "Uh-oh. How much was the offer?"

Beverly told them. "It's lower than I'd hoped for."

"Diane, you're the one who most recently bought a house." Shelley turned to her. "What's the housing market like?"

"If it's about the same as last year, then it's still bad. Beverly, what's the square footage of your house?"

"Forty-two hundred."

Diane started. "Oh my goodness. I knew it was large but I didn't realize it was that big."

"It was custom designed by my husband. I'm selling it with some of the furniture since I don't have room for it here, and much of the furniture was custom ordered for the house."

"What's the neighborhood like?" Shelley asked.

"Quiet. Relatively upscale. Will had wanted the house to entertain clients and special guests, so he didn't skimp on the location or the house."

"If that's the case, the offer seems a little low, but it doesn't seem unrealistic in this market," Diane said.

"That's what I thought," Beverly said.

"Well this might be a sign that it's time to let go of the house," Margaret said. "Maybe you should just accept the offer because it'll finally take it off your hands."

"That is a very tempting thought."

"It might also be the best you'll get," Shelley said. "You don't know for sure if you'll get another offer anytime soon, and in the meantime you're paying property taxes."

"Yes, you should factor that cost in with the lower price," Diane said. "If it takes six or eight months for you to get another offer, you'll also have spent several thousand in taxes for the year, so any new offers would have to cover that expense."

"And there's no guarantee you'd get a higher offer in six or eight months," Margaret said. "It might even be lower, if the housing market doesn't improve."

"So you think I should accept the offer?"

Shelley shrugged. "Personally, I'm not a risk-taker. I'd rather sell now at that price than risk no other offers coming in, and paying all that tax in the meantime."

"I'd sell it now because the housing market is depressed and there's no sign of it improving dramatically anytime soon," Diane said.

"And I'd say for you to sell it now because it's been such a stress on your life that it would be good to finally be able to get it out of your hair," Margaret said.

Beverly smiled. "Those are all great points. My father said pretty much the same things, but he also suggested I ask you three."

"Your father is exceptionally wise." Diane grinned.

"I'm with Margaret," Beverly said. "I'm very glad I have you three in my life."

Shelley winked at her. "We're always willing to help you decide how to dispose of a 4,200-square-foot house."

Beverly laughed. "I do love living here in Marble Cove," she said. "I love being here for my father, and having you all here as my friends."

"Well, we feel the same way," Diane said.

"Hear, hear." Shelley raised a cookie like a toasting glass, then giggled.

Margaret glanced at the time. "I should get home. It'll be time to take Adelaide to the community center soon. Allan might be home any time now, wondering where I am."

"He'll know you're here if he sees Adelaide on the front lawn with Aiden," Shelley said.

"And he'll probably be glad you came to us for some tea and sympathy," Diane said.

"And cookies." Margaret snatched one more before she rose to leave.

"I should get back to work too," Diane rose reluctantly.

"I'll go call my Realtor," Beverly said. "Thanks again for your advice."

As she headed toward her father's home, however, she had to wonder. She'd had a hard time selling Will's art pieces, which didn't have much sentimental value. Despite the years since his death, would it be even harder to sell his house?

CHAPTER FOUR

Shelley hummed as she moved around the kitchen getting dinner ready. She felt almost guilty for being so happy when Margaret had such a terrible thing happen to her, but she couldn't help it.

Dan's apprenticeship seemed to be going very smoothly, and the sight of his paycheck deposited in their bank account had eased a tight knot in her stomach that she hadn't really known was there until it released.

She'd just checked her computer and she had three new Internet orders, which she could mail tomorrow morning. With all the online orders she'd been getting lately, combined with her local customers, she was pulling in a decent income with her baking business, but not so much that she had more work than she could do on her own.

And Aiden was currently sitting in the living room, watching an educational program that had recently become his favorite, which happened to run at the same time each day right at the exact time she needed to get dinner ready.

And today, Emma was content to sit on the kitchen floor and play with measuring spoons and a bowl with a small handful of Cheerios in it. It kept her occupied while Shelley prepared the tuna casserole and popped it into the oven.

She glanced at the clock as she set the timer. Aiden's program was just finishing, and she also heard the front door open as Dan got home.

"Daddy!" Aiden cried joyfully, but Shelley was surprised by Dan's subdued response.

"Hey, buddy."

Emma's head turned toward the kitchen doorway at the sound of Aiden's cry, and she grinned widely and waved her arms. In moments Dan had entered the kitchen and she gave a squeal of delight.

But Dan simply gave her a peck on the cheek. "Hey, baby girl."

Shelley hesitated. What was wrong? Was it bad news?

"Hi, Shell." He gave her a kiss on the cheek also, and she got a clear look at his face. Whereas he usually had a tired smile for her when he came home from work, today his brow furrowed and there were deep vertical lines etched alongside his mouth.

"What's wrong?" she asked.

"Nothing," he said hastily, his eyes sliding away from her. His movement drew his attention to Emma.

"Daddy, Daddy, Daddy!" Her voice rose insistently and she waved her arms toward him. She didn't seem to realize that she still grasped a measuring spoon in one fist.

"Hey, baby girl." Dan seemed almost relieved to turn away from Shelley to pick Emma up. "Are you Mama's helper today?"

"Cheese," she said, waving the measuring spoon and nearly taking his eye out.

He jerked his head back. "Yes, I see." He took the spoon out of her hand and laid it on the table. "When will dinner be ready?" he asked Shelley.

"Thirty minutes."

"You rest. I'll play with the kids." He headed toward the living room with Emma in his arms.

Normally Shelley would have rejoiced at this time to herself, but Dan's subdued mood and evasiveness made her stomach start to cramp again with worry. What was going on? Did it have to do with work? Why didn't Dan want to talk about it?

She cleaned up, but even the sight of a clean kitchen didn't ease her tension. She hated not knowing what was going on, or what she could do about it.

Dan interacted almost entirely with the kids all through supper. He asked Aiden about his day and joked with him about the dog that had gotten loose at the park. He made Emma giggle with his silly faces.

And whenever his eye happened to fall upon Shelley, he looked away quickly. Whenever she opened her mouth to say something to him, he'd quickly say something to Aiden or Emma.

Shelley grew more and more quiet as the meal went on, feeling the hurt squeeze around her heart tighter and tighter.

Finally Dan put the two kids to bed, reading Aiden a story. Shelley expected him to give in to Aiden's pleadings for a second book, but he resisted and instead gave him a smacking kiss on the cheek. "'Night, buddy."

"'Night, Daddy." Aiden curled up on his side, disgruntled that he hadn't gotten his way.

Shelley and Dan were silent as they walked to the living room. He collapsed onto the couch with a deep sigh.

Shelley stood, unsure if he wanted her to sit with him or not, still hurt and slightly miffed that he had avoided talking to her since he'd gotten home. Should she push the issue and ask him what was wrong, or should she give him some time to himself to process things?

He answered her question for her by patting the seat next to him and smiling at her.

She was a little ashamed at herself for how readily she sat next to him. He put his arm around her shoulders even as he picked up the television remote with his other hand.

Shelley didn't want to completely ignore her anxiety about him, but she also didn't want to say something that would make him shut down. So she asked, "Long day at work?"

"Yup." Another long sigh. But then he leaned over and gave her a deep kiss. "But it's good to be home."

He kissed her lovingly again, and Shelley forgot all about her questions and confusion. It must not be bothering him that much, if he felt better in the space of a couple hours. It must be work related, and she didn't want to interfere with his new job and training.

She only wanted him to be happy.

Diane had tried everything she possibly could to help the words flow, but she was stuck as she tried to work on her book.

She made tea, she made coffee. She grabbed carrot sticks to munch on, she opened a bag of potato chips. She lit a soothing lavender candle, and when that didn't seem to help, she lit a candle with an invigorating citrus fragrance. She played music. She turned off the music. She tried working in her office, and when she still couldn't work, she tried moving into the living room. Then the dining room.

She checked the time and realized it was almost dinner. She didn't feel tired—on the contrary, she felt frustrated and annoyed with herself—but she worried that her blood sugar was beginning to dip, so she ate some fruit and some peanuts to tide her over and went for a quick walk along the beach with Rocky afterward.

But when she came back home, she still sat in front of her computer and just couldn't think of what to write. She glared at the cursor blinking snidely from her computer screen, but nothing came to her.

She rested her forehead in her hands and sighed. She had never realized that being a novelist would be so stressful. She thought she'd left the days of stressful writing behind when she retired from being a newspaper reporter. She had somehow thought that novelists would pound out book after book in a haze of creative inspiration.

She never pictured writer's block like this. She'd thought it was a myth simply because as a journalist, she hadn't had the luxury of writer's block—she'd had to write her copy by a deadline or suffer consequences.

Well, here she was, trying to be creative and needing to write these chapters by a deadline, but she was stuck like a dinosaur in a tar pit.

When was her deadline for the first three chapters, anyway? The date had changed a few times, but her editor had given her the final deadline date a few weeks ago. Had it been in an e-mail or on the phone? She couldn't remember. She had intended to put the date into her calendar, but she kept forgetting. She fired up her e-mail to try to find the message.

Instead, she saw the four new interview and guest blog requests from bloggers who were participating in her blog tour. The deadline for the short pieces wasn't for another few days.

But she was obviously stuck and couldn't work on her manuscript, so why not finish these short pieces now? It would be more productive than staring at that gleefully blinking cursor.

She opened the first message, which was from a blogger named Megan.

Dear Ms. Spencer,

I'm so excited to host you on my blog for your blog tour! I'm a huge fan of Agatha Christie and The Lighthouse Goes Dark *was just like a modern version of one of her stories. I couldn't figure out the villain until the very end! Thanks for agreeing to answer these interview questions. I hope you have fun with your answers!*

Megan

Diane couldn't help but smile at Megan's comparison with the great Agatha Christie. How sweet of her.

The questions were mostly the same sort of questions she'd already had from the five other blog interviews she'd done: How did you become a writer? What inspired this book? What do you hope readers will take away from this story? What's your favorite kind of book to read?

The answers were easy for her to write up since she'd already answered them in some form or another on other blogs, but she tried to add something unique for each entry.

After finishing Megan's interview questions, the next blogger was Shirley:

To Ms. Spencer,

Thank you for agreeing to be a guest blogger. I loved your mystery. There was something about the lighthouse that kept drawing me, just the way it drew your main character. You painted the setting so vividly that I felt as if I were there.

Many of my readers love hearing stories about the research behind a novel. Would you be able to write a short 500-word post about some aspect of your research, perhaps something to do with the lighthouse? It can be some historical facts or a story about your research endeavors.

Thank you again for your time.

Shirley

When Shirley mentioned how the lighthouse drew her, Diane couldn't help feeling a spark of warmth in her chest.

It was so wonderful to hear how a reader was emotionally captivated by something she wrote, especially when the lighthouse was such a special aspect of Marble Cove for herself.

She quickly wrote a short post about how she and her friends had spoken to someone who used to live in the lighthouse and rediscovered a hidden door into the old building. She kept out names so that no one would know the truth behind the story, including Edward Maker and the shipwreck off the coast of Marble Cove, but she reviewed her post and thought that the short story would pique her readers' interest in her novel, even though the hidden door wasn't in the published story.

Diane continued reading the e-mails from the various bloggers and answering interview questions. Each message seemed to lift her spirits a little more. Most of the bloggers she'd interacted with so far had read her book and really liked it, which was why they had wanted to host her on this blog tour. It made her feel like she had new acquaintances gathering around her, excited about her debut novel and cheering her on.

After finishing the questions and guest posts she had to write for the day, she saw an e-mail from her agent, Frieda Watley.

Her agent's cheerful message encouraging her to make the most of her blog tour made Diane feel even more positive about her book, and also glad that she had finished that part of her work for today.

The bloggers' messages and her agent's e-mail had given her a boost. She opened up her manuscript document and instead of being frustrated by the balefully blinking cursor, she felt invigorated. She immediately began writing.

She had been writing for a while when she reached a point in her story she had forgotten to research before now, even though she had mentioned it in her synopsis to her editor. She had blithely written something about a coded message but hadn't figured out what code was being used, whether words or numbers or symbols, and she hadn't figured out how long the message was supposed to be. While the character wouldn't know what the message said at this point in the story, she needed to know what the message looked like so the character could take steps to figure out how to decode it.

She opened her Internet browser and began searching for the different types of ciphers. She was overwhelmed by the sheer number of possibilities, but the sight of the different ciphers reminded her of the page from the prayer book that they had copied down.

She got out the sheet that Beverly had given to her and, remembering what they had talked about, she limited her search to ciphers created before the year 1800. She figured that her research would serve two purposes—to decode the prayer book message and then use that cipher for her book.

In looking for what could possibly be the cipher for the message, she saw that there actually weren't that many. Most ciphers were variations of the same cipher—for example, the Caesar and Atbash ciphers were just variations of a simple substitution cipher, where each letter was replaced by another letter, such as X for the letter A, or Q for the letter B, and so on. A mixed alphabet cipher would be a little harder to figure out, but it was essentially still a substitution cipher.

Diane found that since the message in the prayer book was pretty long, she could do the frequency analysis method she found online and try to see if the prayer journal message was a substitution cipher. All she needed to do was figure out how many times each letter of the alphabet was used in the message. It would be easy to say one way or the other if it was a substitution cipher because if there weren't any letters that were used more than others, then it couldn't be a substitution cipher.

She painstakingly tallied how many times each letter was used in the message. After doing the tally and then looking at the numbers, she thought that it just might be a substitution cipher. There were a handful of letters that were used more than others, although according to the article she read, the difference wasn't as great as it usually was with substitution ciphers. She checked her research online, and verified that the message was long enough that she should discover the pattern if it was there.

She continued researching and saw that it might be a transposition cipher. Diane gave a weary sigh and happened to glance at the clock. She yelped. It was already past dinnertime now and she needed to eat. She'd been so fascinated by her research—especially since she had a real-life encoded message to crack—that she'd completely lost track of time.

She headed to the kitchen to warm up some soup. She also ruefully realized she'd worked more on her research than on her three chapters, but since the coded message was the key around which her novel was going to revolve, she figured it wasn't a bad thing. She was just doing some of this harder work ahead of time.

Well, she'd work on the manuscript more tomorrow. She still had plenty of time.

CHAPTER FIVE

Margaret slept very badly the night after discovering the break-in at her gallery, and so this morning she was bleary-eyed and fighting off a low-grade headache. She'd startled herself awake, and then as she remembered the missing painting, a sickening feeling dropped into the pit of her stomach, and she couldn't do more than nibble at toast for breakfast.

Adelaide picked up on her mood and laid her small hand on Margaret's arm. "What's wrong, Mom?" Her face looked worried and stressed.

Margaret immediately regretted letting her mood cause anxiety for her daughter. "I'm just worried about work."

"Do you have a busy day today?" Adelaide asked.

Margaret hesitated. What could she do today? She didn't think her nerves would enable her to paint, unless she were working on some violent piece of abstract art called something like *Inner Turbulence*. Then again, she reflected, that might be a good way to ease the tension inside her.

Allan rescued her from her dilemma. "Why don't you inventory your paintings and consignment items today?"

"That's a good idea." Margaret made sure she kept good inventory records of both her own paintings and the pieces she accepted on consignment, since many of the pieces were sold so quickly during the busy summer months.

"Did you need help?" he asked her.

"No. Besides, I know you need to finish that commissioned table and chairs set. You already spent all day yesterday at the gallery for me. I don't want to take you from your work today too."

"You know I'd do anything I can to help you."

Margaret reached over to lay a hand against his cheek. "I know, and I'm grateful to you. But I have to get back to work sometime, so it might as well be today." Her voice trembled a little as she spoke, but she raised her chin and gave a firm smile.

"Can I come help?" Adelaide asked.

Margaret wavered, but then Allan said, "No, Addie, you've got classes at the community center today, remember?"

Her daughter's face fell, but she nodded slowly.

"You can come help me another time," Margaret said.

"Okay." But Adelaide's shoulders still slumped as she slowly finished her toast.

Margaret was a little surprised, because usually Adelaide was excited about going to the community center. But perhaps her worry about her mother made her want to stick close today rather than keeping with her normal schedule.

Margaret's fingers shook a little as she unlocked the front door to the gallery, but she told herself to buck up. She straightened her back and walked into the gallery.

Everything was quiet and peaceful, which contrasted with the jittery mass of nerves inside her.

She set her purse in her office and then went about her normal routine of opening the gallery, falling back on normal, everyday things. Eventually the ritual soothed her a little, and when a strolling couple walked in a few minutes later, she greeted them with a polite smile. They bought a vase, and the act of ringing them up and packing the vase for them further helped her strung-out nerves to ease up and relax.

But she never quite lost that feeling of uneasiness all day. She did the inventory, and everything except *Sea Breeze* was in the gallery, so nothing but the award-winning painting had been stolen. That was a relief. She expected the news to make her feel better, but it didn't ease her mind as much as she thought it would.

When she had some downtime later that morning and tried to paint, it was as if there were an invisible electric fence between her and the canvas, and she couldn't get past it. She finally gave up, which was just as well, because she had a rush of customers just before lunchtime.

After lunch, Margaret was surprised to see Rita Candleford and Pamela Morgan, members of her Bible study group. The two women entered the gallery and immediately went to where Margaret was just finishing the paperwork on a sale of one of Allan's Adirondack chairs, which the customer had just left with.

"Margaret, we heard about the break-in." Rita's bright blue eyes were worried as they fastened on Margaret. "Are you doing all right?"

"I'm...okay." She couldn't really say she was fine, but she wasn't a hysterical mess or anything like that. "How did you hear about it?"

"Yesterday Detective Little was asking some people at the Cove if they'd seen anything." Pamela tucked a blonde strand of hair behind her ear, but the bob-length haircut kept falling forward in front of her pixie face. "The detective mentioned the missing painting, and so naturally everyone who went to the Cove yesterday heard about it. Have the police found the painting yet?"

Margaret shook her head slowly.

"We're all praying for you." Rita took Margaret's hand in hers. "I know you've probably been too busy, but remember to e-mail or call the Bible study group when you need prayer. We're here for you."

Margaret squeezed Rita's hand. "I'm sorry, I should have told everyone yesterday, but I was just so upset. I went home with Adelaide and talked to some of my neighbors in order to calm down."

"Oh, we completely understand." Pamela also placed her hand atop Margaret's and Rita's. "That's why we came today, to see how you were doing and to see if there was anything you wanted us to do."

"You're already doing it. Thanks for the prayers."

"I wish we could help catch the thief." Rita's eyes flashed, and her graying red curls looked almost like flickering flames in the afternoon sunlight streaming through the windows. Margaret had to bite back a smile as she realized that Rita looked like an avenging fury.

"Do you have any idea who might have taken it?" Pamela asked.

"Not really," Margaret said. "There was one woman who tried to buy the painting here in the gallery a few weeks before the art fair, and then three other people who were interested in the painting at the fair. But I don't know if that really makes them suspects, just because they liked the painting. Anyone could have seen it in the window and wanted it."

"It was a little...odd," Rita said. "Not like your other paintings."

"Yes, it was a new abstract style I'm experimenting with."

"Oh." Rita seemed surprised. "Is there something wrong with your usual style? I like your other paintings a lot." She gestured to a lighthouse painting on the wall, which was slotted to be sold to Matt Beauregard for his Lighting the Way Greeting Card Company. Pamela was nodding her agreement with Rita.

"Oh. Er...the new style won the award at the fair." Margaret's answer sounded rather lame in her own ears.

"That's wonderful! Congratulations," Pamela said quickly.

"Yes, congratulations."

Their words were sincere, but Margaret could tell that they were excited for her success because they loved her, rather than because they were enthusiastic about her new style. Rita and Pamela had both bought original paintings from her, and Rita had bought two *giclée* prints also, so it wasn't that they were being cheerleaders. They were actual fans of her work—her old style.

Margaret realized that she hadn't really considered what her fans would think if she tried to meld her old and new styles together. Would they still like the new style at all? How would that affect her sales here at the gallery? She already knew that Matt liked her old style better—in fact, he'd mentioned at the art fair about how her paintings were good sellers for the greeting card company, but he had made it clear that he would only buy pictures in her old style, not the new one that won the award for best abstract painting at the art fair.

"Please let us know if there is anything we can do for you," Rita said fervently.

The women's concern for her did more to ease Margaret's worry than anything else. "You've done a ton just by coming today to see how I was doing."

"Well, promise us you'll give us a call if you think of something," Pamela said.

"I promise."

They chatted a few minutes more about Adelaide and Allan, and then the two women left. But the warmth of their love for her stayed in her chest like a gentle glow.

Just before closing, she was doubly surprised to see Bernadette Lassiter, a local artist who had helped Margaret paint the mural at the Cannery and whose jewelry she sold here at the gallery. Bernadette's bohemian style always made Margaret a little envious since it was so beautiful and uninhibited, but Bernadette's face was lined with worry as she entered the gallery.

"Hi, Margaret. I heard about the break-in. Are you okay?"

"I'm doing better now," she said truthfully.

"That's awful about your painting." Bernadette brushed aside a long, curly lock of hair that had escaped her loose bun. "I hope nothing else was missing?"

"I just did an inventory, so you don't have to worry. Nothing else was taken."

Bernadette colored. "I'm sorry, I didn't mean my jewelry, even though it must have sounded that way. I meant any of your other paintings."

"Oh." Margaret felt her own cheeks flaring. "I'm the one who's sorry. I shouldn't have assumed . . . Well, nothing else was taken, which makes me feel better."

"I'm sure it's still hard." Bernadette fingered her necklace made of beach glass, obviously from the same line of jewelry she sold at the gallery. "Your lost painting must make you feel like some stranger has tramped through your home and looked in all your dresser drawers."

Margaret straightened in surprise. "That's exactly how I feel."

"It's how I would feel about my paintings." Bernadette's eyes wandered to the paintings on the walls of the gallery. "Each one is a little piece of you, because that's the well you need to tap when you create art. And when it's been stolen, it's like you're a little bit violated."

Margaret nodded. While her Bible study friends' concern had warmed her, she realized that Bernadette, being an artist herself, truly understood what Margaret was feeling at the loss of the painting.

"I just wanted to come by and see if there was anything I could do for you," Bernadette said.

"That's wonderfully kind of you, but I'm okay now."

"I saw the painting a few days ago. It's a new style for you, isn't it?"

"Yes, although it still had that seashore theme."

"I thought it was unique." Bernadette looked thoughtful. "In our profession as artists, we see a lot of different styles, but I can honestly say that your new one was something that stood out. I liked that."

"Thank you."

They continued chatting about normal, artsy things that made Margaret feel almost herself again, and then Bernadette left. Margaret closed up the gallery, being sure to lock the door, and headed home.

There was no one in the house, so she went to see Allan in his workshop. He looked up from sanding a board. "Adelaide's across the street at Shelley's house."

"I'll go get her. It's almost time for supper."

"Margaret..." There was a serious tone to Allan's voice that made her stop and look at him.

He put down his sander. "Have you noticed Adelaide behaving any differently when you see her after her time at the community center?"

"What do you mean?" Margaret thought back to the past week. She hadn't noticed anything, but then again, she hadn't been looking.

"She came back today and seemed a little...grumpy." He raised his eyebrows, seemingly almost embarrassed to mention it.

"Grumpy?" Margaret suppressed a smile.

"Almost like a teenager with too much homework and unfair teachers."

"Did something happen at the community center?"

"I'm not sure. When I asked her, she said nothing was wrong. But she was still grumpy."

"It could be that she herself doesn't really know what's wrong. Maybe she needs time to process it. Or should we talk to Penny Tyler about the special-needs activities?"

"I don't want to make too big a deal of it quite yet if you haven't noticed a pattern during the past week. Maybe she just had an off day."

"I'll keep an eye out the next time she comes back from the community center." Margaret then left to go across the street to Shelley's house.

Shelley smiled as Margaret entered the kitchen. "I hope you don't mind my borrowing Adelaide today."

"Of course not."

Adelaide's face lit up as she saw Margaret—no sign of grumpiness now. "Look, Mom." She held up a fruit tart she'd decorated with slices of fruit and decadent berries.

"That's beautiful," Margaret said.

"I made some too." Aiden held up his own tart, which wasn't quite as pretty as Adelaide's, but Margaret praised it.

"Want some?" Shelley asked. "I have a pot of water heating for tea too."

"Well, I came to get Adelaide for dinner..."

"Oh, please, Mom, can't we have a little?" Adelaide pleaded.

"Well, I'm sure Dad won't mind waiting a little while longer for dinner."

Adelaide grinned and turned to Aiden. "Let's go get cleaned up." She left with him to wash up in the bathroom.

Shelley scooped up a few blueberries that had tumbled off of Emma's plate. The toddler had been given her own tart to decorate, although she seemed more interested in smashing her hand into the creamy filling and stuffing berries into her mouth. She gave Margaret a toothy smile.

"Hello, sweetheart," Margaret said. Then she said to Shelley, "Thank you so much for letting Adelaide help you. That's two days in a row, yesterday and today."

"It was my pleasure, believe me. I wanted to try out a new tart crust recipe, but wasn't sure how to handle the baking and the kids at the same time." Shelley set a slice of tart in front of Margaret and followed shortly after with a cup of tea. Adelaide and Aiden returned with clean hands and sat at the table.

Margaret took a bite of tart. "*Mmm*, this crust is amazing. It's so flaky. But I don't know if it will travel well if you had to deliver it a long way."

"That's what I was afraid of." Shelley sat next to her with Emma and Adelaide on the other side. She took a bite of her own slice of tart. "It's flakier than I had hoped. Since tarts don't have as sturdy a pan as a pie, I wanted to strike a good balance between flakiness and firmness."

"I think it tastes great." Adelaide popped a strawberry slice in her mouth.

"That's because I had great help." Shelley grinned at her.

Adelaide made faces at Emma, making the toddler giggle, while also keeping up a running conversation with Aiden. Shelley took the opportunity to lean closer to Margaret. "While I was baking, I remembered something that might help you with the theft of the painting."

"Oh?"

"Two days ago—the day before the painting was stolen—I was taking Emma and Aiden to the Cove. I was walking past your gallery to get there and I noticed a woman looking at your painting in the window."

"What did she look like? Was she very tiny?" Margaret remembered the short woman who had tried to buy the painting before the art fair.

"No, she was tall and thin. She had long, curly gray hair and she had on a bright magenta silk top and a light yellow-green skirt with pink flowers printed on it, which was why I remembered her so vividly. But also, as I was walking past, she looked up at me and I smiled and said hello. And then she asked me if I'd seen the painting in the window."

Margaret straightened in her chair. "She did?"

"I said that it had won an award at the fair last week, just in case she hadn't seen the little card on the bottom. But she kind of sniffed and said that she'd heard, but she didn't think much of it."

Margaret blinked.

Shelley nodded. "That was my reaction too. At first I thought I must have misheard her, because I couldn't believe anyone would be so blunt about criticizing an artist in front of her gallery. I tried to be polite, but the woman just kept going on about how the style wasn't inspiring at all, while the other paintings you have are so much more ... what was the word she used? Transcendent?"

Margaret snorted in laughter. "I've never heard my work described as transcendent."

"Maybe that's not the right word. But it was some description that struck me as very odd. *She* struck me as very odd, but then again, I've seen so many tourists come through Marble Cove that you kind of get used to the occasional odd bird."

"Was she a tourist?"

"I think so. Before I spoke to her, I thought I might have seen her around town this summer, maybe in the grocery store. She's not a regular resident, but I think she's vacationing here for at least a few weeks. She's not a weekender."

"I wonder if I should have you mention it to Fred Little?"

"If you want me to. I didn't think of it before because it was just a short conversation, since I had to get the blueberry muffins to the Cove."

"It might be worth it. I'll call Fred to come by to talk to you. I already spoke to him about the short woman who tried to buy the painting a few weeks ago, and he said that if I could remember anyone else interested in the painting, I should let him know."

"Sure. I should be home with the kids for the rest of the week."

"We should be getting home. Allan will wonder where we are." Margaret stood. "Thanks for the tart, and the tip about the woman."

"I hope they catch the thief." Shelley gave Margaret a hug.

As Margaret headed across the street with Adelaide, she asked her daughter, "So how was the community center today?"

She shrugged. "It was okay."

"Just okay? Did something happen to make it not as fun as normal?"

"No, it was just like normal." Adelaide's expression didn't give Margaret any indication of what she was feeling.

She tried probing one more time. "You enjoyed it? Or not?"

Adelaide hesitated a moment before saying, "I enjoyed it." But her voice wasn't enthusiastic, and that short hesitation worried Margaret.

But Adelaide wouldn't lie to her about enjoying her community center activities, would she?

CHAPTER SIX

On Wednesday morning, Beverly got off the phone with her Realtor and made an appointment in the calendar on her computer. June twenty-ninth, the last Friday of the month: *House Closing.*

She stared at the words and felt a strange weight on her chest. The house in Augusta was so indelibly Will's—designed by him, the neighborhood and property chosen by him, decorated by him. It was the one place he had been most proud of because it bore his unique stamp all over it.

And now she was selling it.

She thrust the thought aside, although the heaviness remained in her chest. She had to sell the house. Will was gone, and she needed the money from the sale for her new business. She had no more ties to Augusta, so it made sense to sell the house and avoid paying the property taxes on it for this coming year.

But she couldn't shake the tension in her body. If she were still working as a budget analyst, she'd simply have thrown herself into her work.

But, she realized with a smile, she wasn't a budget analyst anymore. And she was working from home in her father's house in Marble Cove, which meant she had the freedom to deal with this tension right now.

She headed downstairs to play on her piano for a while. The music soothed her quickly and more effectively than if she'd thrown herself into her work.

She'd been playing for about twenty minutes when her father appeared, shuffling into the living room with his coffee mug in his hand.

She stopped. "Sorry, did I disturb you?"

"No, no. You don't have to stop. I was just going to get some coffee."

"I'll make you a new pot." She took his mug from him and went into the kitchen.

He followed. "You don't have to do that, you know. I'm old but I'm not quite that old yet." His voice rumbled with grouchiness.

"I wanted some coffee too before I went back to work." She poured water into the coffeemaker.

He gave a smile. "It's nice having you home with me, Beverly."

"I like it too." She remembered the earlier telephone call. "I talked to my Realtor today. The house will close on the last Friday in June."

"That's fast. What do you have to do in the meantime?"

"Sign a few papers, and then clear my things out of the house."

He looked dubiously back at the living room. "How much furniture will you bring back?"

"Oh, not much. Most of the furniture was bought specifically for the house, so I sold the pieces to the new owners. There are a few things I can put up in the attic so you won't need to make room for them in the other rooms."

"You know you can move anything you like in here. It's your home too."

"I know. I just don't have much in the Augusta home that I need to bring back with me."

It seemed so strange that she wouldn't have many things from such a major segment of her life. Was it wrong to get rid of the house when it had so much of Will in it? Was her selling the house cutting him out of her life, her memory?

But maybe it would be good for her to reevaluate her feelings when she went to Augusta to pack up her things. She hadn't felt this way before when she put the house up for sale, but now that it was about to close, the misgivings disturbed her. What if they indicated deeper feelings and regrets? Was she making a wrong decision?

She went back upstairs and started work, which included plans for an end-of-summer special that the Sand Dollar, a B and B in Pemaquid, wanted to run in August. Beverly crunched numbers for most of the morning, stopping only to make a sandwich for herself and her father at lunchtime, and finishing in the early afternoon.

She stretched in her chair, glad the work was finally done because the weather outside looked lovely. She was about to leave her office when she realized it would be perfect to sit out on the front porch with her laptop and her copy of the cipher from the prayer book.

She went downstairs, tiptoeing because she could hear her father's snores coming from his library, and stepped out into the front porch. The bright sunlight slanted across the cream painted floorboards, and a light breeze fingered through her hair. She sat in a wicker love seat with her feet propped up on the railing and opened her laptop.

She'd done some research into ciphers already but had been dismayed by how many there were. The easiest had been the substitution cipher, and a quick frequency analysis had shown that it might be it. She started doing more online searches for other ciphers and was relieved to find out that some ciphers were simply too recent to be the one used in the prayer journal. Still, there were a lot of possible ciphers, including a lot of different substitution ciphers she could try. Perhaps it would be best if she made a list of which ciphers the message could be encoded with, and then divide them up among the four friends who wanted to help crack the code.

"Hey, neighbor!"

Beverly looked up to see Diane returning from a walk with Rocky. She returned Diane's wave. "Had a good walk?"

"The beach was amazing today, even better than yesterday, because the breeze makes it just comfortable without being cold." Diane walked up to the front porch and peered at her computer. "Oh, I'm sorry. I'm not interrupting your work, am I?"

"No, not at all. I've actually been working on the cipher from the prayer book."

Diane's eyes lit up. "I was doing that yesterday. I thought it might be a substitution cipher—"

"That's what I thought too. I did a frequency analysis and there's a strong chance it could be that. Of course, it might be a bunch of other things too."

"I did a frequency analysis too. We should coordinate our efforts so we're not repeating each others' work."

"True." Beverly pointed to her computer screen. "Some of the older ciphers are still pretty complicated. There are a few polyalphabetic substitution ciphers that people used, and if they combined it with a transpositional cipher, it made it easy to encrypt and decrypt if you knew the keys, but hard for anyone else to crack."

"How about we divvy up these substitution ciphers we haven't tried yet?"

They went down the list, and Beverly said she'd e-mail Diane's "assignments" to her.

"I don't know about you, but I always loved word games." Diane's eyes glowed. "I loved the challenge."

"I liked the number puzzles more than the word puzzles, but I like puzzles in general," Beverly said. "When I was younger, Mother had a book of puzzles that she and I would do together." It had been something she did only with her mother, because her father had laughingly said that the puzzles made his head spin.

"Maybe the writer of this encoded message did puzzles a lot with whoever this message was meant for. That might explain why it was written in the prayer book—it would have been something just between the writer and the recipient."

"Yes, I could see that. It sounds like something fun Mother might have done for me—leave me an encoded message and expect me to figure it out."

"So how are things going with your house?"

"We've just set the closing for the day before the Founders Day celebration."

"That's great. I suppose you need to move all your stuff out before then?"

"Only some personal stuff. Most of the furniture was sold with the house."

"Did you need help?"

"No, I'll be fine. But thanks for offering." Beverly smiled at Diane, thankful once again for the good friends she had made here in Marble Cove.

Yes, selling the house would be a good thing, after all. Because although she'd grown up in Augusta, this place felt more like home to her.

Shelley saw Diane heading toward her home with Rocky, and impulsively headed out the front door. "Diane!"

"Hi." She waved and detoured toward their house.

"I hate to ask you this, but would you be able to watch Aiden and Emma for a little while this evening after supper? I'll feed the kids, but I want some time to talk to Dan without the kids around." Even as she asked for the favor, Shelley's hands shook. Would Dan open up to her? She hoped she was doing the right thing in forcing him to talk to her.

"Of course." Diane reached out to touch her shoulder. "Is everything all right?"

"I'm…I'm not sure."

"Is it serious?"

"I don't think so, but…" Memories of Dan's grim face made her continue. "For the past two nights, he's come home looking a little down. Last night he was even a little snappish to me. He plays with the kids and then he's fine, but I just know something's bothering him. He won't talk to me, especially with the kids around, and last night he was so tired he just wanted to go straight to sleep after we put the kids to bed."

"Why won't he talk to you?"

"That's what worries me. It could be that it's something he thinks is minor and he doesn't want to worry me about it, but it's still making me worried." Shelley thrust her hands up in frustration.

"Do you think it has to do with your relationship? Or the kids? Or his family?"

"I think…" Shelley bit her lip. "I think it might have to do with work, because it's always when he comes home, and a couple nights ago, he seemed fine after dinner. But I wasn't as worried about it then, so I didn't say anything to him. But when it happened last night too, I'm really starting to be concerned about him." She looked at Diane sheepishly. "And when I saw you from the living room window, I just made up my mind right then and there to talk to Dan if you're able to watch the kids tonight. Just for an hour or so."

"Of course I'd be willing to help."

"I know you're terribly busy, with those interviews and your chapters due soon."

"But you're a friend, and I will always have time for you."

Her words warmed Shelley like direct sunlight on her shoulders. "Thanks, Diane."

They agreed upon a time for her to come over, and Shelley hurried back in the house. She felt guilty that she'd left Aiden and Emma alone in the house, even though she'd only been a few steps outside the front door, but she found them still playing together in miraculously perfect harmony on the floor of the living room, with Prize rolling on her back alongside them.

Shelley made Dan's favorite, meat loaf, which was also quick enough to throw together while Aiden and Emma played. She popped it into the oven a little early so that she could have everything ready to eat when Dan got home.

Shelley told Aiden, "After dinner, Miss Diane will be coming over to play for a little while. I want you to make sure to behave for her."

"Okay," Aiden said, not paying much attention. "Maybe she'll play spaceship with me."

"I'm sure she'd love to play anything you want. It's almost time for Daddy to come home. Why don't you get your basket and put away your toy cars?"

He started to protest, but changed his mind and went to his bedroom to get his toy basket.

Shelley sighed. Emma was still busy playing, so Shelley left her for a moment while she went to finish setting the table. Just then she heard Dan enter the front door.

"Daddy!" Aiden called to him. "Miss Diane is coming over after dinner to play spaceship with me!"

Dan looked perplexed, but he gave Aiden a bear hug and asked, "How's my little man?"

"Good." Aiden replied, hugging back.

Dan rumpled his hair. "Shell, what's up?" He turned to her with a peck on the cheek.

Shelley tried to put on a bright face, but she worried she only looked pained. "I, uh, asked Diane to come over and watch the kids after dinner so we could go for a walk together."

Rather than being pleased, he looked wary. Not a good sign.

Shelley led the way to the dining table. "I made your favorite."

Emma saw him and gave him a wide smile.

But Dan didn't respond as she'd hoped. "What's going on, Shell?" He kept his voice pitched low so that Aiden wouldn't hear as he scrambled into his chair at the dining table.

Now that he was standing in front of her, tired lines around his eyes and mouth, confused and worried, Shelley realized she couldn't just accuse him of being bad-tempered when he came home from work. It would only make him feel worse, and regardless of how she felt, he was doing his best for their family.

So she gave him a sweet smile. "You've been working really hard, and Aiden was a little cranky earlier today. I thought he might be cranky after dinner too, and I didn't want it to make you more tired after coming home from work. I thought it might be nice to go for a walk, nothing that'll keep you from the kids, but just a little together time. I hope it's a good end to your day."

He returned her smile and gave her a hug. "You're the best. *Ooh*, meat loaf?"

"Daddy!" Emma screamed, banging her fork against her plastic plate.

"Oh, I can't believe I neglected my little girl." He swooped in and gave her a loud, smacking kiss that had her giggling.

They sat down to eat and Dan said grace. They chatted with the kids and Shelley was careful not to bring up any reference to work. Aiden was only too happy to chat about the spaceship adventures he'd gotten into that day, although Shelley couldn't think about how he had the time to do half of what he boasted about.

Aiden was a little mutinous when Diane came over. "I want to go with you and Daddy," he said.

"Why don't you show Miss Diane your new cars?" Shelley suggested.

"I don't want to," he said with a pout.

"Aiden," Dan said in a heavy voice. His face looked more tired than ever as he looked at his recalcitrant son. "Please obey your mother."

Aiden hesitated, his face screwed up in a pre-tantrum expression, but then he stomped off to the living room.

"I'm sorry," Shelley said to Diane.

"Don't be. Enjoy your walk." Diane waved them off from their front door.

As Shelley and Dan headed to the beach, he gave a deep sigh. "You were right about Aiden being cranky. I don't know that I'd have had the patience for him tonight."

"Was work busy today?"

"Work's been...kind of tough."

Oh no. Had this been the wrong career move for Dan? Was he already disliking his job?

Shelley told herself to be calm and take a deep breath. In fact, she took two. "Is the work difficult to learn?"

"Oh, nothing like that." He gave her a quick smile. "I actually really like it. It's different from anything I've done before, and it's rewarding when the job is done and everything's working properly."

Shelley smiled at the spark of enthusiasm in his voice. "That's wonderful, Dan."

They walked in silence for a minute or two, taking the path that led to the lighthouse. Then Shelley asked, "Is there something else about the job that's making it tough for you?"

Dan heaved a long, slow sigh. "Wayne has been kind of crusty."

"Your boss?"

"Yeah." Dan fell silent.

"Crusty, how?"

"Oh, I dunno." Dan's shoulders hunched. "He's kind of a stickler. Nothing I do is good enough for him."

Shelley bristled at this criticism of her wonderful, hard-working husband, but she kept her voice even. "I'm sorry, Dan. That must make it hard for you to do your job."

He stopped and reached over to briefly cup her cheek. "You're the greatest, Shell. You always understand me."

"I wish I could do something to help you."

"It's just nice to come home to you and the kids." But he gave another long sigh.

"I'm sure things will get better soon." They continued walking and Shelley made her voice positive and upbeat. "You know how there's always a learning curve when you start something new."

"But I worry that I'm even learning things right. Wayne's pretty critical."

"Does he tell you when you do something right too?"

"Well, sometimes the only way I know I've done something right is if he doesn't have anything to criticize about it." Dan kicked at a clod of sand. "Is this really the right path for me to take? I don't want to be kidding myself if I'm not cut out for this."

"Oh, Dan, I've never heard you sound as excited about any other job—even working for Allan—as you do about this one."

"But just because I like it doesn't mean I'm going to be any good at it," he said gloomily.

"It's only been about a month. You can't know if you'll be good at this or not with only a few weeks under your belt."

He nodded. "I guess you're right."

"Of course I'm right. I'm your wonderfully brilliant wife."

He smiled then, and the worry began to melt away from his brow.

"Just stick with it," she said. "I'm sure things will start to get better soon."

But even though she gave him a cheerful look, inside her stomach twisted in knots. What if this wasn't the right career direction for him? What if he wasn't as good at the job as he needed to be? What would happen then? How would it make Dan feel? How would it affect all of them?

Shelley couldn't help feeling just a slight tremor of fear.

CHAPTER SEVEN

Fred!" Margaret hurried toward Detective Little as he strode toward his blue pickup truck, parked in his driveway. It really was quite convenient to live next door to him, although she deplored the reason she had to talk to him.

"Margaret, I'm afraid I don't have time to talk right now." He got into his truck so hastily that the top of his graying buzz cut nearly brushed the top of the door frame.

"I only wondered if you've found out anything about my missing painting."

"I'm afraid not."

"Did you investigate the people who were interested in the painting at the fair? How about the woman who looked at it in the gallery window?" Even as she said it, she realized they were rather weak leads. "Or how about the short woman who had tried to buy my painting?"

"My officers know to keep an eye out for that short woman, but to be honest, Marble Cove is full of tourists right now." He started up his engine. "I'm sorry, Margaret, but I have to go. There's been a report of smuggling a little ways down the coast."

"Oh, goodness." Margaret gave a little wave as he drove off. She supposed smuggling was somewhat more important than a stolen painting, especially since nothing else in the gallery had been touched.

She saw Diane heading back to her house after walking Rocky along the beach. Diane waved and headed toward her. "Are you okay? You look a little sad."

"I'm impressed you could see that from across the street."

"It wasn't so much your expression as the forlorn little wave you gave me." Diane did an imitation that looked like a sea lion waving a flipper.

Margaret laughed. "I guess it did look a bit like that. I was just talking to Fred Little. He hasn't found out anything yet about the painting."

"Oh, that's too bad. What about the woman who tried to buy it?"

"He said that policemen are 'keeping an eye out for her,' but he's apparently pretty busy. He left in a hurry because of something about smuggling down the coast."

"Uh-oh." Diane sighed.

"I just don't know if Fred is able to devote any time to my little theft when there are smugglers to catch."

Diane gave her a small shake. "It's not a 'little' theft. And there's nothing that says you can't do anything yourself."

Margaret gave a half smile. "Shall I go around Marble Cove investigating like a private detective?"

"Well, why not?" Diane flung her arms out. "You're as smart as any private detective. And you already have a good relationship with most of the business owners in town. If anyone can chat them up and dig for information, it's you."

"What in the world would I dig for? 'Did you happen to see a thief taking off with a large painting sometime between 5:00 PM June third and 8:00 AM on June fourth?'"

"You could do what the police may not have the time to do—check up on that short woman who tried to buy your painting. She's the most suspicious character you've got so far."

Margaret didn't know why she hadn't thought of that before, especially after Fred had made it clear the Marble Cove police department had other cases besides hers to investigate. She couldn't really expect him to get his officers out in the town, interviewing people about a woman who might or might not be a suspect.

But Margaret could.

"Diane, you're brilliant."

Diane laughed. "Not brilliant, just practical."

"Well, I could use your practical mind when I talk to people. Will you come with me? I could use your help. You might think of questions I wouldn't have thought of."

Diane hesitated, and Margaret remembered what she'd said a few days ago. "Oh no, never mind. I had forgotten about how busy you are—your interviews and things." Except she really had hoped for Diane's help. She would always walk away from a conversation and later think of questions she should have asked or things she should have said.

But then Diane smiled. "Of course I'll help you. It's only one day. Plus I didn't have any other blog interviews or guest posts to write today, so I can work on my chapters tonight."

"Oh, thank you, I'm so glad. I really do need your help."

"Let me put Rocky inside, and then we can head downtown."

"Great."

A few minutes later, Margaret and Diane were strolling down Main Street.

"Where should we start?" Margaret asked. "Maybe we should check out the local hotels. But what if she's renting a cottage? So maybe the Realtor?"

"How about we first talk to the store managers of the places near the gallery? If that woman stopped at your gallery, there's a good chance she stopped at the stores nearby. Then we can head to the real estate office on the next street."

They stopped at the Cove, next door to the Shearwater Gallery. Brenna McTavish glanced up as they entered and smiled. "Heya, ladies. If you're looking for blueberrah muffins, we're all out already." Her heavy Maine accent was perfectly suited to the worn pine floors, wood-paneled walls, and dim interior of the coffee shop, which had once been a fisherman's pub. Margaret immediately smelled a fresh pot brewing in the machine.

"Actually, if you have a minute, could we ask you something?" Margaret breathed deep of the rich coffee aroma. "And I'll also take a cup of coffee to go. Want one?" she asked Diane.

"*Mmm*, you bet."

Brenna grinned. "If ya wait a couple minutes, the pot'll be done."

"That's what we're hoping for."

Brenna finished serving a ceramic mug of coffee and one of Shelley's Danishes to a customer, then turned to Margaret and Diane. "What did ya need to ask me about?"

"You heard about the break-in?" Margaret asked.

Brenna winced. "Yeah, I'm so sorry about it, Margaret."

"You might be able to help the police. There was a woman who came and wanted to buy the painting a couple weeks ago. She was very tiny, almost as small as a child, with straight brown hair with bangs."

"Hey, did she dress kind of…starchy, like?" Brenna asked.

"Yes, that's her." Margaret's heart beat faster.

"She came in here asking for tea. I showed her our tea bags and she stuck her nose in the air and walked out."

"Have you seen her since then? Or maybe around town?"

Brenna shook her head. "I only remember her coming in that one time and I haven't seen her around town."

"Oh." Maybe the small woman had only been a visitor to town that one day.

"Which painting got stolen?" Brenna asked.

"It was the painting that was in Margaret's gallery window."

"Oh, was it that one with the strange-looking starfish? I didn't even realize that was yours, Margaret."

Margaret found that she was disturbed by the fact Brenna hadn't really thought the painting was hers. "It's a slightly different style for me."

Brenna gave a small shrug. "I didn't like it as much as your other stuff. My mom really likes the lighthouse print I got for her for Christmas."

Another customer came up to the counter, and Diane said, "Sorry to keep you, Brenna."

"Let me just get your coffees." She hastened back with their cups, and they paid and left the Cove.

"Well, that wasn't very helpful," Margaret said.

Diane laughed. "This isn't like television. We're not going to walk into a store and have the staff give us a name and address."

They continued to the store next door to the Cove, which was the Mercantile, but the young teen manning the counter couldn't give them any information. They met with the same dead end at the shoe shop next to the Mercantile, and on the other side of the shoe shop, they stopped at Captain Calhoun's Crab and Lobster House.

Margaret grasped the handle and pulled to open the door, but it wouldn't budge. "I completely forgot the time!" she laughed. "Captain Calhoun's probably doesn't open until closer to lunchtime."

"Let's go to some of the other stores, and we can stop back here when they open."

But they ended up speaking to merchants all morning. They went to the Crow's Nest and the Hermit Crab, all with no luck. They even stopped off to try to talk to the teenagers working at the Tastee Freeze, but the teens looked at them as if they were deranged. They didn't make it back to Captain Calhoun's until almost one o'clock. "Let's get something to eat while we're here," Margaret said.

They pushed open the heavy wooden door and immediately smelled the pleasantly sharp scent of seafood, mixed with a little wood smoke from the old fireplace in the corner, even though it was unlit at this time of year. They were greeted by Kirsten Morgan, the college-aged daughter of Pamela Morgan, who was in Margaret's Bible study group.

"Hi, Mrs. Hoskins." The tall, thin young woman had her mother's straight blonde hair, worn in a ponytail, and sunny smile. "Two for lunch?"

"Yes, please, Kirsten."

She sat them in a corner booth that was open since the heaviest lunchtime rush was starting to pass. They each ordered crab cakes and iced tea.

"I can't understand how a woman so unusually short wouldn't be noticed by those students working at Tastee Freeze," Margaret grumbled.

"You can't really blame them. They're only teens and college students who are working over the summer months, and they serve so many tourists that the faces probably all blur together."

Kirsten brought their iced teas and promised their crab cakes soon, then whirled away to wait on another table.

"I wish more people working in the Marble Cove downtown stores had seen that woman. It seems we didn't find anything useful about her," Margaret said.

"We sort of did." Diane stirred her iced tea with her straw. "She didn't spend a lot of money on eating out. I thought we'd got a hit when the grocery store checker remembered her. I was so disappointed when she'd paid cash for her toothpaste."

"Well, since you're familiar to Kirsten, you can ask her if she remembers the woman."

Margaret saw Kirsten bustling around, serving tables. "Let's wait until after our lunch. I don't want to interrupt her when she's too busy."

The crab cakes were excellent, as usual, and by the time they finished, the restaurant had emptied to about half the people who had been there when they arrived, and Kirsten looked a little less harried. Margaret waved the young woman over to their table.

"Can I get you something else, Mrs. Hoskins?"

"Kirsten, we're wondering if maybe you could help us."

"Me?" Kirsten's blue eyes widened.

"Well, you or anyone else who's been working here this summer," Diane said.

"I'm only part time," Kirsten said. "I've been working for about six weeks—since I came home for the summer."

"How do you like school?" Margaret asked. "What are you majoring in?"

"Psychology." Kirsten grinned. "I'm driving my brother nuts because I'm doing all my homework on him, asking him weird questions."

Diane and Margaret laughed.

"So what did you need to know?" Kirsten asked.

"We want to know about two women who showed interest in the stolen painting," Diane said. "We're not accusing them of anything, but we'd like to talk to them."

"One was a very short woman who saw the painting a couple weeks ago. She was about this high." Margaret held her hand up to less than five feet from the ground.

"Oh, I remember her. She had her hair in this short bob cut, right? And glasses?"

Margaret nodded quickly. Would Kirsten give them some useful information?

"She came in a couple weeks ago on my shift," Kirsten said. "I remember her because she looked a little unusual. But then she complained about the lobster roll, said it had too much sauce." Kirsten shrugged. "I got the manager for her, and he comped her meal, so she didn't give me any tip."

Diane frowned but didn't say anything.

"The thing is, she didn't raise her voice or anything," Kirsten said. "She was kind of solemn about it all. After she ate almost all of the lobster roll, she called me over and said it had too much sauce, like she was discussing the weather. Most people who don't like their food get kind of upset."

"How about when she talked to the manager?" Diane asked.

Kirsten shook her head. "Didn't raise her voice then, either. By far the most polite complaint I've ever seen."

Margaret remembered the woman in her gallery, with her somber expression despite the rather aggressively stated low-ball offer to buy *Sea Breeze*.

"You didn't get her name, by any chance?" Diane asked.

"No..." Kirsten suddenly squinted at the cash register behind the front desk. "But she did fill out a feedback form—the manager asked her to do it when he comped her meal. Maybe she put her information down."

Margaret and Diane abruptly looked at each other. Diane's eyes glowed.

Kirsten went to the front desk and rummaged below it, finally coming up with a small shoebox with perhaps a couple dozen small white cards. Kirsten brought the box over to their table and pulled out the first one. "Here it is. We haven't had a complaint in a few months so it was right up front." She handed it to Margaret.

The woman had written in spidery handwriting exactly what Kirsten had said, that the lobster roll had too much sauce. However, she'd checked "Excellent" for the wait staff, which surprised Margaret since the woman hadn't tipped Kirsten.

And at the bottom was the name Agnes Dillwater.

"Bingo!" Margaret showed the card to Diane, who read the card and squeezed her friend's arm.

Agnes had also given a telephone number, which had a Marble Cove area code. Diane immediately punched it into her cell phone and called.

After a few seconds, Diane's eyebrows rose. "Oh, hello, Victoria. It's Diane Spencer."

Victoria? Margaret mouthed to Diane.

"Do you mind if I come over right now? I have something to ask you about a guest. Thanks." She disconnected the call and told Margaret, "That was Victoria Manchester, who owns the Landmark Inn."

"Is that where Agnes was staying?"

"I think so, if she gave the Landmark's phone number on this card." Diane pointed to the feedback card still in Margaret's hand.

Margaret turned and gave it back to Kirsten, who was watching them with a curious expression. "Thank you so much, Kirsten. We think we've found our mystery woman." She also gave Kirsten some cash for their lunch, brushing away Diane's attempts to dig into her purse to help pay.

"No problem, Mrs. Hoskins." Kirsten headed back to the front desk to return the box and take care of their bill.

Diane and Margaret headed out from Captain Calhoun's. "I'll drive," Diane said.

"Do you still keep in touch with Victoria after helping her out on Valentine's Day?"

"Once in a while I'll see her in town and chat, or I'll go out to lunch at the Landmark Inn. She always gives me a discount." Diane winked.

"I'm not sure she's able to give out information about her guests."

"She could certainly chat about people in town, though, especially with a couple friends."

They were walking down the sidewalk along Main Street when Margaret heard her name called. She turned to see the person least likely to speak to her—Harriet Malcolm, an art critic who had a column in the local paper.

As when she'd attended Margaret's gallery opening, Harriet was dressed in a rather smart suit, this one a rich mahogany, but the effect was again completely spoiled by her white sneakers. Harriet's sharp nose looked like she'd inhaled a whiff of strong vinegar.

At first Margaret thought she must have heard wrong, because no way would Harriet want to speak to her. In her newspaper column, she'd castigated Margaret's paintings as "typical Maine fare" that "lacks seriousness and depth." Margaret's steady sales belied the critic's lukewarm review, but the words still stung.

Margaret was about to turn away when Harriet again said, "Mrs. Hoskins."

Why would Harriet want to speak to her? "Ms. Malcolm," Margaret said coolly. She could sense Diane stiffen next to her as she also recognized the woman.

"I heard about the theft of your painting." Harriet's voice sounded strangled, almost as if she couldn't believe someone would steal it.

Margaret didn't reply at first, but when it was obvious Harriet wasn't going to express any kind of sentiment about it, she said, "The police are looking for it."

"Do they know why it was stolen?"

"I'm afraid not."

"Art theft is so rare in Marble Cove," Harriet said.

Margaret gave her a neutral look. She guessed that Harriet was wondering why Margaret's unoriginal little painting was taken as opposed to other pieces of art on display in galleries up and down the coast.

"The thief obviously saw that Margaret's painting was special," Diane said in a freezing voice.

And then Harriet completely shocked Margaret by saying, "Yes, that was a good painting of yours."

Margaret was sure her mouth was hanging open, but she couldn't close it.

"It was different from your usual style," Harriet went on. "It showed a little more imagination."

It was a rather backhanded compliment, but Margaret was surprised that opinionated Harriet had ventured to say *anything* positive about her work.

"Perhaps that's why it won first place in the abstract category at the Port Clyde Art Fair last week." Diane's tone was sweeter than Shelley's sugar cookies.

Harriet's penciled eyebrows rose toward her hairline. "Did it?" she asked faintly.

"We're especially worried about the theft because someone had already bought it," Diane continued. "The buyer will be very upset that someone *else* wanted it so much that they'd steal it."

Margaret nearly choked while trying to hide her laughter as her friend gave Harriet a bright smile that showed a lot of teeth.

"Well, we won't keep you. We need to get going. Good-bye!" Diane pulled Margaret away and they continued down the sidewalk.

Margaret gave in to her laughter as they turned onto Newport Avenue. "Diane, you scamp."

"I knew you weren't going to say anything about the painting, so I did. It felt good to throw that award at her when she'd been so rude in her review of your gallery."

"She actually did say some positive things about the painting, you know."

"In a rather lukewarm fashion. She said it almost grudgingly."

"It's interesting that she said it about this painting, though. It was different from my normal style."

"It was obvious from what Brenna said that there are people who like your old style too."

"Brenna wasn't as enthusiastic about that new style, was she? Neither were Rita and Pamela when they came to see me at the gallery the other day."

"Which just goes to show you that your old style is wildly popular even without Harriet Malcolm's dubious stamp of approval."

"The problem is that I'd been planning to meld my old style with the more abstract style I used in *Sea Breeze*."

Diane hesitated, then said, "You should paint what makes you happy. But speaking practically, you should also paint things that sell, like the seascapes and lighthouse paintings. The question is, what makes you happy?"

Margaret still loved doing seascapes, but she also loved her new style and exploring where that took her. After winning the award at the art fair, she had thought melding the two styles was the answer, but now she wasn't so sure.

Really, what would make her happy?

CHAPTER EIGHT

Diane hurried inside to grab her purse and car keys so she could drive them to the Landmark Inn. She caught sight of her laptop where she'd left it on the coffee table in the living room, and felt an uncomfortable squeezing sensation around her midsection. She really should work on those first three chapters.

At the same time, Margaret had really been thrown for a loop by this theft, understandably so. Going with her to try to discover information about these two women seemed to help ease her worry. It was something Margaret was able to *do* about the situation, as opposed to sitting at home or trying to work at the gallery.

Ultimately, Margaret was more important right now. Diane knew she could write fast and she could work more on her book tonight.

She stifled a yawn. Or maybe she'd go to bed early and work on her book tomorrow. She certainly felt tired today.

She went out to the car and saw Margaret already there, gazing off toward the beach. The stress lines on her face only confirmed Diane's decision to spend this time with Margaret.

Her expression lightened when she caught sight of Diane. "Allan has been filling in for me today, but I do need to get back in an hour or so. He has some orders to finish up today."

They drove out to the Landmark Inn, a stately old building that, according to everyone in town, had been elegance itself back in the day. It had fallen into disrepair, but then Victoria Manchester had inherited it and fixed it up, with Beverly's help, and brought it back to its former glory.

It certainly looked glorious now, with the sun shining off the picture windows that overlooked the water. Trees shaded the walkway up to the front double doors, which opened into a spacious front foyer lined with antique velvet-cushioned chairs against the wainscoted walls.

Victoria stood behind a small square podium-style desk that sat discreetly beside the wide staircase leading to the guest rooms on the second floor. She was dressed with her usual elegance in a cream-colored suit and low pumps, her liquid gold hair pulled back in a chignon. She smiled when she caught sight of Diane.

"Welcome." She came forward and gave Diane a brief hug. "I haven't seen you in a while."

"I've been terribly busy, but I've been meaning to make a dinner reservation as soon as my work schedule eases up."

"It was nice to see you and that handsome veterinarian here a few weeks ago." Victoria winked a smoky eyelid. "I hope you'll come back for another romantic dinner soon. I'll always give a fifty percent discount to my favorite kitchen helpers."

Diane smiled ruefully, remembering the Valentine's Day when she, Leo, Beverly, and Jeff had helped in the kitchen to prevent the Landmark's opening night from becoming a complete disaster.

"I don't think I've introduced my friend Margaret to you, Victoria."

Victoria gave Margaret a hug too. "I've heard all about you from Beverly. We always have a nice chat over tea when she comes out here on a consultation for me."

"Have things been going well?" Diane glanced through the open doorway to the dining room beyond. There were a few tables occupied by inn guests lingering over lunch but the rest of the room was already prepped for the dinner crowd that would come in a little less than two hours. Antique linens covered the tables, which gleamed with silverware and hurricane lamps that held tiny votive candles. Fresh flowers also sat in tiny glass vases, and for the summer, huge vases of flowers stood in the elaborately carved fireplace.

"Beverly has been a miracle worker." Victoria gestured toward the sitting room opposite the dining room, which was filled with beautiful antique furniture that had been cleverly restored, and up toward the crystal and brass chandelier that tinkled softly. "The rooms are at one hundred percent capacity right now, and even for the autumn months, I've got enough reservations that I'll be at seventy-five percent.

And the dining room is completely filled six out of seven nights this summer."

"That's wonderful."

"Come on into the dining room and we can have tea and scones." Victoria led the way and sat them at a table near the fireplace. Diane could smell the scent of the freesias in the vase nearest her.

Victoria signaled to a waitress, and Diane was pleased to see it was Suzette, who'd been working at the Landmark ever since that first Valentine's Day dinner. "Hello, Suzette. It's nice to see you."

The young woman dimpled. "Hi there, Mrs. Spencer."

"Suzette, could you please get us tea and scones?" Victoria asked.

"Sure thing." With a swirl of her black skirt, she headed toward the door into the kitchen.

Victoria sat back in the plush velvet dining room chair and rested her hands on the scrolled arms. "On the phone you mentioned you wanted to ask me something?"

"Yes. Did you hear about Margaret's painting being stolen from the window of her gallery?"

"Yes, that was horrible." Victoria leaned toward Margaret. "Have the police caught the thief yet?"

"No, and right now they're busy with something to do with smuggling down the coast."

Victoria's lips thinned. "Forget smugglers! They should deal with the crime right here in town."

"We thought we'd give them a hand," Diane said.

"A couple weeks ago, a woman came to the gallery and wanted to buy the painting," Margaret said. "I couldn't sell it to her because it was supposed to be displayed at an art fair, and she left. I never got her name, but I found out she left a feedback card at Captain Calhoun's, and she put the Landmark's telephone number down."

"What was her name?" Victoria asked.

"Agnes Dillwater."

"Why, she did stay here."

"Did? So she's gone now?" Diane asked.

"She left at least two weeks ago. I could go check."

"Are you allowed to do that?" Diane asked delicately.

But Victoria just waved her hand. "She's gone, and she might be a potential thief." Victoria went back out to the front foyer to check on the computer set up on the small podium there, then came back to the table and sat back down. "Yes, she checked out two weeks ago, on May twenty-third."

"Oh. She left Marble Cove a day or two after she spoke to me at the gallery." Margaret's shoulders sagged.

"Here you go." Suzette arrived with blackberry scones and a pot of tea. She poured cups for all of them and then left to wait on one of the other tables in the dining room.

When she was gone, Victoria leaned closer to Diane and Margaret. "I was rather glad Agnes finally left. She complained about everything, but not in an angry or whiny way. She just very coldly said that her dinner was too salty— after eating most of it—or that her breakfast was too oily, after leaving only a sliver of egg. I must have given her half her meals free."

Margaret gaped at her. "Why, she did that at Captain Calhoun's too."

"Sounds like a pattern for her," Diane said. "Maybe she didn't have much money."

"She had plenty," Victoria said. "She reserved the most expensive room and then tried complaining about it, but I refused to give her any rate discount. If she really didn't have the money, I don't think she'd have risked being forced to pay the full price."

"She offered to buy the painting for a very low price," Margaret said. "I wonder if she was just saying that to see if I'd sell it to her."

"Like how she complained about her food. Maybe she was just trying to see how far she could take it," Diane said. "I knew a couple coworkers who were like that. They were very assertive, always trying to see how much they could push people to give them free things."

"Well, I never." Victoria looked sourly at her half-eaten scone. "I wish I hadn't given her any freebies."

"Even though she left two weeks ago, is it possible she could have come back?" Diane asked.

"I don't think so," Victoria said. "Before I figured out her game, I had given her a coupon for thirty percent off any future meal here at the inn, and she never used it during her stay. I think if she did come back into town, she'd definitely use it."

"I think you're right," Diane said.

"So...she's probably not a person of interest?" Margaret laughed. "Now I sound like a police officer."

But Diane saw Margaret's tiny sigh and knew that her friend had hoped they'd found the woman who might have stolen the painting. "Thanks for the tea and scones, Victoria."

"And for the information," Margaret said with a last sip.

"Anytime. I hope you recover your painting."

Diane and Margaret went back to Diane's car. "Margaret, we're not giving up just yet."

"We're not?"

Diane shook her head. "No. We'll find out who took your painting. Don't lose hope."

"You're right. I should pray more about it. Surely God knows how important this painting is to me."

"I'm sure He does."

After Margaret had walked back to her house, Diane entered her cottage and grabbed Rocky's leash. They went for a quick walk, then she put some soup on the stove to heat for supper while she checked her e-mail.

She was dismayed to find four messages that had to do with the blog tour. She appreciated the kind words the bloggers had about her book, but the thought of the two interviews and two guest blog posts she had to write made her stomach churn with stress. She had so much to do. Maybe she shouldn't have gone with Margaret today...

Tomorrow she really had to buckle down and work on her three chapters.

CHAPTER NINE

As Beverly drove up the sweep of driveway to her house in Augusta, the beauty of it took her breath away, as it always did. Cream-colored walls in dramatic lines, windows in unusual shapes and peeking out from places that enhanced the design of the architecture.

Will had planned it that way. This was his masterpiece. Should she really sell it?

She had to. What choice did she have? Why was she waffling about this?

Beverly unlocked the front door, which was a large red circle with a slightly Asian motif around the outside edges. It was there to enhance the drama of the house design, and it made a statement without standing out like a sore thumb, but Beverly had always felt a little strange walking through it.

Today, however, she remembered the first time Will had showed her the finished house, and he'd playfully picked her up and carried her through this door. She'd run her fingers along the carved Asian designs on the scarlet wood and felt like she was being carried into a fairyland out of *A Midsummer Night's Dream*.

Beverly ran her hand over the wood again now and acutely missed the lively, excited expression on Will's face as he unveiled his creation to her.

The house seemed more welcoming to her now than it had before. She'd sometimes entered and felt cold because the house had been so meticulously designed and decorated for effect and not for homeyness. Once the effect wore off, all that was left was the chill of fashionable pretension.

She decided to go room by room and remove her things. She'd already taken most of her small kitchen appliances with her to Marble Cove when she first moved into Father's house, so she started there.

The buyers hadn't wanted anything except furniture, the few art pieces that remained, and the major appliances like the refrigerator, stove, and washer and dryer set. But as Beverly fingered the silverware and china, both modern and specifically chosen to match the house, it seemed a shame to her to have to take these. Even though her father's silverware was old and mismatched, it fitted the tidy Victorian house they lived in. The chinaware they used had been her mother's set.

These... She picked up a plate, irregular in shape and of a strange color that managed to be both peach and sage at the same time, but somehow pleasing to the eye in its uniqueness. She couldn't see her father ever using these, or the silverware with the modern sculpted handles.

She supposed she could sell these on eBay and get a good price for them, because she never knew—she might need every dollar in the coming months as she built her business.

She packed away the silverware and china in a box that she labeled "sell" and continued throughout the kitchen.

She found some party trays and serving utensils that she only used for large parties where she needed to use a buffet to feed everyone. They'd thrown a Christmas party each year for Will's prestigious clients and she'd bought the serving items for those occasions.

But what use did she have for them now? She put them in the "sell" box. She might even be able to sell these things directly to some of her own clients.

Beverly was dismayed to find that there weren't many things she could simply donate to a thrift store or throw away. Will had always insisted on the best quality in whatever he bought, so they hadn't bought many disposable items.

She happened upon a small silver box in a kitchen drawer and realized she'd forgotten it was there. It had been a wedding gift, a simple little jewelry box that Beverly hadn't really needed since she had a larger jewelry box that Will had bought for all the expensive, flashy pieces he'd given to her. But whenever she'd washed dishes, she never had a place to put her rings, watch, and any bracelets she might have been wearing, so she'd tucked the box in this drawer for her to drop her jewelry into while cooking or washing.

She pulled it out now and lifted the heavy, sculpted lid. Inside, nestled against the velvet lining, sapphires winked up at her, almost invisible against the dark cloth.

She lifted out the bracelet. She remembered Will giving this to her as an engagement gift. She remembered the unusually vulnerable expression as he clasped it around her wrist. The sapphires glimmered alongside the smaller diamonds in the vintage gold setting, but their beauty ran deeper, in the images conjured up in her mind.

She sighed and dropped the bracelet back in the silver box, then packed it in the "keep" box. If she turned maudlin over every item she came across, she'd never get the house emptied before the closing date.

She worked steadily, pausing only to eat the turkey, lettuce, and tomato sandwich she'd made before heading to Augusta this morning. By the time the clock showed four o'clock, her back hurt and she was amazed at the amount of dust that her cleaning had kicked up.

Beverly had already arranged with Mrs. Peabody to cook and serve dinner for her father, so Beverly didn't need to be back in Marble Cove by any particular time, but she felt the urge to escape these walls with their neutral and earth-tone colors and modern finish. She longed for surroundings that were old-fashioned, casual, lived-in. Like her father's house. How amazing that only a few months living there had changed her view of what was comfortable for her.

She packed up the car with the boxes and was about to head back to Marble Cove when she wondered if perhaps Edward Maker would want to have dinner with her. The idea appealed to her—she hadn't seen him in a while. She called him on her cell phone.

"Hello?" His voice sounded gravelly, reminding her that, despite his youthful vigor, he was even older than her father.

"Hi, Mr. Maker. This is Beverly Wheeland-Parker."

"Beverly, hello there." His voice lightened, and it was obvious he was pleased to hear from her.

"I'm in Augusta right now and wondered if I could take you out to dinner."

"You don't need to get back to take care of your father?"

"No, tonight Mrs. Peabody's making one of his favorites, chicken pot pie."

"Why are you in Augusta?"

"I'll tell you over dinner."

"I'd like me a little chicken pot pie too." His wistful tone made him sound years younger.

She laughed. "How about Kara's Kitchen on First Street? I can pick you up in a few minutes."

She swung by his two-story bungalow home, admiring the variety of flowers in his garden. He smacked his lips as he got into her car, his full salt-and-pepper hair brushing the top of the door frame. "I can taste that chicken pot pie already."

Beverly drove to the small hole-in-the-wall diner, which boasted a menu rich in comfort food and an atmosphere saturated with good cheer and the smell of cooking oil. Since it was still a little early for dinner, they managed to find a small table and ordered—chicken pot pie for Mr. Maker, and lobster mac-and-cheese for Beverly.

He made a face as the waitress bustled away. "Lobster mac-n-cheese? Separately, fine. But together?"

"My mother made it for me a lot while I was growing up. She and I loved it. My father didn't like it, so there was always plenty for me." She grinned.

Mr. Maker waved a hand gnarled and tanned from his long hours in his garden. "You young people. Jeff still likes to eat lobster rolls with ketchup. I didn't raise his mother that way, that's for sure."

Now it was her turn to make a face. "Ketchup in lobster rolls?"

"I think he did it just to see how disgusted I'd be. He was a rascal that way."

"He was a rascal when he was younger? He doesn't seem like he was the wild type." Beverly deliberately pushed aside the insidious voice in her head that questioned why she was so interested in Jeff's childhood.

"Well, you have to understand, his mother was my only child, and he was her only child. The boy was spoiled six ways to Sunday. He and I liked to tease each other a lot." His intense blue eyes crinkled as he remembered.

Their meal came, and Beverly tucked into the creamy macaroni and cheese tempered by buttery lobster pieces. Mr. Maker made another good-natured face at her and broke the flakey crust on his chicken pot pie with his fork.

"Was Jeff always into photography, even as a boy?" She tried to sound casual as she asked the question, but as soon as the words came out of her mouth, she realized how nosy she sounded, and how obvious it was that she wanted to know more about Jeff's childhood.

Mr. Maker noticed too, if the dimple in his cheek was any indication. "Well, now, there wasn't much Jeff *wasn't* into when he was young. He wanted to be an astronaut one day, and a race car driver the next, and a doctor the day after that, and by next Tuesday he had decided to be a travel writer in China."

"Don't all boys want to be astronauts and race car drivers?"

"When they're five. Not when they're twenty-five."

Beverly paused in taking a bite of mac-and-cheese. "He wanted to be a race car driver when he was twenty-five?"

"Actually, probably more like twenty-three." Mr. Maker winked at her.

"Now you're pulling my leg."

"No, he really did have a year where he wasn't sure what he wanted to do. He'd just dropped out of medical school—"

"Jeff went to medical school?" The question burst out of her before she could rein in her astonishment. It seemed so unlike his personality that the news surprised her.

"For a year. He figured out pretty quick that it wasn't what he wanted to do."

"For all you're telling me about what a rascal he was, he was apparently a rascal with very good grades."

"He had a grandmother who'd nag him to death if he slacked off on his schoolwork. He was also very smart," Mr. Maker added in a slightly more serious tone. "He could have done anything. But in the end, he decided to follow his heart and he went back to school for photography. He also interned at the local paper and worked part-time at a photography studio downtown. When he goes after something, he likes to go after it with gusto."

His words hit a nerve. Jeff did like to go after things with fervor. He'd been earnest in wanting to see more of

Beverly since they'd met again several months ago, and she constantly struggled with how close to get to him. She didn't realize that she'd grown silent until Mr. Maker said, "You never told me why you were in Augusta."

"Oh." Somehow, talking about the house was like trying to talk with a mouthful of saltwater taffy. "I'm selling my house." She knew she ought to say more, explain more, but she had a hard time figuring out what to say.

He mistook her silence for overwhelming emotion, and reached across the table to touch her hand. "It's hard, is it?"

She wanted to say "not really," but her mouth still wasn't working. Why couldn't she explain how she felt about selling the house? What exactly did she feel about it?

Thankfully, Mr. Maker changed the subject. "How's your father doing?"

She had no problem answering him when the topic wasn't the house. "He's doing well. Reading as much as ever and keeping me on my toes," she replied.

Mr. Maker chuckled. "Sounds like the Harold Wheeland I know. Please tell him I asked about him."

The rest of dinner was pleasant, and Beverly drove Mr. Maker back to his home. The last of the sunlight turned the sage green paint almost a burnt orange color.

"Come on in for dessert." Mr. Maker was already halfway out of her car. "I have a blackberry cobbler that my neighbor's wife made from my blackberries."

Beverly had been about to head home, but he seemed to expect her to come inside. And a part of her was reluctant to leave him. Their conversation had been...interesting. Without looking too deeply into it, she got out of the car and followed him up the porch steps into the house.

He started the coffee—decaf, at her request—and dished up the blackberry cobbler. They'd just sat down in his living room when his phone rang.

Beverly took a few bites of the cobbler as he answered the phone, but she froze when she heard Jeff's name.

"Oh, nothing much. I had dinner with Beverly." The bright blue gaze Mr. Maker turned to Beverly as he said this made her look away in embarrassment. She could imagine Jeff's slow smile as he heard she'd been visiting his grandfather, and the vision warmed her insides even though she felt faintly guilty to have been pumping Mr. Maker for information about Jeff.

"She took me to Kara's Kitchen," Mr. Maker said in the phone. "Why haven't you ever taken me there, huh? I would have liked it better than that sushi place you dragged me to before."

Beverly couldn't help grinning at the teasing note in Mr. Maker's voice.

"Oh, this and that," Mr. Maker said, and Beverly guessed Jeff asked what they'd been talking about.

"Sure," Mr. Maker said. He held the phone out to Beverly. "Jeff wants to say hi."

Her fingers trembled a little as she took the phone from him. "Hi," she said awkwardly.

"Hi, Beverly." The way he said her name told her he was pleased she was there. "I hope my grandfather hasn't been talking your ear off."

"Of course he has." She grinned as she glanced at Mr. Maker.

Jeff laughed. "Thanks for taking him out to dinner. You're in Augusta to pack up your house?"

"Yes."

His voice softened. "How's that going?"

"Okay..." She remembered the sadness as she'd packed up things that reminded her of her marriage, but also of her need to escape the sterile, modern feel of Will's house. "I feel conflicted. Does that make sense?"

He laughed. "Perfectly. I can call you later to talk about it if you want."

"I think...I think I'd like that."

They said good-bye, and after chatting with Mr. Maker for a few minutes longer, she soon took her leave.

She was amused at the things she'd learned about Jeff that night and determined that when next they spent time together, she'd ask Jeff himself about his past. After all, although they were taking things slowly, he had said he wanted her to be honest with him, even about her feelings in regard to the sale of Will's house. Why would she be afraid to ask him about his past? What was she afraid of?

Herself, she realized. Because she was caring for Jeff more, talking to him more, wanting to know more about him. And in packing up Will's house, she was beginning to realize that moving on was a complicated process.

CHAPTER TEN

On Friday, Margaret intended to hold down the gallery all day since Allan had taken over for her yesterday when she and Diane had traipsed all over Marble Cove in their vain search for the elusive Agnes Dillwater.

The morning and early afternoon were slow, but then a couple entered the gallery. They looked like they were simply strolling along Main Street, and their eyes passed casually over the paintings on the wall.

Margaret approached them with a smile. "Welcome to Shearwater Gallery. Have a look around, and if you have any questions, just let me know."

"Hey, look at this." The young man's awed voice drew the other three to a table in the corner that Allan had just completed a few days ago, with different colored wood inlaid in the edges.

"That's made by my husband," Margaret said. "He made all the wooden furniture in the gallery, and the display stands and frames."

"I'd love something like this on a larger scale." The young woman drew her hand along the edges of the inlaid table. "Does he do larger projects?"

"Yes, he'll do larger orders. When did you want it done by?"

"How long would it take him to do an eight-foot table?"

Margaret bit her lip. "I'm actually not sure. I can give him a call, if you'd like."

"Also, would he be able to do dining room chairs?"

"I'll ask him." Margaret had moved to the phone to dial the house when she saw Allan walking up to the gallery. "Actually, there he is."

Margaret held the door open for him as he maneuvered a chair inside. "These people have some questions about a larger order."

"Great." He turned to smile at them. "Give me a second to set this up."

"I can do that for you," Margaret said.

"Actually, it's nearly time to pick up Adelaide from the community center. Did you want to do that for me and I'll stay here?"

"Sure." She knew it would give him a chance to answer any questions the couple might have about their order. She hoped they'd go through with it. She knew many people had questions about a custom order, but then never actually placed one. However, the young woman and her husband seemed fairly serious. They were dressed casually, but Margaret saw that their clothes were designer, and the young man had a very expensive watch, so they could probably afford the custom table and chairs.

Margaret headed to the community center to pick up Adelaide. Usually her daughter had an excited expression on her face as soon as she saw Margaret, and was full of stories about what she'd done that day.

But today, she saw Margaret and seemed almost relieved. She left the table where she'd been working on some sort of papier-mâché project and immediately went to wash her hands. She smiled at Margaret as she said, "Hi, Mom. I'm ready to go."

And on the way home, when Margaret asked her how her day had been, Adelaide gave a small shrug and said, "It was okay."

Her noncommittal answer made Margaret look sharply at her. "Did anything bad happen?"

"No, nothing bad happened."

And yet Adelaide didn't seem to have enjoyed her time at the community center today. Why not?

Adelaide immediately went to her cats in the living room when they got home. Margaret was debating whether she should talk more to her daughter when she got a call on her cell phone. She was surprised to see it was Penny Tyler, the director of the special needs program at the community center.

"Hi, Penny."

"Margaret, I'm sorry I didn't speak to you when you came to pick Adelaide up, but I didn't want to talk to you in front of her."

"Oh?" The tension in Penny's voice sent Margaret's senses on alert.

"Would you and Allan be able to meet with me tomorrow sometime? Without Adelaide."

She could ask Shelley if she'd allow Adelaide to help her with the kids tomorrow. "Sure. Let me get back to you on the time."

"Anytime in the afternoon is fine."

Margaret said good-bye and stood a moment, staring at the phone in her hand. What would Penny need to speak to them about? They had just recently spoken about the quality-of-life skills classes Adelaide was taking and had moved her into a more advanced money and budgeting course that she seemed to be enjoying. But maybe something else was going on there. Had there been some sort of incident at the community center that involved Adelaide? Is that why she'd seemed so unenthusiastic about her time there today, and why Allan had mentioned that she seemed a bit down over the past week?

She knew that if it had been serious, Penny would have told her right away over the phone, but it didn't prevent Margaret from feeling a flutter of worry in her stomach.

Shelley heard Margaret's voice at the front door as she washed green beans at the sink. "In the kitchen, Margaret!" She cast a quick eye out the kitchen window where Aiden was still playing with Prize and Emma in the green grass of the backyard. He had a smear of dirt across his cheek that he'd acquired sometime in the past five minutes since she'd looked outside, and Emma had a correspondingly muddy hand.

"Hi, Shelley." Margaret looked a little worried, and Shelley immediately left the sink.

"What's wrong?"

Margaret blinked. "How could you tell?"

Shelley shrugged. "You just looked a little tense. Is there something I can do for you?"

"I got a call from Penny Tyler from the community center." Margaret sighed. "She wants to meet with me and Allan tomorrow afternoon."

"What does she want to talk about?"

"That's what's worrying me. I really don't know. Adelaide has been rather quiet after coming home from her classes for the past week or so. Allan noticed it first, then I saw it today. I'm really worried that something might have happened."

"I don't know if you really want to borrow trouble. And I can't believe I'm the one telling you this, because it's Diane's line." Shelley smiled, and Margaret gave a small smile in reply. "But really, you don't know what Penny wants to talk to you about, so try not to worry too much until you speak to her. It'll just give you indigestion."

Margaret laughed as she touched her stomach. "True. I don't even realize I'm worrying, sometimes. So could Adelaide come over tomorrow afternoon?"

"Of course. But what about the gallery?"

Margaret's mouth dropped open. "I didn't even think of that."

"Maybe Diane or Beverly can hold down the gallery for you for an hour or two."

"That's a good idea. I'll ask Beverly, because I know Diane's been busy lately. Besides, she spent all day with me yesterday."

"I don't think Beverly's home yet."

"Where did she go?"

"I saw her this morning on her way out. She's in Augusta packing up her things from her house. I was going to talk to her too, but her car still isn't in the driveway, so I think she's not back yet."

"What did you need to talk to her about?"

Shelley tried to put on a cheerful face, but she found her voice wavering as she said, "Oh, I got a couple e-mails today from customers."

"What kinds of e-mails?"

"Oh, Margaret." Shelley swallowed the unexpected lump in her throat. "I sent two pound cakes to two different people yesterday, and they both e-mailed me today to say that they arrived in terrible condition."

"What did they mean? Were they wet or something?"

"No, they were in pieces. They both sent me pictures." The memory of them made Shelley's stomach cramp with worry the way she'd just described to Margaret. One cake had split into three pieces, and it looked like crumbs had exploded all over the inside of the padded box. The other cake had been better, but it had still had a large dent in one corner.

"To two different customers?"

"In two different parts of the country too. I had to refund their purchases and the postage costs, which were expensive since they had to be sent overnight shipping."

"Oh, Shelley." Margaret laid a hand on Shelley's arm. "How distressing. Do you know why the cakes didn't arrive intact?"

"Well..." Shelley wrung her hands. "Postage prices increased earlier this year, but I forgot to change my shipping and handling prices on the Web site. Then Beverly helped me do an analysis of my financing, and she showed me that I was losing money on my Internet orders because I wasn't charging enough for postage and handling. People already have to pay a lot because the pastries have to be mailed overnight mail. In fact, the customers who bought the cakes paid almost as much for postage as for the cake. So I thought I'd keep my postage and handling prices the same, but instead buy cheaper padded boxes to make up for it."

"Ah." Margaret nodded. "So it looks like the cheaper packaging isn't strong enough to keep the cakes from being damaged in transit. There's no way you could have known that in advance."

"I know, but I feel horrible for these customers, and I'm sure they'll never order from me again."

"Should you hike your shipping prices, maybe?"

"I probably will have to, but I don't want to. I think the shipping prices already deter some people from ordering from me."

"You already make pastries for a few local places. Can you eliminate your Internet orders?"

Shelley shook her head. "The Cove is a regular customer, but the caterer is only sporadic, when they need pastries for an event they're catering. And Alexander's, the upscale restaurant in the next town, canceled their standing order because they found someone local, so they don't have to drive all the way to Marble Cove to pick up their desserts. I'm just so worried my new business is going to tank if I can't ship my pastries safely and for a decent shipping cost."

"I'm sure Beverly will have some good advice," Margaret said. "She's so smart."

"That's true, and she's been helping me so much with my business."

"I know it's bothering you right now, but my suggestion is to wait for Beverly to get back from Augusta and speak to her tonight or maybe tomorrow morning."

"I think you're right."

"I better get home to start my dinner too. Thanks, Shelley."

"Anytime, Margaret."

Shelley finished washing the beans and popped a casserole into the oven to bake just as Aiden and Emma finished watching a TV show. "Mama, can we play in the front yard?"

Well, she had already finished preparing for dinner, and while she had intended to clean up the house, she wanted a little fresh air and time with her children. "All right."

She headed out to the front yard and sat in the grass with Aiden while he explained the intricacies of his latest spaceship adventure, which somehow involved his dog Prize, and six of his toy cars, but her mind kept wandering because she was worried about the pastries.

She suddenly jumped when she realized Diane was standing next to her. "Shelley, are you all right?"

"Oh, I'm fine."

"I called to you twice and you didn't respond, so I was worried." Diane smiled. Rocky was with her on his leash, but she had let it go so that he and Prize could play together. Aiden and Emma were delighted.

"Are you coming back from a walk?" Shelley asked.

"No, just going out for one. I've been working all day."

"You've been busy with your deadline, haven't you? How's it going?"

"Actually, I'm avoiding another round of blog interviews."

"Are they very difficult to do?"

"Not difficult. Sometimes they're even fun, but they take a long time to do. I've been at it all day because they're due tomorrow."

"Tomorrow? They didn't give you much time, did they?"

"Actually, the messages were sent to my agent's generic e-mail address by mistake instead of directly to me, and my agent doesn't check that e-mail address more than once a week. She didn't forward them to me until this morning. That's why I'm scrambling to get them done." She paused to smile at Rocky and Prize. "How's Dan's new job going? You mentioned that he had problems with his boss?"

"Yes, thanks again for taking care of the kids so I could talk to him. Wayne was apparently pretty critical of him."

"It could be that they're feeling each other out. It can take time to iron out the kinks in a working relationship."

"That's what I thought too. I told Dan to stick it out for a little while longer and see how things go. I hope they get their issues resolved soon. When Dan comes home from work, I can tell he's super-stressed."

"It's good that he talked to you about it. He could have tried to keep it from you so you wouldn't worry, or he could have been too proud to share what he was feeling. He's a good guy."

"I feel blessed every day that we're together."

"Well, I'd better take Rocky on his walk."

"I'll be praying you get your work done."

Diane squeezed Shelley's shoulder. "Thanks so much. I really appreciate the prayers."

As Shelley watched Diane head toward the beach, she noticed that her friend's steps weren't as lively as normal, and her eyes had been shadowed with fatigue. She hoped Diane wouldn't let the workload overwhelm her. Shelley knew what it felt like to be overwhelmed, and how paralyzing and frustrating it could be.

Lord, please help Diane get her work done.

Luckily, Diane was almost done with all the interviews and blog posts she had to write today. Maybe the exercise would help her feel less tired, and she intended to only go for a quick walk.

When she'd seen the rash of e-mails in her in-box this morning, including her agent's apologetic message about not seeing these requests until today, she'd panicked about being able to get everything done by tomorrow. Now that it was suppertime and she was almost finished, she was able to breathe a little easier.

The only problem was that she hadn't been able to work on her book all day today. She'd gotten some good work done last night, but she'd had a headache—probably caused by her not eating regularly enough, making her blood sugar to swing a bit more than it should.

And to top it all off, she had that sense of urgency to figure out the cipher in Jeremiah Thorpe's prayer journal. Since she and Beverly had divvied up which ciphers to try, Diane had unfortunately not had time to try any of them. But the Old First Founders Day celebration was at the end of the month, and they wanted to figure out the cipher soon. If the cipher had something to do with the treasure, they could use that treasure to save Old First.

She got home from the walk, heated up some chicken casserole and nibbled at it while finishing up her interviews. She happened to need to look up a date, so she opened the calendar on her computer.

She gasped. She'd completely forgotten about a telephone call tomorrow morning with a podcaster who wanted to interview her. He had said in his e-mail that it would probably take a couple hours, if she wanted to do retakes of some of her answers to the questions. He'd sent the questions to her, and she had intended to write out answers to them so she wasn't going into the phone interview cold.

She grimaced. She'd have to work on that tonight too. She'd had half an idea of working on her book for a little while before bed, but the need to write out answers to the interview questions threw that hope out the window.

She sighed. She'd have to first finish the blog interview she was doing, then go to work on that. She glanced at the clock.

Looked like it was going to be another late night.

CHAPTER ELEVEN

After her morning run Beverly called the Landmark Inn.

"Landmark Inn, this is Victoria."

"Hi, Victoria, this is Beverly Wheeland-Parker."

"Hi, Beverly. Did we have a consult this week?"

"No, I'm actually calling to ask for a favor."

"You've done so much to help me with my business, I'd be happy to do anything for you."

"It's kind of an unusual request. I have some serving items that I bought when my husband was alive and we did a lot of entertaining, but I don't have any use for them anymore. I wondered if you might be willing to look at them to see if you'd like to buy them."

"Sure. That would be great."

"I can drive the box over to you anytime this morning." Margaret had called earlier to ask if Beverly would help out at the gallery for a couple hours this afternoon while she spoke to the woman at the community center about Adelaide, and Beverly had said yes, knowing she could bring her laptop and get some work done at the gallery in between customers.

"Can you come by right now? There's a little bit of a lull between breakfast and lunch, and I'd like my chef to take a look with me."

"That's a good idea. Sure. I can be there in thirty minutes."

"See you."

Beverly headed downstairs to make sure everything she wanted to show Victoria was in the right box. As she was sorting through the boxes she came across the silver box with the bracelet. She removed it and held it up to the sunlight streaming through the living room windows, remembering when Will gave it to her.

The dull thud of a shoe hitting a box interrupted her thoughts.

"Sorry." Her father had accidentally shuffled into one of the boxes littering the floor of the living room.

"No, I'm sorry. I'll get these boxes out of your way soon. Some I'll take to the thrift store to get rid of, and other stuff I'll put up in the attic."

"What's that?" He gestured to the bracelet she still held.

"Oh." She looked down at it. "Will gave this to me. I'd forgotten I had it, but I found it again when I went to clean out the house yesterday."

"It's pretty." He came closer to get a good look at it. "I like it better than some of the other jewelry he gave you."

Beverly did too. "It belonged to his mother. He gave it to me when we got engaged."

"That's where I saw this before. I think I remember you showing it to me when you told me about the engagement."

It was the least flashy of all the jewelry Will had bought for her, and it meant a great deal to her because Will hadn't spoken about his mother very much. The memories of her were painful, and he always managed to turn the subject.

But when he'd given her the bracelet, he'd said, "My mom would have been so happy to see you have this."

"Why?"

"Jill—my previous wife—never believed in me or my architecture firm. She kept telling me I dreamed too big. But my mother never lost faith in me. She said that whatever I went for I could do."

He clasped her hand in his. "But you have faith in me. You always did. Mom never liked Jill because she thought Jill was trying to hold me back. But Mom would have liked you." He looked down at the bracelet glittering against her skin. "I never could convince myself to give Mom's bracelet to Jill. Now I'm glad I never did, and I can give it to you. It's as if you and Mom have a connection to each other. You both believe in me. And when I build that house in Augusta, it'll be as if you and Mom are there with me, because you both only wanted me to be my best."

Even though they'd had some struggles in their marriage, she had once loved him very much, and he had loved her just as much, she knew.

Maybe that's why she had lingering misgivings about selling the house. It was almost as if she were trying to erase the good memories by selling his house. She knew that wasn't true, but it felt that way.

Was this too soon? Should she just eat the costs and not sell the house just yet?

Was she really ready to get rid of this last physical aspect of her marriage to Will?

Shelley rang Beverly's doorbell and waited a little anxiously. She hoped she wasn't interrupting her in the middle of something really important.

But Beverly greeted her with a smile when she opened the door. "Come on in. Sorry about the mess. I brought some boxes back with me from Augusta last night."

"You're not in the middle of something, are you?" Shelley stepped into the bright living room, filled with comforting, old-fashioned furniture and the smell of lemon oil and Old Spice. There were also boxes spread across the floor, some half open with what looked like fancy, modern dinnerware.

Beverly headed into the kitchen. "Not at all. Want some coffee? I just put on a pot for me and Father."

"No, I don't want to take up more than a few minutes of your time."

Beverly turned to face her. "Shelley, we're friends. You should never feel you can't come talk to me, no matter what I've got happening."

Shelley gave a guilty smile. "Thanks, Beverly."

She turned to pour some coffee for her. "What did you need to talk to me about?"

Shelley explained about the broken cakes, the postage price increase, and the cheaper packaging she'd used.

"And I need the Internet orders," Shelley continued. "My local vendors are scaling back, except for the Cove, and the caterer I work with is great, but the business they give me isn't consistent."

"*Hmm.*" Beverly stirred cream and sugar into her mug of coffee. "Well, there are a few things I can think of for you to do."

Beverly's calm good sense and confidence made Shelley breathe a sigh of relief.

"First of all, do a little more research about packaging. There might be packaging like what you were using before that's lower in price."

"Okay, I'll look again. I had thought I'd done a good job searching, but maybe I missed something."

"What you can also do is order several different packages to test them with different products. Had you shipped a pound cake before?"

"Yes, a few times. And I've shipped muffins before, which are kind of the same weight and heft."

"And the customers who ordered the cake and muffins never said anything about them arriving damaged?"

"No. But now that I think about it, if it were me, and the goodies weren't too badly damaged, I probably wouldn't have said anything."

"That might have been what happened, but it could also be that they arrived perfectly fine," Beverly said.

"I hope so."

"I also think you should do an experiment."

"Experiment? I didn't do very well in science in school."

Beverly laughed. "Nothing difficult. Send some pound cakes to someone through the mail so you can see how they arrive. You can try different packaging. I know!" Beverly snapped her fingers. "Mail some pound cakes to my home in Augusta. It's far enough away that you'd be able to see how the cheaper packaging really holds up in the postal service."

"Okay, that's a good idea." Shelley sighed. "Thanks for the advice, Beverly."

"Don't thank me yet. I didn't really solve your problem for you."

"But you had advice about what I could do about it. I was frustrated because all I could see was the problem and I couldn't figure out where to go next."

"Well, sometimes you just need someone outside the problem to look at it from a different perspective."

"I'll come to you for your perspective anytime." Shelley glanced at the boxes scattered across the living room floor. "How's the housecleaning going?"

"It's going quickly." But Beverly sighed.

"Is it hard, packing up your old home?"

"That's the thing, it never really felt like my home. It was Will's house, not mine. But it's harder than I expected it to be."

Shelley put her arm around Beverly. "I think you're doing the right thing in selling the house."

Beverly hugged her back. "Thanks, Shelley. I guess I need people to keep telling me that."

After chatting a few minutes more, Shelley headed across the street with a lighter heart. Now she had a plan of action for her baked goods.

She just hoped the ultimate solution would be easy to find.

Adelaide was thrilled to spend part of the afternoon with Shelley and her kids. They had phrased it as Shelley needing help with the kids, and Margaret would pay Shelley back for the money Adelaide would "earn" today.

Beverly had said she was more than happy to hold down the gallery for a couple hours. She'd even brought her laptop with her so that she could do work if no one came in.

Despite all her plans coming together so well, Margaret felt frazzled as she and Allan went to the community center to meet with Penny Tyler. Allan seemed less tense than she did, but there were some worry lines in his brow as he drove.

"Do you know what Penny needs to talk to us about?"

"Margaret, that's the third time you've asked me today." He smiled at her reassuringly. "Let's not worry too much about it yet, okay?"

"You're right. I'm sorry."

"Don't be sorry. I'm wondering too."

When they arrived, instead of heading to the main hall, they walked toward the back where the offices were. The office door was unlocked, and when they walked in, Margaret was surprised to see Penny's teenage son Sam Tyler at the reception desk.

"Hi, Mr. and Mrs. Hoskins," he said.

"How have you been, Sam?" Margaret had mentored him last year, but their mentoring had tapered off this year as he got more involved in football and also the school glee club.

"Things are going well. This summer, I'm filling in for the receptionist while she's on maternity leave, and Mom's even paying me." He grinned.

"Good for you," Allan said.

"You can go into Mom's office. She's expecting you." Sam nodded toward the short hallway lined with office doors.

"Thanks, Sam." Margaret and Allan went to the third door, which had "Penny Tyler, Special Needs Program" on a nameplate. Allan knocked and turned the handle.

"Come in." Penny looked up and saw them. "Hi, Margaret, Allan. Have a seat." She gestured to the two seats in front her cluttered desk. Her face was cheerful, which made Margaret's shoulders ease slightly as she sat.

"I didn't realize until I was talking to Sam today that my message yesterday might have alarmed you." Penny winced. "Sorry about that. Let me first say, this meeting isn't about anything too serious."

Margaret let loose a breath she had been holding.

"I didn't really notice this until this past week," Penny continued, "but I'm a little concerned that Adelaide might be bored with the activities we're doing here at the community center."

Margaret and Allan looked at each other. "Bored? But she hasn't been bored before."

"We've been changing up our curriculum, because anyone would be bored doing the same things, but Adelaide has still seemed not very interested in most of the activities. She hasn't said that in so many words, and I'm guessing she hasn't spoken to you two about it?"

"No."

"She may not yet realize herself why she doesn't find the classes as interesting as she used to. Even the finance and budgeting course doesn't seem to be the right fit for her. But she's grown a great deal in the past year—had her first crush, met some friends living in a group home and thought about living independently for the first time." Penny leaned forward. "I think the two of you should think about perhaps allowing Adelaide to take some other types of classes or participate in other activities outside the community center. Things that she hasn't done before."

Margaret and Allan looked at each other. "But what kinds of classes and activities?" Margaret asked.

"What kinds of things could she do?" Allan asked.

"You two would know best," Penny said. "Talk to her, mention a few options. She might have an idea of what kinds of new experiences she'd like to explore. Or maybe something you mention to her might spark her interest."

"Do you mean..." Margaret was trying to think. "Music classes? Or art classes? Or...?"

"Anything. You never know what Adelaide might be interested in unless you ask her, or unless she tries."

"Would she still come to the community center?" Allan asked.

"Oh yes, of course. She has a lot of friends here. But if she has another outlet that's stimulating her in a different way, then the time she spends here can be more social than instructive for her."

"Where could we find classes appropriate for her?" Margaret asked. "How would we know she can handle them?"

Penny's face became thoughtful. "You might need to go through a bit of trial and error. I'd talk to her, as well, to let her know that it's okay if something is too difficult—or maybe even too easy—for her, that she should just talk to you about it."

Penny's answers sounded reasonable, but Margaret still felt like a boat adrift. There was so much Adelaide would never be able to do, and so many people in the world who wouldn't understand her—or want to understand.

They stood to leave. "Thanks, Penny." Allan ushered Margaret toward the door. "We'll think about what you said."

Penny nodded. "If you want to run anything by me, just give me a call."

When they were driving home, Margaret said. "This is so difficult. The choices we make for Adelaide could be great for her, or they could throw her into a situation she's not prepared to handle."

"We'll ask Adelaide what she'd like to do," Allan said, "and we'll also pray about it so that we can try to make the right decisions for her."

"I'm so worried about letting her do something that's wrong for her."

"I am too, so we won't go into this impulsively or unprepared." Allan turned into their driveway. "I'll do some research into this, and you talk to Adelaide and nudge her to see what she might be interested in doing. Don't ask her outright, but put out a few feelers."

"Okay, that sounds like a plan."

But even as she got out of the car, Margaret wanted to throw her arms around her daughter, not ask her about other types of classes or activities. What if Adelaide wanted to go rock climbing? Or take flying lessons? How could Margaret bear breaking her daughter's heart by saying no?

And yet, with Adelaide being bored with the community center activities, how could she hold her back?

CHAPTER TWELVE

Diane breathed a sigh of relief as she finished the first chapter of her book. It had taken her so long, and she had a sick fear that the rest of the book would take just as long. But some of her online critique partners had mentioned that often the first chapter was the one that took the longest, and that they sometimes went back and rewrote or even deleted the first chapter after they were done with the book. While Diane was used to revisions from her job as a newspaper reporter, the idea of deleting this chapter that she'd spent so much time working on seemed horrific.

She was exhausted. She hadn't even started working on her book until after lunch because she'd had the podcast interview in the morning. It had been fun, but it took a little over two hours. She'd felt physically drained, even though she hadn't done much but talk on the phone, but that was probably because she hadn't been getting enough sleep lately.

She also attended to several blog requests. She'd considered ignoring them since they weren't due for a couple days, but items in her in-box had always distracted her so much that she couldn't focus on other things she needed to complete until she could clear them out. So after staring at the blinking cursor for an hour, she'd finally given in and worked on her interview questions, finishing them in only a couple hours. She'd had a late lunch, and then started work on her manuscript, finally. And finished chapter one—which gave her a good feeling.

But now she had the greater problem of figuring out which direction she wanted the mystery to progress. She'd been toying with ancient Roman coins as a plot device, but had only kept the idea on the back burner because she didn't know much about Roman coins to begin with.

But now that she was fully into the book and about to start chapter two, she realized she needed to make a decision about whether she was going to use the Roman coins plot device or not. And she couldn't make that decision until she started researching the ancient coins more thoroughly.

She realized she was dreading opening her Internet browser because then she might be tempted to check her e-mail. She knew it was all too likely she'd find more blog tour requests in her in-box.

"That's silly," she told herself firmly. "You're a grown woman with a job, not a teenager trying to avoid doing homework."

Rocky, lying on the floor at her feet, lifted his head to look at her with questioning eyes.

"Yes," she told him, "you're probably wondering why your owner is talking to herself like a crazy person. Well, Rocky, this book is starting to drive me crazy."

She determinedly opened her browser and started doing a Web search for Roman coins. It seems many of them had Caesar's head on them, so she also did a search for "Caesar."

She was surprised to find that one of the resulting links was colored differently on her browser, meaning she had visited that link once before. She clicked on it and realized it was about the Caesar cipher, one of the substitution ciphers she'd found out about when looking up ciphers to decode the message in the prayer book.

She skimmed the page again in case there was more information about Caesar, who had supposedly used this cipher for his secret messages, and suddenly saw a small reference near the bottom about a Vigenère cipher. What was that? She clicked on it.

It was a type of substitution cipher that used a series of Caesar ciphers. And Diane's interest was caught when she saw that the cipher dated from the year 1553.

The Vigenère cipher was something called a polyalphabetic substitution cipher, and it made the message harder to crack than a regular substitution cipher. If a message used a Vigenère cipher and someone used the frequency analysis like Diane and Beverly did with the message, it would still look similar to a simple substitution cipher, because certain letters would still be used more than others. However, with a Vigenère cipher, the difference in frequency between letters wouldn't be as great.

Diane had been spending a few minutes each night before bed trying out different substitution ciphers and even trying some of the transpositional ciphers on the message, but hadn't had any luck. It was becoming more and more frustrating, but now she wondered if this was why she hadn't been able to crack it.

If it was a Vigenère cipher, she was missing a vital element in the cipher: a secret key word that was used to unlock the code. The key word was something known only between the message writer and the recipient, not something written down. But with the use of the key word, the cipher was easily translated.

She kept reading and found that one way to figure out if a message was a Vigenère cipher was to look for repeating letter fragments and to count how far apart they were.

Diane had always been good with word-search puzzles, so she got out her copy of the coded message and began scanning it.

It took her a while, but she finally found four different three-letter fragments that repeated each other.

She looked on the Web page, but there was a complicated mathematical formula describing the Vigenère cipher that made her eyes cross. She read further to find out how to solve the cipher if there were repeats, but she wasn't quite certain about the mathematical example.

She stared at the page, unsure what to do next. Then she slapped herself on the forehead. Beverly had been a budget analyst—she'd know and understand the math behind this cipher.

Diane gave her a call.

"Hi, Diane," Beverly answered the phone.

"Beverly, I have a theory about what the cipher might be. Have you heard of a Vigenère cipher?"

"That sounds familiar. Hang on, let me look it up online." There was the sound of clicking keys on a keyboard and a few moments of silence. Finally Beverly said, "Yes, I briefly looked at this, but I dismissed it because it said that Vigenère ciphers hid the fact that certain letters are used more often than others."

"But the Web page I read said that while the Vigenère cipher masks that effect, which we saw when we did the frequency analysis, it doesn't erase it entirely."

"Yes, I'm seeing that now. I hadn't read that far down the page. If you did a frequency analysis on a message coded with the Vigenère cipher, the results would still look a little bit like a simple substitution cipher. Do you think this message uses a Vigenère cipher?"

"Well, I read something about how you can figure out the key word if you look at repetitions in the message."

"Yes, I'm reading that now."

"I went ahead and looked for them, and I found four repeating patterns."

"What are they?"

Diane told her about the four letter fragments and how many letters apart each repetition was.

"Diane!" Beverly nearly shouted into the phone. "Do you realize what you discovered?"

"Uh...no."

"380, 230, 100, 170, and 180. The only common denominators are two, five, and ten."

"Common denominators?" Diane vaguely remembered the term from high school math classes.

"It means that this probably *is* a Vigenère cipher and that the key word for this message has to be either five or ten letters long."

"Really?" Diane was dumbfounded. "You sound very certain."

"I am. When you have four different letter fragments repeating like this, it's probably not coincidence."

"But what would the key word be for this message?"

"Well, let's assume that it would be something to do with Jeremiah Thorpe. "

Diane glanced at the clock and realized it was supper time. "We should see if the four of us can meet to talk about this—maybe after supper tonight?"

"That sounds good. But we can't meet at my house—I have boxes of things from Augusta all over my living room. My poor father keeps tripping over them."

"We can meet at my house. How about seven thirty?"

"Sounds good."

Diane then called Shelley and Margaret, who both said they could make it.

After a short walk with Rocky, Diane made dinner for herself—a real meal rather than the sandwiches and soups she'd been heating up for the past week or two. She boiled some whole-wheat pasta and made a quick spaghetti sauce with turkey sausage, garlic, onions, and bell peppers, spiced with some fragrant oregano and thyme.

Her three friends arrived right at seven thirty, just as Diane was washing the last of her supper dishes. She opened the door for them and put the kettle on for tea.

Shelley followed her into the kitchen. "Since Adelaide helped take care of the kids for me this afternoon, I made Danishes and brought some with me."

"Perfect."

Shelley laid the goodies out on a plate and carried it and small dessert plates into the living room. Diane made the tea and carried the pot and cups.

"I'm dying to hear what you discovered." Margaret sat back with a Danish and a cup of tea.

"Diane cracked the code," Beverly said.

"Actually, Beverly had to tell me I had cracked the code because I had no clue what I'd done," Diane laughed.

"It's a cipher that needs a five- or ten-letter key word," Beverly said. "It would be a secret word that only the message writer and the recipient would know, and you need that key word to decode the message."

"What kind of key word?" Shelley asked.

"Probably something personal to Jeremiah Thorpe."

"Or it could involve Old First," Margaret said.

Diane was counting letters on her fingers. "Jeremiah is eight letters long. Thorpe is six letters long. So it's not either of those."

"Old First is eight letters long," Shelley said.

They brainstormed for a few minutes, but no one could come up with any key word that was exactly five or ten letters long.

"So our homework is to try to figure out what the key word could be," Beverly said.

"I'll talk to Augie on Monday," Diane said. "He might know something, or maybe he knows people connected with the Thorpes."

"I'm scheduled to meet with Frances Bauer tomorrow to talk over the Old First Founders Day celebration," Margaret said. "She's been a church member for so long, she might know something about Jeremiah Thorpe or Old First."

"Tomorrow's Sunday. Should I ask Reverend Locke?" Beverly said. "He might know something about Old First that wouldn't be in a history book."

"Let's not ask him anything at this point," Diane said. "He's already suspicious of us and we don't want to annoy him."

"Yes, I think you're right."

"Excellent." Diane beamed at them all. "We've got an action plan."

"I feel like we should be doing a football huddle." Shelley grinned.

"Margaret, how did the meeting with Penny go today?" Beverly asked.

Margaret seemed to deflate a little. "It went fine. There wasn't anything seriously wrong."

"That's good, right?" Shelley asked.

"I'm just frustrated." Margaret's hands tightened on her teacup. "Penny said that she thinks Adelaide might be bored at the community center, and that she might want to take other classes or try other activities."

"What exactly can Adelaide do?" Beverly asked.

"That's the thing—I really don't know." Margaret's eyes were wide and anxious. "How do we know what's too difficult for her, or what would put her in a bad situation? How do we support her and yet protect her at the same time? How do we know what she's capable of?"

Diane laid a hand on Margaret's knee. "I'm sure you're much more knowledgeable about that than you think you are."

"It's very stressful, and I feel overwhelmed," Margaret said. "Allan and I are going to do more research into it, and maybe then I'll feel like I have a better handle on what to do, and what to say to Adelaide."

"That sounds like a good plan."

"Thanks to both of you," Margaret said to Shelley and Beverly, "for helping with Adelaide and taking over the gallery this afternoon."

"Not a problem. You can thank Adelaide for giving me time to make these Danishes." Shelley held one up in a mock toast.

"And the gallery was a breeze," Beverly said. "I brought my laptop and got some work done in between customers."

"How is everything going with your house?" Diane asked her.

Beverly looked at her teacup for a moment before answering. "It's fine, I think. It's making me more emotional than I thought it would because there are things about the house that stir up old memories. I keep remembering Will and missing him."

Shelley shifted so she could put her arm around Beverly's shoulders and give a quick squeeze.

"I still have some time before the closing date, so I'm clearing the house out slowly." Beverly gave them a quick smile. "It's fine. I'll be okay, especially when it's all over."

"That reminds me. When are you going back to Augusta again?" Shelley asked.

"Tuesday, probably. I have a client call on Monday but nothing on Tuesday."

"Could I mail a few packages of pastries to your Augusta house?"

"Sure. You mail them overnight, right? If you mail them on Monday, I'll be at the house on Tuesday to accept them, and I can tell you Tuesday night how they came out."

"I hope this will help me figure out what to do." Shelley's brow furrowed. "I really need my Internet orders, but if the pastries keep breaking, I can't afford to give refunds and lose disgruntled customers at the same time."

"How are you doing with your manuscript?" Margaret asked Diane.

"I finished chapter one today."

"Hooray!" the other women cheered.

"When are the three chapters due?" Margaret asked.

"Mid-month. They kept changing the date, but I have it written down on a piece of paper at my desk." That reminded her, she needed to find that paper and make sure it was in her calendar on her computer. She should have done that earlier this month.

"I'd better go." Shelley rose reluctantly to her feet. "I have to tuck the kids into bed."

"Thanks for letting us meet at your house tonight," Beverly said to Diane.

"This was great to just catch up a little," Margaret said.

"It was also good to figure out in what direction we need to go with this cipher," Beverly said. "Now that we'll all be looking into Jeremiah Thorpe and Old First, maybe we'll have the key word soon."

"I hope so too," Diane said.

As she stood in her doorway and waved good-bye, she couldn't help feeling a bubbling excitement in her chest. If they could decode the cipher, maybe it would point to Jeremiah Thorpe's rumored treasure. And if they could find that treasure, maybe, just maybe, it would save Old First.

How wonderful it would be to have a treasure from the past rescue the grand old church in the present—especially if they could find it in time for the Founders Day celebration.

CHAPTER THIRTEEN

Diane yawned as she got home from Sunday service, feeling guilty that she hadn't heard much of the sermon. She'd had a bad night because she had tried to work on her manuscript after her friends had left, but had gotten stuck on a plot problem and hadn't made much headway into chapter two. Plus speculation about Jeremiah Thorpe kept seeping into her brain, distracting her from her writing.

They were so close to solving the cipher! Maybe she should just put some effort into it so they could solve it faster. Then she wouldn't be distracted when she was supposed to be doing her other work.

She promptly gave August Jackson a call. He answered on the seventh ring. "Hello?"

"Hi, Augie, this is Diane Spencer."

"Hello there. Let me guess: you've got another historical question for me."

"I hope it's not always that obvious," she said with chagrin.

"Oh, don't worry, I love to talk about history. I'm busy today—got the checkers club meeting at the park, and we're usually out there until supper time. Tomorrow ... *hmm*, it's Senior Morning at the Cove."

"Senior Morning?"

"Once a month, from five to eight, they have free coffee for seniors. I always go to that. Why don't you meet me there?"

"Er ... at five?"

"Gosh, no. Who in the world gets up at five? Well, maybe Odessa," he mumbled.

It took Diane a moment to remember Odessa Karpenko, the oldest Marble Cove resident at one hundred and seven— or was she one hundred and eight by now?

Augie continued, "How about you meet me at seven thirty? I have a doctor's appointment at nine, and at noon, my daughter's picking me up. I'll be going to her home in Bangor for a couple weeks."

Diane certainly didn't want to wait a couple weeks to talk to Augie when he might have important information about Jeremiah Thorpe or Old First, which could crack that coded message. "Tomorrow morning is fine for me."

"See you there. You're buying the coffee." He cackled at his own joke and hung up.

Diane yawned again. She really needed to get better sleep tonight so she could be up bright and early to meet Augie at the Cove.

She thought about checking her e-mail, but decided against it. She'd been working hard for a couple weeks now and didn't want to work on a Sunday. Any blog interviews could be taken care of tomorrow.

She wouldn't get on the computer to work on her manuscript today, but she might go for a long walk on the beach. She hadn't gone for a good walk in quite a while, and she might be able to figure out that tricky problem keeping her from continuing with chapter two. She fixed herself a hearty lunch of soup and a sandwich. Then she tucked a couple energy bars into her pocket to take with her, as well as a water bottle.

"Rocky!"

Her dog bounded to her side immediately, tail wagging eagerly.

"I guess you're ready to go for a walk, aren't you?"

At the magic *W* word, Rocky's mouth fell open and he began to pant. He looked like he was grinning.

Diane clipped the leash to his collar and headed out the front door. She saw Frances Bauer's SUV in Shelley's driveway and figured Shelley's in-laws were over for lunch after church today.

Or maybe Frances was making lunch? Frances appeared from around the SUV with a full grocery bag, a few leafy stalks of celery peeking out the top. She was heading into the house when she caught sight of Diane.

Diane waved, but was surprised when Frances veered away from the front door and headed across the street to her.

"I'm so glad I saw you." Frances was a little breathless from hurrying across the street with the grocery bag still in her arms.

"Do you need help with the groceries?" Diane asked.

"Oh no, there's only this one bag. I'm dropping this off for Shelley to make supper for all of us, and then Ralph and I are taking the grandkids to the park for the afternoon."

"That sounds like fun."

"I have a favor to ask you."

Normally Diane would be happy to help if she could, but today, with the thought of the work she still had to do for the blog tour and manuscript, the request caused a lead anchor to drop in her stomach.

But she put on a polite smile. "What do you need me to do?"

"Founders Day for Old First is in a couple of weeks, and we're putting together a commemoration booklet," Frances said. "I was wondering if you might be willing to write a short history of Old First and Jeremiah Thorpe. We'd of course give you access to any type of records you'd need to write the piece."

Diane's first inclination was to say no, but the name Jeremiah Thorpe and the offer of access to old records made her realize that this might be an excellent opportunity to find out more information that could lead to the key word for the cipher.

"I'd be happy to," Diane said. "What records do you have?"

"There's a collection of old pieces kept in the Maine Room at the Thorpe Free Library," Frances said. "But also, when we put out the call for items to display for Founders Day, the

Courier looked in their 'attics,' so to speak, and found a box of random old pages and pamphlets. They found a couple things about Old First—there's a photo from the 1920s that they said was in the box—and I told them I'd look through it to see if there was anything else we could use. If you want to look through it with me, we could get through it faster."

"That would be wonderful." Inwardly, Diane was salivating at the prospect of reading old records that might have information about Jeremiah Thorpe and Old First.

"I know this is a bit last minute, but do you have time tomorrow afternoon?" Frances shifted the grocery bag in her arms. "The *Courier* sent the box to the library, and I've already scheduled with the librarian to let me into the Maine Room at one o'clock. If you can't make it tomorrow, I can talk to the librarian about another day to let you in."

"Tomorrow is fine." Diane could meet with Augie in the morning, get some work done over lunch, and then go to the library. She didn't want to wait to look at the box because that would give her even less time to write the short piece for the commemoration booklet.

"Great. We'll meet at the library a little before one, then?"

"Sure."

"Thanks for doing this for us, Diane." Frances gave her a brief smile before heading back across the street with her groceries.

Diane headed to the beach, and as she stepped onto the sands, she closed her eyes briefly as she felt the salty, crisp air in her face and smelled the scent of warm sand and briny rocks. Just one of the many reasons why she loved Marble Cove, this wonderful shoreline.

She unleashed Rocky and let him chase the seagulls circling the mirrorlike sands as the waves rippled farther out. She nodded at a few tourists and smiled and waved at some Marble Cove residents who were out walking.

Her steps gravitated toward the Orlean Point lighthouse in the distance, majestic against the rocks and ocean foam. Jeremiah Thorpe had built that lighthouse when a mysterious light led his ship into Marble Cove, and then he'd founded Old First. If they could find his treasure, it would be as if Jeremiah were saving his church from beyond the grave.

They'd already found out some things about Jeremiah, especially thanks to his granddaughter's stories. The thought made Diane's steps slow for a moment. *Edith Mauer*. Ten letters. Maybe that was the key to the cipher? She vowed she'd try it as soon as she got back home.

Perhaps she could also interview Odessa Karpenko. There might be some stories she could remember about Jeremiah that would lead to the key for the cipher.

Diane also reflected that Frances might know something as well. She resolved to ask Frances tomorrow if she'd be willing to be interviewed. Since she'd asked Diane to do the piece for the commemoration booklet, there wouldn't be anything strange about the questions Diane would ask her.

Suddenly her cell phone rang, and a grin pulled at her mouth as she saw that it was her daughter Jessica. "Hi, sweetheart."

"Hi, Mom. Good news, I can come on Wednesday and stay a few days. And Martin will come with me. Is that still okay?"

"Of course, if he doesn't mind sleeping on the couch."

"No problem. I'll drive down and see you early Wednesday morning, okay?"

"See you then."

As Diane hung up the phone, she couldn't help heaving a happy sigh. It would be so wonderful to see her daughter again and spend some quality time with her. Since Jessica had only briefly visited her at Christmas, Diane hadn't felt like she'd had enough time with her.

She didn't care how much work she had—she'd take advantage of every moment she could spend with Jessica.

Margaret knew she needed to open the gallery on Sundays during the tourist season, but this Sunday was especially hard for her. For the past few days, she'd been worried about Adelaide and hadn't had much leisure to think about the missing painting. She'd also been busy at the gallery so she'd spent a lot of time talking to customers and artists and hadn't touched her paints.

But now that she and Allan had talked to Penny Tyler and they were starting to look into classes or clubs or activities for her daughter, Margaret found herself mulling over the theft more and more.

She wished there was something she could do about it besides sitting here in her gallery, trying to paint while waiting for customers to come in. She had always figured that lots of foot traffic meant more sales, while fewer customers meant more time for her to paint. But today, the lack of customers was wasted on her because she could only stare at her canvas and think of *Sea Breeze*.

She knew she had done as much as she could. She had investigated—if she could call it that—Agnes Dillwater, but that had turned out to be a dead end, in all probability. She couldn't look into the three people at the art fair who'd wanted to buy the painting because she simply didn't have the resources or the ability to try to find them.

And there had been dozens of people who had looked at *Sea Breeze* while it hung in her gallery window. Lots of people who had come in to ask about it, to congratulate her on the award, even one or two who had asked if she intended to paint anything else similar in the near future.

Of course, there had also been one or two who mentioned that they would always like her soothing lighthouse seascapes best.

But now it didn't matter because the painting was gone. She also knew that since the police still had no leads on the theft, she had to call and tell the buyer about its being missing. The thought sent ripples of nausea through her.

And then her telephone rang, and her heart sank as she read the name on the caller ID. It was John Wilson, the buyer of *Sea Breeze*.

Oh my goodness, oh my goodness. She took a deep breath. *Just remain calm.* "Hello?" Her voice shook just the tiniest bit.

"Hi, Margaret, this is John Wilson. I bought your painting *Sea Breeze* at the art fair a couple weeks ago."

"Hi, John."

"I'm calling to let you know that I'll be able to pick the painting up earlier than I had planned. Maybe sometime next week."

"Um, I was just about to call you about that." Margaret swallowed. "The gallery was robbed."

There was a stunned silence, then he asked, "What?"

"I'm afraid that *Sea Breeze* was stolen from my gallery window."

He let out a gust of air. "Stolen?"

Margaret went on in a rush, "I reported the theft to the police and they're looking into it, but so far they haven't had any leads. I have the incident report number here and the Marble Cove police department number, if you'd like them."

"They haven't found anything?"

"I gave them the descriptions of a few people who had expressed interest in the painting at the art fair, but since I didn't get any names, they've had a hard time tracking them down. And I even went investigating here in Marble Cove after a woman who had tried to buy the painting before the art fair, but it turns out she wasn't even in town when the robbery happened. I'm so very sorry about this. I'll issue you a full refund, of course."

"Thank you, I appreciate it." The way he said it seemed as if he were speaking mechanically. "I can't believe someone robbed your gallery."

"I can't, either."

"Do you think you'll be painting anything similar to *Sea Breeze* anytime soon?"

"I'm definitely going to try." She couldn't confess that she hadn't been able to paint since the robbery. Would she ever recover enough to recapture the inspiration behind *Sea Breeze* again?

"Well, if the police do find the painting, please let me know," he said. "I hope they catch the thief."

"I do too."

"And please let me know if you paint anything else like it. Do you have an e-mail newsletter?"

"Uh . . . not yet, but I'm in the process of setting one up." *Starting right now.*

"Please sign me up." He gave her his e-mail address, which she noted on a piece of paper. She'd talk to Beverly today about how to set up an e-mail newsletter. She had seen other galleries with newsletters, and they didn't send them out more than a few times a year. She realized, in talking to John, that it would enable fans of her work to be kept abreast of any new pieces she did that they might be interested in. After hanging up with John, she gave up trying to paint and instead started jotting down ideas about what she might be able to do in an e-mail newsletter. She received them herself, but hadn't considered doing one for the gallery. She could take digital photos of her latest pieces, perhaps, or list giclée prints she had available. She might even be able to do a giclée print sale. That was an idea that had her writing out possible plans.

Soon it was time to close the gallery, and she headed home. The smell of baking bread greeted her when she walked in the door.

"*Mmm.*" She gave Allan a peck on the cheek as she peered at the bread machine on the kitchen counter.

"I'm trying a new bread recipe," he said. "It's got a little Parmesan cheese, basil, and black pepper."

"Sounds intriguing."

"I found it when I was searching the Internet this afternoon. Which reminds me." He stopped chopping carrots, laid down the knife, and turned to face her. "I was doing some research about classes Adelaide could take."

"I did some last night—looking at clubs in the area and things, but Allan, I just don't know..."

"That was my problem too—I didn't know what would be good for Adelaide. So instead, I did a search about other kids with Down syndrome and what kinds of things they've been able to accomplish."

"Oh. That's a good idea." She hadn't thought of that route.

"I thought I'd mostly come up with examples of a child's limitations, but Margaret, what I found was amazing."

His enthusiastic tone made her stare at him in surprise.

"For example, there was one young woman who was in Special Olympics."

"But we've tried that. Adelaide didn't care for sports at all."

"This young woman didn't just participate in Special Olympics—she raised money for a local charity, and then with her parents' help, she created a foundation to financially help special needs children participate in Special Olympics."

"She did all that?"

"And there's another story about a boy with Down's who went to college. There are also kids who go to acting school and get parts in shows and programs."

"Yes, I had heard about that, but...for some reason I hadn't thought about our Addie doing any of that."

"Margaret." Allan placed his warm hands on her shoulders. "After looking online today, I realized that maybe we've been too overprotective of Adelaide. Maybe there's so much more she could do, but we've been the ones holding her back."

Tears filled Margaret's eyes. "I never thought of that. I've only ever wanted to keep her safe, to help her feel loved and supported."

"I think we've done that, but she's getting older. Maybe it's time we let her spread her wings just a little bit."

"What do you think she'd like to do?"

"We can ask her. All I know is, I want to help her reach her true, full potential."

Margaret took a shaky breath. "It'll be hard to not be overprotective."

Allan kissed her on the top of her head. "I know. Me too. We'll help each other, okay?"

She nodded. She suddenly saw a whole new, scary world open up for her daughter. College classes? Would she want to do something like that?

But Margaret also knew that her darling daughter could do anything she set her mind and heart on. And wherever that went, Margaret vowed she'd be her number one cheerleader.

CHAPTER FOURTEEN

On Monday morning, Shelley was up earlier than usual to do her baking for the Cove and also an order of cupcakes for one of the local caterers. But she also did a batch of pound cake that she intended to use today for her "grand experiment." At least, that's what she called it in her mind.

After delivering the pastries, she returned home and boxed up the cakes. She was using three different kinds of mailing material—the old packaging she used to use before the postage price increase, the cheaper packaging she'd used with the broken cakes from a few days ago, and also some new packaging she'd bought that had been recommended online. She was sending these "test subjects" to Beverly's house in Augusta to see how the three compared.

At last she was ready to round up her children for a trip to the post office, with the three parcels balanced on Emma's stroller. Aiden amused himself by looking for bugs along the sidewalk, which made Shelley feel faintly sick but which kept him occupied while they waited for the post office to open. Emma toddled beside him, although she wouldn't touch the creepy crawlies he picked up.

Finally, the post office opened at a minute past eight o'clock.

"You're here early," remarked the post office clerk who unlocked the front door.

"I've got these three boxes to send Express Mail. Come on, Aiden, Emma. Aiden, put down the earthworm."

"Off you go," she murmured as the post office clerk carried the packages into the back to be picked up for the Express Mail truck. She hoped this experiment would be useful and help her figure out what to do about her Internet business.

"Mom, can I have hot chocolate?" Aiden looked up at her with brilliant blue eyes that never failed to melt her heart.

Shelley looked around at the sunlit street. It was only a little after eight, but it was already heating up into a warm day. "It's hot out."

"That's why I want one now, before it gets too hot."

"Choc'late," said Emma with a toothy grin.

Shelley hesitated. She didn't want to spend money on things she could make at home, but she didn't have any hot chocolate in the house, being summertime. However, Brenna over at the Cove always gave her free hot chocolate for the kids. Shelley didn't like to take advantage of her generosity, but she hadn't brought them into the Cove very much this summer so far.

"Okay," she said.

"Yay!" Aiden zoomed along the sidewalk toward the Cove, Emma chasing after him as fast as her little legs could carry her.

"Aiden, wait!"

He did come to a screeching halt before approaching the door, which was a good thing. A customer came barreling out of the coffee shop, his cup of coffee in one hand and his cell phone in the other as he read something on the tiny screen, paying scant attention to anyone he might run over in his haste.

"Good job, Aiden," Shelley said as she caught up to him. "You stopped when I asked you to."

"I didn't want to run into the man." Aiden pointed to the back of the customer, who was rapidly walking down the sidewalk in the opposite direction.

As they entered the Cove, Shelley saw that it was packed with early-morning coffee drinkers, and wondered if maybe she shouldn't have brought the children here. She debated between breaking her word with her children or braving the crowd when a voice called, "Shelley!"

She turned and saw Diane sitting at a table with Augie Jackson, waving her over.

Shelley parked the stroller under the countertop, where Brenna said she was welcome to leave it, and after picking Emma up, headed toward them. Aiden had already bounded over and was chatting with Augie.

"Hi there," Shelley said.

"Hi. And hi there, cutie." Diane tickled Emma's roly-poly tummy, making the little girl giggle.

"And I found an earthworm this big." Aiden thrust his hands out two feet as he talked to Augie, whose eyes twinkled behind his tiny black-framed glasses.

Shelley realized that while she'd met Augie before, she couldn't remember if her children had ever met him. "Aiden, did you introduce yourself to Mr. Augie?"

"Miss Diane did."

"Don't worry, I like kids," Augie said. "I even eat them once in a while."

Aiden laughed.

"I don't want to interrupt you two," Shelley said.

"You're not. I was asking Augie about Jeremiah Thorpe and Old First. Want to join us?"

Aiden tugged at Shelley's pants. "Mom, can I get my hot chocolate?"

"Diane, can I leave the kids with you while I order?"

"Of course." Diane's face lit up as she reached her arms out for Emma. "Any excuse to spend more time with this sweetie."

"I didn't tell you about the grasshopper I found," Aiden said to Augie.

Shelley went to the counter and asked Brenna if she'd mind getting two hot chocolates for her children.

"No problem," Brenna said with a grin, and soon gave Shelley two small cups. "I made one of them a mite cooler for your younger one."

"Thanks."

When Shelley returned to Augie and Diane's table, she was mortified to hear Aiden ask Augie, "Why do you have that white stuff on your mouth? It looks weird."

"It's called a mustache," Augie said, unperturbed.

"Does it hurt?"

"No, but it sometimes tickles." He leaned in and twitched it close to Aiden's cheek, and he squealed at the sensation.

"Have a seat," Diane gestured to one of the two empty seats at their table.

Shelley hesitated, realizing she was inserting two small children as well as herself into the conversation. "Are you sure? I don't want to bother you."

"Of course not. Besides, I don't intend to give up your daughter until you do." Diane winked at her.

"Here's your hot chocolate." Shelley put the cup in front of Aiden as he climbed into the other chair. "Don't spill it."

"I won't, Mom," he said in his snootiest I'm-all-grown-up voice. Shelley had to hide her smile.

Augie said, "I was telling Diane that we don't know a lot about Jeremiah Thorpe because he came to Marble Cove more than two hundred years ago."

"No one ever wrote about him?" Diane asked.

"Some of his descendants, but none of them were very prolific writers."

"We read some stories that Edith Mauer, his granddaughter, wrote when she was young," Diane said.

"The Thorpes weren't very prominent community figures. Jeremiah was the reverend of the church, and he and his wife only had two children that I know of, a girl and a boy."

"What were their names?" Diane asked eagerly. Shelley knew she was thinking that one of the names might be the key to the cipher.

"I don't know, but I remember his wife's name was Evangeline. She died on the ship on her way to Marble Cove."

"We know he founded Old First," Diane said. "And he built the lighthouse. Was there anyone else involved in all of that? A friend of his or someone who played a significant role in the building of either of them?"

"Not that I know of. But most of what I know is just from what I've read or picked up from talking to residents."

Diane continued to pick Augie's brain, but he couldn't give them any other names he could recall at that moment. "But I'll think about it, see if I can remember any other historical figures from that time. I'll double-check the contents of *A Pictorial History of Marble Cove* and see if I come up with anything."

Augie looked at his watch. "I better skedaddle. I need to walk to my doctor's office."

"Did you want me to drive you?" Diane asked. "I can get my car."

"No, it's just down the street. Well, you two ladies take care." And with more energy and speed than she'd have expected of a man in his eighties, Augie left the Cove, his bright purple shirt standing out against the more sober colors of the other people in the coffee shop.

"Well, that wasn't as helpful as I'd have hoped," Diane said.

"Well, hello you two," said a cheerful voice, and Shelley saw Mrs. Peabody heading toward them.

"Hi, Mrs. P," Shelley said. "What are you doing here?" She rarely saw her in the Cove, mostly because Mrs. Peabody's finances were tight and, like Shelley, she didn't often indulge in drinks or snacks she didn't make herself.

Mrs. Peabody waved a small gray card. "I came in for blueberry muffins the other day and they didn't have any, so Brenna gave me a voucher for a free pastry. My sister's coming to visit me today so I thought I'd get something instead of baking it myself."

Aiden began rocking in his chair. "Aiden, sit quietly, please." She should probably take the kids home now— though they'd been exceptionally good while they were chatting with Augie. She turned to Diane and Mrs. Peabody, intending to politely say good-bye, but Mrs. Peabody asked, "Can you believe about Margaret's painting being stolen? I'll bet it was that woman I saw looking at it the day before."

Diane's eyes were wide. "What woman?"

"That tall, thin woman. Long gray hair like a wild woman and a bright pink shirt."

"Oh, I saw her." Shelley remembered the odd conversation she had with the woman when she had been on her way to deliver the extra tray of blueberry muffins to the Cove the morning before the theft.

"The woman needed a hairpin. Or a dozen." Mrs. Peabody sniffed.

"Did you catch her name?" Diane asked.

"No, I never got a chance to get a word in edgewise. And goodness gracious, she certainly had forceful opinions about art. I don't know much about it, but she was quite willing to give me an earful, whether I wanted to hear it or not."

Shelley had to suppress a smile, since Mrs. Peabody herself would often ramble on in conversation to people.

"She would have kept me all night if I hadn't had to go home to fix supper," Mrs. Peabody said.

It took Shelley a moment to realize what Mrs. Peabody said, but then she did a double-take. "Supper? What time did you see her, Mrs. P?"

"Oh, around five."

"In the afternoon?" Diane's voice clearly showed her amazement, and Shelley knew that Diane had also realized what Mrs. Peabody was saying.

"Of course in the afternoon. I don't walk around Marble Cove at blessed five in the morning."

Diane met Shelley's eyes across the table. Mrs. Peabody had seen this woman in the afternoon, but Shelley had seen this same woman in the morning.

Why would this woman visit Margaret's gallery twice on the same day, the day before the painting had been stolen?

CHAPTER FIFTEEN

Diane managed to excuse herself from Mrs. Peabody as quickly and politely as she could, and she and Shelley exited the Cove.

When they were on the sidewalk, Shelley asked, "Do you think this woman had something to do with the painting being stolen?"

"I don't know."

"I told Margaret about the woman earlier, but I didn't really think she had anything to do with it. I mean, lots of people stop and look in Margaret's gallery window."

"But how many people look at the window twice on the same day?"

"It's especially strange since the painting was stolen that night."

"We need to tell Margaret," Diane said. "And we need to tell Detective Little too."

"All we have is a description of her," Shelley said. "We don't even have a name."

"But we have a very clear description, and I'd think her behavior is strange enough that the police would look into it. After all, they haven't been able to figure out much else about the case."

"And I've definitely seen her in Marble Cove earlier this summer," Shelley said. "So there's a good chance she's a summer resident. We might see her again around town."

They headed to Margaret's house since it was too early for her to be at the gallery. As soon as Aiden saw they were going to the Hoskinses' house, he gave a whoop of joy. "Can I play with the kitties, Mom?"

"You'll have to ask Adelaide," Shelley told him.

"Kitties," Emma said, drooling a little.

Their knock at the door was immediately answered by Allan, who greeted them with a smile. "Good morning."

"Hi, Allan. Sorry to come over so early, but we discovered something important we have to tell Margaret."

"Sure, come on in. Hey, Aiden," he said. "Want to play with the kitties?"

"You said the magic word," Shelley said as Aiden darted into the living room, where Adelaide was playing with the cats on the floor. Shelley let Emma down, and the little girl toddled over to them.

Margaret was finishing up a cup of coffee at their breakfast table, and she looked up as they entered the kitchen. "Good morning."

"Do you remember when I told you about the tall, thin woman I saw looking at the painting the morning before the theft?" Shelley sat across from Margaret, her eyes shining with excitement.

"Yes, I think so."

"We just talked to Mrs. Peabody," Diane said as she also sat down. "And she saw the same woman, but this time in the afternoon, looking at the painting again."

Margaret's face froze. "In the afternoon? On the same day?"

"Only a few hours before the painting was stolen," Shelley confirmed.

"Are you sure it was the same woman?"

"Mrs. P described the same hair, and also the same magenta blouse," Diane said.

"And she also told us about the woman's rather forceful opinions," Shelley said, "just like when that woman was talking to me."

"Oh my goodness." Margaret stared at her coffee cup for a moment before suddenly rising to her feet. "Would you two be willing to come with me to the police station? We need to tell Fred Little about this."

"You bet." Diane also rose to her feet.

"Can Adelaide watch the kids for me?" Shelley asked.

"Of course." Margaret went into the living room to speak to Allan and Adelaide, then returned with her purse. "Let's go. I can't believe this. After that dead end with Agnes Dillwater, I pretty much lost hope we'd find the thief. But this woman's behavior is so suspicious."

"Exactly," said Diane.

They went to the police station, but Detective Little wasn't there. Another officer took down Margaret's information about the woman instead. Shelley was able to add a more detailed description, and the officer said they'd try to find her.

"Are you sure she didn't give a name?" the officer asked.

"Sorry," said Shelley.

"It'll be hard to find her without a name," the officer said. "There are a lot of tourists here in Marble Cove this summer. A tall, thin woman with wild gray hair really isn't that unusual when you've got so many different people around."

Personally, Diane thought that the woman seemed sufficiently unusual that they should be able to ask around about her, but she also realized that Detective Little was probably still investigating the smugglers, or maybe some other crime, and a missing painting with only vague leads was probably low on his to-do list.

Margaret seemed disheartened by his words, so Diane said, "Thank you for your time," and led the way out of the police station.

"What we'll do is ask around the Marble Cove stores again," Diane said to Margaret as soon as they had left the police station. "I'm busy for the next few days, but I'll go with you this week."

"Do you really think we can do any better than the police?" Margaret asked.

"We found Agnes Dillwater, didn't we? I'm sure we can find this other woman." She didn't add the fact that they probably had more time to do it than the overworked police department.

Also, they had more motivation to find this mystery woman. If they didn't... Diane didn't want to think what that would mean for Margaret's award-winning painting.

"Hey, stranger!" Diane waved to Shelley as she headed toward the front door of the library.

Shelley grinned. "Gosh, we haven't seen each other in a whole two hours."

"You're here for the storybook hour?"

Shelley nodded. "What are you here for?"

"Your mother-in-law asked me to write a short piece on the history of Old First for the commemoration booklet. She bribed me with a chance to view a box of old papers in the Maine Room."

"What old papers?"

"I don't know. It's a box that the *Courier* found. From what Frances said, it sounds like the papers aren't just about Old First, but I'm hoping there might be something that'll give us some information on Jeremiah Thorpe."

"*Ooh*, makes me almost wish I were with you." Shelley winked.

They separated just inside the front entrance of the library, Shelley heading to the children's book section with a wave to Frances, who stood waiting for Diane.

"Thanks again for writing this piece for the booklet," Frances said. "Shelley mentioned last night how busy you were."

Her words sounded almost like an accusation, but Diane tried to remember that this was simply Frances' direct way of speaking. "I am busy, but I'm also happy to help Old First any way I can. It's an important historical part of the town."

Frances led the way up the stairs to the Maine Room on the second floor of the building. "Gilda Harris gave me the key so we can let ourselves in."

The scent of dusty, slightly moldy old paper hit Diane as she entered the room. There were shelves on each wall, bookcases at the far end of the room, and a card catalog to her right. On the long reference table that ran down the center of the room sat a severely browned cardboard box that had obviously had some weather damage.

"And there's the box," Frances said. "Gilda said she'll catalog these pieces this week when she has more time, but she was very gracious to allow us to look through the box right now, especially when I reminded her that the Founders Day service is in only a couple weeks' time."

Diane followed Frances down the length of the table and they stood catty-corner to each other with the box between them. "Do you know what's in here?" It looked like a bunch of old black-and-white photos, pamphlets, single sheets of paper, and thin booklets had been crammed into the box without any concern.

"Since it's from the newspaper, probably lots of photos that were never used, and some informational papers or flyers about events. The *Courier* used to do pieces on every sort of social event in Marble Cove, especially when it was smaller."

"Is it okay for me to take digital photos of the pages if I don't use a flash?" Diane had thought to tuck her digital camera into her pocket.

"I don't see why not. Just be sure the flash is turned off to protect the age of these documents. You don't want any accidental flashing going on," she said with a hint of reproach. Diane smiled, thinking she finally knew how Shelley must feel.

"What did you need to look at?" she asked Frances.

"There's a black-and-white photo of Old First that was taken by the newspaper in the twenties. Someone from the *Courier* said that they'd seen it in the box when they went through it, but they shoved the photo back in. I'm hoping to be able to get it copied so we can put it in the commemoration booklet."

"That should be a wonderful picture to include."

"It might be the oldest photo of Old First in existence." Frances began picking things out of the box and laying them on the table and Diane followed suit.

Diane found that she couldn't search the pages very quickly. They were all very old and brittle, but also for many of them the printing was faint, and she needed to squint at them under the dim ceiling light in order to read what they were about.

She didn't know who had decided which papers were shoved into this box. Some things weren't what she'd personally have taken so much time to preserve—she found a ship's log of how many barrels of fish they had in

1835, and also an electric bill for the *Courier* building from the 1920s.

"Why in the world did they put all this in this box?" Diane wondered.

"I have a theory." Frances squinted at a black-and-white photo. "These look like miscellaneous sheets that must have been lying around the offices, and someone wanted to clean up one day so they put everything in this box and shoved it in storage."

"You might be right." Then she remembered what she had wanted to ask Frances. "For the historical piece, would it be all right for me to do a short interview with you?"

Frances' mouth widened in a smile. "Me? I'm flattered."

"Your family has been in this town for many generations, and you certainly know a lot about the church."

"Certainly, I'll do an interview. We can set up a time for you to come over and we can have tea."

"Great. I was also thinking about interviewing Odessa Karpenko. Since she's the oldest resident in town, she might know something her family heard from the older town residents who had known Jeremiah Thorpe when he arrived in the cove."

"Perhaps," Frances said slowly. "But Odessa hasn't been a regular churchgoer at Old First, and neither was her family, so she may not be as well versed about the church itself."

"Oh." Diane resolved to call Odessa anyway and see if she could do a short interview, since the older woman might know things specific to Jeremiah Thorpe.

Then Diane discovered a small, almost overlooked pamphlet that read, "Re-Dedication of Old First Church, September 1775. Programme of Events."

"Look at this." Diane eagerly set it on the table. "It's a program for the rededication ceremony for the church."

Frances peered at it. "This must have been when the congregation outgrew the original structure and a new wooden one was erected."

After two hymns, accompanied by pianist Meredith Erlich, there was a Scripture reading by a Captain Reginald Burgess. Then a message by Reverend Thorpe—Jeremiah, she surmised. Another hymn, sung by the children's choir, and the closing prayer by Reverend Thorpe.

Diane frowned. Nothing very interesting. She flipped it over.

There was a list of names, apparently the children who sang in the choir. And near the bottom was printed "Elisabeth Thorpe" and "John Thorpe."

Thorpe! Hadn't Augie mentioned that Jeremiah had two children, a boy and a girl?

"Are these Jeremiah Thorpe's children?" She pointed to the names.

Frances squinted at them. "Elisabeth and John. *Hmm.* Perhaps. How old would they be?" She thought a moment. "Reverend Thorpe left his wife and children behind when he sailed to Marble Cove in, I think, 1761. His family sailed to America to join him, but his wife died onboard the ship during the journey, leaving him a widower with his two children."

"That means his children had to have been born in 1761 or earlier."

"For this rededication in 1775, Elisabeth and John would have been at least sixteen, seventeen years old."

"I suppose they would qualify as 'children' for the children's choir? But wait—how could Edith Mauer be Elisabeth's daughter? She would have been too old to have a daughter born in 1815." Diane noted.

"Perhaps."

Diane silently counted the letters of their names. Elisabeth had nine letters and John had four, but John Thorpe had ten letters. Perhaps this was the key for the cipher? Diane resolved to try it as soon as she returned home. She took a photo of the program and kept sifting through the box with Frances.

Diane also discovered an old church program from a special Easter service in spring 1934—again, she wasn't sure why this paper had been archived as opposed to others. It welcomed all visitors to Old First and listed the name of the pastor, a Reverend Grant. It also listed some church events like the women's Friday night social and the young men's group meeting on Wednesday night. It ended with a caution to parents to avoid the back stairs, which were unsafe. She also found the photo Frances was looking for. "Frances, is this the photograph of Old First?" She held out the fragile page to her.

Frances' face lit up. "That's it." She carefully secreted it in a special envelope she'd brought in with her. "This was the only thing I came for, but there's still so much stuff in the box to go through," she said in that curt way of hers.

"If you need to leave, I can lock up the room behind you," Diane offered.

"If you're sure you don't mind..." Frances handed her the key to the Maine Room. "Just give that to the librarian before you leave. I hope you find some other useful things for your historical piece."

Frances left, and Diane continued searching through the archived papers. She did eventually find a small tourist booklet from 1950. It had short blurbs for several of the businesses and buildings in town. Diane smiled to read about a bicycle-renting stand along the harbor and an artists' community center that had apparently stood where the current community center now stood. The *Courier* might have received the booklet so they could write an article on the tourism in Marble Cove, or perhaps on the businesses in town.

What interested her was also a page about Old First, which included a truncated history of the building. It had been built in 1761 by Jeremiah Thorpe, who claimed a light along the shore guided his ship to Marble Cove in 1761. The church built a new structure in 1775. The sanctuary burned in a fire in 1789, but the fire happened to save the lives of the people aboard a passenger boat when the lighthouse beacon was extinguished that night during a storm due to a broken glass pane. In 1790, the church was then rebuilt with stone around the remnants of the old structure, and that was the historical building still in use "today"—in the booklet, 1950.

This short history was dry, but Diane knew she could embellish it using the story of the church fire written by Jeremiah Thorpe's granddaughter, Edith Mauer, in her juvenile essays that they had found a few months ago. And maybe she would figure out how Edith Mauer could be Elisabeth Thorpe's daughter. That just didn't make sense.

Diane took a photo of the page, although she guessed she'd need to do some photo manipulation on her computer to be able to read the page with the dim light of the archive room. She checked her watch and was shocked to find it was almost five o'clock.

She hadn't found exactly what she was looking for, but she'd found some things. She'd start on the history tonight—she might even finish it—and then she'd try some of the names in the coded message to try to crack the cipher.

CHAPTER SIXTEEN

Diane was surprised to receive a phone call at eight the following morning. It was a New York number.

"Hello?"

"Hi, Diane, this is Jane Veers."

Her editor at the publishing house in New York! Suddenly Diane had a hunch that this wasn't just a social call. "Hi, Jane."

"I was wondering if you've finished the first three chapters of your book yet? They were due yesterday."

She'd completely missed a deadline! The magnitude of what she'd done slammed into her like a blow to her stomach, and she couldn't breathe for a moment. "Oh my goodness, I'm so sorry, Jane. It completely slipped my mind. I'm so embarrassed."

Diane began scrambling around her desk, searching for the Post-It note that had the deadline scribbled on it. She had kept forgetting to input the date into her calendar on her computer. For some reason she'd thought she had more time, that the deadline was closer to the fifteenth of the month.

"I know we changed the deadline a couple times," Jane said, "but I'm almost sure that the last time we talked, we set it for the eleventh."

Diane found the note just as Jane said the date, and sure enough, she'd scrawled, "3 chps due June 11."

"You're right. It was the eleventh. I'm so very sorry to have missed the deadline. I'll work on the chapters today and get them to you by tomorrow morning." She'd get those chapters done, even if she had to pull an all-nighter. She couldn't believe she'd missed it!

"Tomorrow morning would be great."

"I'm so sorry to disrupt your schedule this way." Diane had worked for a newspaper long enough to know that deadlines were set in stone, and a missed one meant everything was pushed back, in a domino effect.

"Don't worry, Diane, it's only a couple days. It doesn't interrupt things too badly."

"I'll send you the chapters as soon as I'm done with them."

"I look forward to reading them. Thanks."

Diane hung up and buried her face in her hands. How could she have missed a deadline? She was so blessed to be able to be a professional novelist—so she needed to act like one and make her deadlines.

Now was not the time for useless recriminations. She had to prove she was a real writer—writer's block or not—and get those chapters finished.

She headed to her office and fired up her laptop.

Shelley had never before dreaded a new Internet order, but this morning she stared at the order on her computer and groaned.

The order was for a dozen of her chocolate chip cookies, which were becoming a customer favorite. She made them extra large, a full six ounces, and chock-full of chips and walnuts.

She wondered if maybe the large size of the cookies might have kept them from being damaged during shipping. Was that why she hadn't gotten complaints about broken baked goods before this?

Come to think of it, maybe the muffins and unfrosted cupcakes she shipped also stood up better than the cake that had broken in three pieces?

At that moment, the telephone rang. "Hello?"

"Hi, Shelley, it's Beverly."

"Oh, what good timing. I was just wondering how the cakes arrived."

There was a slight hesitation, which made Shelley's insides squirm.

"First of all, there wasn't much damage," Beverly said. "But all three boxes looked a bit banged up."

"Oh no."

"I'm glad you numbered the boxes. Box number one was banged up a lot and the cake split in two."

Shelley groaned. "That's the new, cheaper packaging I bought."

"Box number two was a little better, but there was still a section of the cake that crumbled."

"That's the packaging I just bought but haven't used in my business yet."

"Box number three had only one dent on the side, and the cake was a little squashed on that corner but otherwise okay."

"Oh no," Shelley moaned. "Box number three was the old packaging I used to use before I bought the cheaper stuff. I didn't realize that even it wasn't protecting the cakes well enough."

"Remember, it's only pound cake we're talking about. You didn't try mailing muffins or cookies."

"I was just thinking about that. I wondered if maybe I didn't get complaints about broken goodies because I mostly ship muffins and cookies, and they might travel better than a pound cake."

"Before you got these two complaints, how many pound cakes had you shipped?"

"Let me check." Shelley tapped on her laptop computer and found her order summary table that Beverly had helped her create. She was able to sort it by item type. "I shipped three other pound cakes, and they were all within Maine."

"Maybe the customers didn't want to complain, or maybe those cakes happened to ship better than these did."

"I don't know." Shelley sighed. "I just got an order for cookies today. What am I going to do?"

Beverly thought for a moment. "My suggestion is to use the old packaging. It's more expensive, and you'll lose money because the customer already paid the shipping and handling fee, but the old packaging worked the best at protecting the cakes, and I think that's most important."

"Yes, I think you're right."

"You also might want to think about taking down your Internet orders temporarily."

"I'll...I'll think about it." There was a part of Shelley that was very resistant to just giving up such a good source of income. Maybe the cookies would ship fine. She'd pack them with extra bubble wrap or something.

"I'll keep thinking about it too, Shelley," Beverly said. "Maybe there's a solution to all this that we haven't thought of yet."

"I hope so." But she felt miserable. And defeated. What would happen to her business if she couldn't get enough orders? Dan and his father had just built this lovely kitchen specifically for her baking business. How could she justify the expense and effort they gave to her when she couldn't get enough business?

She knew Dan would always love her, but she didn't want his belief in her to be repaid with only failure.

She wondered if maybe Diane would have some ideas about what she could do. She gathered up Emma and asked Aiden, "Want to go see Miss Diane and Rocky?"

"Yeah!" He bounced up, then darted to the corner to pick up an old ball. "Can I give this to Rocky? I think he'd like it."

"Let's ask Miss Diane first."

They headed across the street and knocked on the door. At first Shelley was a little alarmed because it took so long for Diane to answer, and then she took in Diane's white, tense face when she finally did swing open the door.

"Diane, what's wrong?"

"Oh, Shelley, I'm so upset at myself."

Shelley hadn't heard Diane's voice take on such a miserable tone before. She turned to Aiden. "Why don't you and Emma play with Rocky." Once the kids were occupied, Shelley turned her attention back to Diane.

"I'm sorry, I didn't mean to upset your kids," Diane said.

"There's nothing to be sorry about. What's wrong? How can I help you?"

"There's nothing you can do. I'm just so mad at myself. I missed my deadline yesterday for turning in my three manuscript chapters."

"Oh no! I didn't realize they were due so soon."

"I kept thinking I had until the fifteenth. It's my own fault because I wrote it down on a piece of paper, but I kept forgetting to find it and put it into my calendar. And then the date just passed without my realizing it." Diane wrung her hands. "I never miss deadlines. I can't believe this."

"What do you have to do?"

"I'm going to work all day and all night if I have to. My editor is expecting the chapters in her e-mail tomorrow morning."

Shelley laid a hand on Diane's shoulder. "I know you can do it. You always work so hard."

"I've been so distracted lately with the blog tour and with the research into Jeremiah Thorpe. I've also been suffering from a little writer's block. I should have been able to block out the distractions and focus on the chapters, to just plow through and get the work done."

"I'm sure you can do it."

Diane took a deep breath. "I have to. When I was a newspaper reporter, I found I worked better under pressure. Maybe that's what's been missing—the sense of urgency."

"Is there anything I can do for you?"

Diane bit her lip. "You can pray for me. And maybe ... "

"Anything, Diane."

"Could you walk Rocky for me? He doesn't really take much time from my day, but he still needs to go for his walk this morning, and then he needs to be walked again in the evening."

"Done. Aiden will be thrilled. Did you want me to bring Rocky over to my house for today? Would that help you?"

"Oh yes, thank you so much." Diane looked immensely relieved. "He isn't really that much work, but it would make me feel so much better to not have to think about anything else but my chapters for today."

"Show me where his dog food is, and I'll pack some to take with me, and I'll bring his dog bowls too. And we'll grab his leash so we can walk him right now."

Bustling around, Shelley realized that Diane always seemed to be helping her, and she relished this opportunity to help Diane. She cared deeply for this woman who had come into her life and formed a close friendship with her.

"Now." Shelley paused on Diane's doorstep with Rocky on a leash, Aiden skipping around the front yard, and Emma toddling after him. "I've got all of Rocky's things, and we'll take care of him for you today. And I'll tell Beverly and Margaret so all of us can be praying for you." Shelley gave Diane a quick hug. "It'll all be fine."

"Thank you so much, Shelley."

"What are friends for?"

Margaret had hoped that an early-morning walk along the beach would help her regain some emotional equilibrium. She'd just sent off the check to John Wilson to repay him for the lost painting, and the ending balance in her bank account made her want to weep. She hoped anyone noticing her would attribute her watery eyes to the salty ocean breeze.

Best not to think about it, she told herself. After all, she had her health and her family.

She remembered what Allan had said about the Internet articles he'd read. Could Adelaide really do something like what those people did? Would she want to try?

Or would Margaret and Allan be setting her up for failure?

With the waves foaming in between her toes and the sunlight glinting off the water, she was reminded that God had His hand over all these things—Adelaide too. Was she not trusting Him enough?

She'd always done her best to protect and nurture her daughter. But maybe, like Abraham, she needed to realize that her daughter belonged to God, not to herself.

Impulsively, she turned around and headed home. She still had an hour or so before she needed to open the gallery. She had just enough time.

She said good-bye to Allan and Adelaide and got in the car. She headed to Evergreen, a community college in Bramford.

Evergreen had a serene campus with lots of green grass, dotted with trees. The classroom buildings were built in a rambling fashion over the grounds, making it look like a little town rather than a college campus.

Margaret parked in the parking lot and followed the signs to the administration building, which ended up being a darling little Victorian house that had been renovated and converted into offices. Margaret climbed the front steps to the tiny porch and let herself in the front door, which had been changed to a framed glass panel, but with an old-fashioned brass doorknob.

The front foyer was dominated by a receptionist's desk, and a young woman with chic black-rimmed glasses looked up pleasantly at her.

"I'm wondering about your class schedule for my daughter." Margaret hesitated, wondering what she should disclose, then plunged ahead. "She has Down syndrome, but we think she might be interested in taking college classes."

"Oh." The young woman smoothed back her sleek black hair and adjusted her glasses. "You probably want to speak to Mrs. Castle. Let me ring her up for you."

She picked up the phone and pressed a few buttons. "I have a woman here who has a special needs child and she'd like to speak to you about classes her daughter could take. Okay." The woman hung up and smiled at Margaret. "Mrs. Castle has a few minutes free right now. Head upstairs and her office is the second door on the right." She pointed toward the narrow staircase just beyond her desk.

Margaret climbed the stairs, her footsteps muted by the rich red carpet laid down over the refinished hardwood steps. The second floor of the building probably had been bedrooms but now there were four doors lining the narrow hallway. Margaret knocked tentatively on the second door on the right, and a brisk, "Come in!" made her turn the knob and enter.

The office was tiny, barely large enough for the oak desk, a filing cabinet, and a tall bookshelf. The woman behind the desk was a stout woman with rosy cheeks and short gray curls, who stood and thrust her hand out to Margaret. "Eleanor Castle. Nice to meet you."

"Margaret Hoskins." Margaret sat in the small wooden chair opposite Eleanor.

"So your daughter is special needs?" Eleanor asked without hesitation or reservation.

"Down syndrome."

Eleanor smiled. "My son has Down syndrome too."

Margaret blinked at her for a moment. "Oh. Does he go to this college too?"

"He used to. He occasionally still takes classes that interest him, like a new painting class or sculpture class. We had local sculptor Beka Banks come and teach last semester."

"I've seen her work. She's very good."

"What kinds of classes is your daughter interested in?"

Margaret bit her lip. "I don't know. Penny Tyler at the community center in Marble Cove suggested we look into other classes and activities for her because she fears Adelaide might be bored with the classes there."

Eleanor nodded. "Sometimes that happens. We never know our children's potential until we let them try something new."

"Does Evergreen have classes that would be appropriate for Adelaide to take?"

"Tons." Eleanor rummaged in a desk drawer and pulled out a thin booklet, which she passed to Margaret. "This is the class schedule for the fall semester. The summer semester is already started. The classes show the requirements for students. Your daughter can pretty much take any class where she meets the requirement. There are lots of options for special needs students."

"Are there many special needs children on the campus?"

"Right now, only a couple, but there will probably be more come fall. We had about four last year."

"I didn't realize there were so many."

"Not all the students had Down syndrome. We also had a couple students with high-functioning autism."

"What kinds of classes would you suggest for my daughter?"

Eleanor shrugged. "She can take anything she's interested in. My son took a lot of art classes. There are also sports classes she could take which don't have requirements. We have a couple cooking classes she could also try. There are some child development classes and child care courses we just started this past year with small class sizes and lots of one-on-one attention."

"Maybe the cooking. Or the child development classes, if they're not too difficult—she likes taking care of children."

"She might think about being a teacher's aide or a nursery school teacher. It depends on what classes she's already taken and where her interests lie."

Margaret flipped through the courses list. "I hadn't realized there were so many options for her."

"There are a lot more options for our kids now than there used to be." Eleanor grinned. "I admit, I've pushed for more options because of my son, but we also have a very strong community of parents in this area who have special needs kids, and the school wants to support them."

Eleanor nodded at the class list. "Look through that, and then talk to your daughter about what she might want to take. You may be surprised."

"Thank you." Margaret stood and shook hands with Eleanor. "You've given me a lot to think about."

Eleanor gave her a business card. "If you have any questions, just give me a call."

Margaret drove home in a daze, and when she walked in the house, was glad to see Adelaide busy in her room. Margaret went out to Allan's workshop and told him about her conversation with Eleanor Castle.

Allan flipped through the course list. "It was one thing to read about this online, but it feels strange to be looking at this book to actually figure out which classes might be suitable for Adelaide."

"It feels a little scary," Margaret said, "but at the same time, now I can actually see a glimpse of all the new opportunities there are for her."

"Let's look at this tonight together. We can talk to Adelaide about it tomorrow," Allan said.

"That's a good idea." Margaret squeezed his hand. "It won't feel so scary if we're all in this together."

Chapter Seventeen

Margaret walked into the kitchen the next morning and looked around, but only Allan sat at the breakfast table. "Where's Adelaide?"

"She went over to Shelley's house. They kept Rocky all night and so they're all playing with him."

"I wonder how Diane is doing? I called her yesterday before dinner to remind her to eat despite her stress, and she sounded focused but fine."

"You can go over this morning and find out. I'll be happy to go to the gallery for you for a few hours."

"That might be a good idea, but what about Adelaide? Will she go with you or stay home?"

"She might stay at the Bauers'. Shelley said she'd be happy to feed her breakfast."

Margaret laughed. "Adelaide probably prefers that. She loves Shelley's breakfast goodies."

"So we'll talk to Adelaide tonight about the classes?" Allan asked.

"Sounds goo—"

The sudden loud, urgent ringing of the doorbell broke into her conversation. Over and over it sounded, hastening Margaret's steps to the front door.

Diane's daughter Jessica stood there, her face white, with an unfamiliar young man standing behind her. "Jessica, what—?"

"It's Mom." The young woman's blue eyes were watery with tears. "I came to see her this morning and I found her in the living room."

Margaret was out the door in a flash and racing to the house next door. She entered the open doorway and saw Diane sprawled out on the sofa in the living room.

"Diane." Margaret knelt in front of her, lightly slapping her cold cheeks.

"Ma...Mar..." Diane was conscious, but seemed very woozy.

"Jessica, call the ambulance," Margaret said.

"I already did." Allan stood in Diane's open doorway, holding his cell phone.

Margaret headed to the kitchen and yanked open the fridge. She pulled out a carton of orange juice and poured it into a glass.

"I'll give it to her." Jessica grabbed the glass and headed back into the living room.

Margaret saw the open bag of bread on the counter and went to close it. She then saw a piece of toast in the toaster. It was cold.

Had Diane forgotten to eat last night, despite Margaret reminding her?

"Margaret," came Jessica's strangled voice from the living room.

She went to Diane and Jessica on the sofa.

"It's not kicking in. The orange juice." Jessica's hand shook as she held the glass of juice.

Margaret took it from her and eased it to Diane's lips. "Take a sip, Diane."

With unbearable slowness, Diane opened her lips and sipped a little. It was as if the effort to move was too great for her.

Jessica started to quietly sob, and the young man put his arms around her and held her close. This must be Martin, Jessica's boyfriend. His scared brown eyes met Margaret's over Jessica's bent head.

"It'll be all right." Margaret didn't know if she was saying that for Jessica's sake, for Martin's, or for her own.

The paramedics came only a few minutes later, but it seemed like a lifetime. "You told the dispatcher that she was hypoglycemic?" one of them asked Margaret.

Allan must have told them. Margaret nodded.

The paramedics immediately checked Diane's blood sugar levels, and the grim expression on his face told Margaret more than the numbers on the tester he held. "We're going to give her a glucagon injection," he told them.

Margaret backed away and stood with Allan against the wall, to give the paramedics room. He put his arm around her and squeezed tight.

Margaret began to silently pray. *Dear Lord, please help Diane. Please let her be okay.*

They waited while the paramedics did various things Margaret didn't understand. She watched Diane's pale face, the half-lidded eyes.

Then slowly, Diane began to seem more alert. She blinked and looked at her daughter, who also watched her anxiously. "Jessica?" she asked in a faint voice.

Jessica gave a sob but couldn't approach her mother because of the paramedics.

The paramedics asked Diane various questions and she began to answer them with more conviction as they went along.

"We need to take you to the hospital," one of them said to her.

"Oh, do I have to—?" she began to ask, but then Jessica said firmly, "Yes, Mom, you do."

Even though Diane was still pale, Margaret could tell she was horribly embarrassed by all the fuss being made about her.

The paramedics insisted on carrying her out in the stretcher, and Jessica seconded their decision with a firm look at her mother.

Once outside, Margaret told Jessica, "We'll follow you to the hospital."

"No, I think she'll be all right now." Jessica laid a hand on Margaret's arm. "Thank you so much."

"Of course. We'll come by later today to see her."

"I think she'll like that, after she gets over the mortification of needing to go to the hospital." Jessica's voice was dry, but her worry still came through in the lines around her mouth.

Margaret watched as the paramedics drove away, Jessica's car following.

Allan remarked, "One thing's for sure. Diane will never again forget to put a deadline in her calendar."

"Allan, I don't know whether to slug you for that remark or start crying."

He put his arm around her again and squeezed her tight. "She'll be fine."

"Yes, thank goodness."

⌒

Diane's bed was extremely cushy and comfy, but she had never felt more uncomfortable in her life.

Part of it was the hospital gown they'd made her wear, despite the fact she insisted she felt fine now and wanted to go home.

Part of it was the fact that Jessica and her boyfriend Martin were in the hospital room with her, looking at her with concern. Their looks made her want to crawl under the bed and hide with embarrassment.

"I promise I'm normally not this forgetful about eating," Diane said.

"I heard you a hundred times ago, Mom." Jessica's eyes twinkled at her.

"I'm just so embarrassed—"

"I heard that about two hundred times ago. Relax, Mom." Jessica leaned forward in her chair to grasp Diane's hand where it lay on the cover. "It's not that big a deal."

"Yes, it is a big deal. What a terrible first impression for Martin."

He gave a half smile. "Not a big deal, Mrs. Spencer."

"Diane," she insisted.

"Sorry, forgot." Another half grin.

Jessica turned a smiling face to him, and her joy at being with him shone out of her.

Diane, however, hadn't really formed that much of an impression of Martin. He had talked about safe things like the weather, his job as an information technology manager in Boston, his family in Ohio, his new BMW, the men's Bible study he had joined at his church. To be honest, he was as exciting as vanilla.

But Jessica apparently loved vanilla because she sat and talked with him easily when she wasn't chatting with her mother.

At that moment, Jessica's cell phone rang, but after looking at the caller ID, she grinned and handed the phone to her mother. "It's for you."

"What?" Diane answered the call. "Hello?"

"Mom, are you all right?" Justin's concerned voice crackled over the phone.

Her embarrassment rocketed through the roof and she gave Jessica a stern look. Her daughter simply smiled serenely at her. "I'm fine," Diane told her son. "How are things with you?"

"Don't try to distract me, Mom," her son said. "We're going to start thinking we need to put you in a nursing home."

"Nursing home?!" Diane yelped. "Justin Spencer, you—"

But Justin was laughing, and so was Jessica. "The pair of you are going to put me in an early grave," Diane complained to her son.

"Mom, you worried us," Justin said, his voice quiet.

Diane sobered too. "I'm sorry, sweetheart."

"We want you to promise us you'll take better care of yourself."

"I promise." She couldn't blame her children for being worried about her. After all, she'd gone through the cancer treatments with the two of them and Eric beside her. "So how is your Officer Candidate School course?"

This time, he allowed himself to be distracted and they talked about his training course for a few minutes before he had to hang up. When he did, Diane immediately missed having him near, even though she was also proud of him for taking control of his career.

"Hello!" Margaret's voice at the door made Diane perk up.

Not just Margaret, but also Shelley and Beverly walked into the room.

"How are you doing?" Shelley asked.

"I'm fine," Diane said.

"When do you get out of here?" Margaret asked.

Diane frowned. "I keep telling them I feel fine, but they won't let me leave for another couple days. They said they want to monitor my blood sugar levels."

"I think that's very wise of them." Beverly gave her a mock-stern look. "You gave everyone a scare this morning."

"I'm sorry about that."

"Did you at least get your three chapters done?" Margaret asked.

"Yes, I finished them in the wee hours of the morning and e-mailed them off as soon as I finished." Diane remembered getting up from her office chair and feeling woozy. She'd sat down on the sofa and then the next thing she knew, there were paramedics all around her and Jessica's anxious face hovering over their shoulders.

"If it's all right with the nurses, I'll bring the kids to see you tomorrow," Shelley said. "Aiden has been asking after you all day. 'When's Miss Diane coming back? Is she okay? I want to go see her.'"

"Aww." Diane was touched that Shelley's son would miss her so much.

"What have you been doing all day?" Margaret asked.

"Nothing."

Her friends laughed at the miserable note in Diane's voice.

"Tell us how you really feel," Shelley said with a grin.

"And you're going to continue to do nothing," Jessica said sternly. "You've done way too much in the past two weeks, if what you're telling me is true."

Diane felt the heat rise up her neck and into her cheeks. She'd blithely talked to Jessica about everything that had been going on, but her daughter had been appalled at how packed her days had been.

"You always complain to me that I'm working too hard, Mom. But you should listen to yourself."

"You have been pretty busy," Shelley said. "I'm sorry for always coming to you for help. I should have let you alone so you could get your work done. Then you might not have missed your deadline."

"I came to you for help too." Margaret's brow was furrowed. "You helped me all day when we were searching for Agnes Dillwater, and that didn't even come to anything."

"This wasn't anyone's fault but my own," Diane said.

"It doesn't matter who's to blame," Jessica said. "While I'm here, Mom is going to slow down and take better care of herself."

Diane knew her daughter loved her and was concerned for her, but she couldn't help but worry that there was so much for her to do. She still had the blog tour, including some interviews and guest posts that were now overdue. She'd called her editor earlier today to explain, and Jane had promised to tell the PR firm handling the blog tour so they could let the bloggers know about the delay, but it didn't mean Diane still didn't have to do the work eventually.

And the Founders Day service for Old First was scheduled for the end of the month. How wonderful it would be if they could find some sort of information about the treasure to try to save the historic church in time for the service. They seemed so close to solving the message, and Diane just knew that it had something to do with the treasure.

But she was stuck in this hospital bed, although Jessica had said that she'd get her laptop for her tomorrow. However, knowing her daughter, she'd probably only allow her to spend limited time on it.

But she truly was grateful for her daughter's presence, and her friends around her. If not for Margaret and Allan, she might have been more seriously ill.

"Is there any news about your stolen painting?" Diane asked Margaret.

She shook her head.

"We still need to go around town asking about that tall, thin woman," Diane said.

"Not right now, you're not," Jessica said.

"That can wait," Margaret said at the same time.

"I did ask Brenna at the Cove about her," Shelley said. "She said that she's seen her around town this summer, but not lately. She promised to keep an eye out for her and to tell me right away."

Well, at least that was some headway into the case.

"Don't worry about any of this." Margaret reached out to clasp Diane's shoulder. "After what happened this morning, none of that seems very important to me anymore."

"Of course it's important. It's your award-winning—"

"It's only a painting. You're my friend. Just concentrate on getting better. We can go talk to every merchant in town when you're out of here."

Margaret smiled at her, and Diane relaxed back against her pillows. It sounded like she was worrying more about the painting than Margaret, which was silly of her.

Chapter Eighteen

At dinner, Margaret asked Adelaide, "So how did you enjoy the community center today?"

To her surprise, Adelaide bent her head and started pushing her asparagus around her plate. "Oh...it was okay."

"What's wrong?" Margaret was on high alert now.

"Nothing's wrong." But Adelaide gave a huge sigh.

Allan laid a gentle hand on Margaret's wrist as if to remind her not to assume the worst. "Did something happen today that upset you?" he asked.

"No, nothing happened." Sigh.

"Did someone say something to you that upset you?" Margaret asked.

Adelaide paused.

"What did that person say?"

"It was my friend Chloe."

Chloe was a young woman with Down syndrome who lived in the group home, Bayview House, with her identical twin sister Cassie. Margaret remembered Chloe was a bubbly personality. "What did Chloe say?"

"She was excited because she got a part in a play." Adelaide's mouth worked as if she wanted to say more, but wasn't sure how to phrase it.

"Where's the play?" Allan asked.

"Chloe and Cassie both tried out for it. It's a theater group in Augusta. Only Chloe got a part, though."

"Was Cassie disappointed?" Margaret asked.

Adelaide nodded.

"What did Chloe say that made you upset?"

"Not upset." Adelaide paused, as if choosing her words. "She's my friend. I want to be happy for her. But I feel kind of sad."

Margaret wondered if she was a little jealous. "Do you want to try out for a play too?"

"No. But..."

"Maybe you feel sad because you want to try something new and exciting like that too?" Margaret guessed.

Adelaide nodded. "Yeah, I think so, Mom."

This would certainly make sense in light of what Penny had said to them earlier. "Adelaide, do you think you might want to take college classes?"

If Margaret had had any doubts about the idea, they were wiped away by the brilliant look of joy on her daughter's face. "Really?"

Margaret nodded, then went up to retrieve the college booklet she and Allan had looked through last night. They'd marked absolutely every class that Adelaide would be able to take, not sure which ones might interest her.

Margaret gave the booklet to Adelaide, who accepted it with a little squeal. "I could really take classes at college?"

Margaret and Allan exchanged smiles as they nodded. "What kinds of things would you like to learn?" Margaret asked.

"I don't know." Adelaide slowly leafed through the booklet. She suddenly looked up at them. "Do you think I could be a teacher?"

"I think you could be anything you want to be." Margaret fought the tears tightening her throat. Her little girl was actually a young woman.

"When can I start?" Adelaide asked.

"These classes are for the fall semester," Allan said. "You can start in September if you want."

"I think you'd make a great teacher," Margaret said. "You're already so good with Aiden and Emma."

"I like kids." Adelaide grinned at them.

Allan reached for her hand and gripped it tightly. She knew what he was feeling. Their daughter was definitely growing up and moving toward independence.

It made Margaret sad, but she was also proud of Adelaide. She knew that her inquisitive mind and courage would take her far.

As Beverly drove up the driveway to her house in Augusta, the morning sun happened to catch the sparkling windows and cast a brilliant orange glow over the walls. The beauty of it should have awed her.

But Beverly realized that the beauty only left her cold. The house left her cold. Just the sight of it seemed to dampen her spirits.

Maybe there was a part of her that was happy to be getting rid of the house. She'd been spending so much time second-guessing her decision to sell. Had she overlooked any feelings of relief that the house would be out of her hands?

The thought made her pause before opening the front door. Then she shook off the wayward thoughts and unlocked the door.

This would probably be the last load of things that she'd take from the house. She only had her bedroom and the bathroom left, and most of those things had already been taken back to her father's home in Marble Cove.

She started in the bathroom and found a bunch of old cosmetics she'd needed when she had to dress up for special parties that Will would throw or events he'd go to. The more dramatic colors of her eye shadows, lipsticks, and blushes seemed garish to her now. She hadn't used these colors even when she'd had to make her face up for work at the State House in Augusta, because they were too dark, too vivid.

As she dropped the cosmetics into a trash bag, she felt a sense of freedom in being able to throw them away. She wouldn't have to go to any large, fancy dinners again if she didn't want to. And Jeff certainly didn't go to them oft—

She stopped herself midthought. How strange that she'd thought of Jeff.

But it was true. He didn't care for those types of fancy events, and luckily his job didn't require him to attend many of them. And now, neither did hers.

She packed some of her regular toiletries to take back with her—the extra shampoo and soap she had kept at the house for her own use. But she found a lot of things from her old life with Will that she no longer needed, and they were all pitched in the trash bag with a strange, immense satisfaction.

She went to her wardrobe next, where she knew there were some old dresses that she hadn't needed in Marble Cove. Several glittering dinner dresses, a ball gown or two. A soft floral gown she'd worn to a wedding of one of Will's associates.

She had liked the floral gown, and figured it would come in handy if she had to go to another wedding. She set that aside to take with her.

But the other gowns, with their excess of sequins, their slightly daring necklines, their figure-skimming shapes— she looked at them and didn't want them.

She grabbed the gowns a bit more forcefully than she intended to and dumped them all unceremoniously in the box labeled "sell." Some of them were worth thousands of dollars, and if she sold them at a clothing consignment store she wouldn't get even a tenth of their worth, but she didn't care. It felt as if she were hastening to free herself from shackles.

The last gown in the wardrobe was bulky and soft, covered in a thick plastic garment cover. Her wedding gown.

She'd bought her dream gown. A gown that made Will's eyes light up when he saw her. She remembered the tender look in his face as he watched her walking down the aisle.

She pulled the garment bag out of the wardrobe and laid it on the bed. Her fingers hesitated over the zipper. A part of her wanted to open the garment bag to look at the dress again, to feel its soft satin folds, the rougher texture of the embroidery at the neckline and cuffs, the whisper of lace and tulle.

But another part of her didn't want to see the gown again. It cringed away from the memory, wanted to shove the gown back in the closet and lock it up tight.

It had been one of the happiest days of her life. But the memory of it also made her sad, because she hadn't had as many happy days in her marriage as she had hoped for starting out.

Will hadn't been a bad man, but their marriage hadn't been a fairy tale. It was why she'd had so much guilt when she'd been enjoying talking to Jeff on that boat as Will had died. She almost felt as if she needed to suffer more because of how her husband had died.

But she realized that she'd spent too long punishing herself. That this house, in a sense, was punishing her.

And she suddenly knew it was time to let it go.

She picked up the garment bag with the wedding gown and laid it in the "thrift store" box. And didn't feel a single qualm about it. If she did get married again, she'd want a simpler gown, a dress more to her current tastes rather than this elaborate, expensive gown.

She finished clearing out the house and carried the boxes to her car. She locked the door firmly, for the last time.

As she drove away, she glanced back at the house in her rearview mirror. The afternoon sunlight glinted off the windows in a way similar to that morning.

And as the house grew smaller and smaller in her mirror, she could feel her spirits lift.

Yes, that was definitely a sign.

The house and the memories saturated in it had become an emotional burden to her. And now that Will was gone and she was moving on in her life, it was only causing her stress that was adding to the worries she already had about her new business, her father... and her burgeoning relationship with Jeff.

Yes. It was time to let go.

CHAPTER NINETEEN

On Thursday afternoon, Shelley stared down at the broken cake in the box. It was one of the pound cakes she'd mailed to Augusta on Monday, and Beverly had brought it over to her yesterday so she could see the extent of the damage.

Last night, her family certainly hadn't minded the damage. They'd attacked the cake with gusto. Dan had even joked that since it was already broken, they might as well "break" it further.

While she'd understood his joking, it had still gnawed at her that she couldn't mail her cakes without damage. What was she going to do? She still didn't have a solution.

"Hello?" A voice at the front door made her look up.

"Meemaw!" Aiden shouted, and headed to the door.

Shelley let her mother-in-law into the house. Frances was all smiles as Aiden and then Emma came up to her for hugs and kisses.

"I came to see the grandkids," she said to Shelley.

A part of Shelley was annoyed that Frances assumed it would be fine for her to drop in anytime she wanted, but she realized that was petty. Frances was a loving, attentive grandmother to Aiden and Emma, and they enjoyed having her around as well.

"We were going to have cake, Grandma." Aiden grabbed Frances' hand and pulled her toward the kitchen. "Let me get my new rocket to show you." He darted off to his room to look for his new toy, Emma toddling after him.

"Cake? You made cake for them?" Frances' eyebrows rose as she looked at Shelley.

Shelley tried not to bristle. She took a deep breath first, then said, "It's left over from an experiment I did."

"Experiment?"

Shelley hesitated. She shouldn't have mentioned the experiment to Frances, because she didn't really want to have to explain about her problems with her Internet orders. She always felt like she was walking on eggshells with Frances, expecting some new criticism about her home-based business.

"I mailed a couple pound cakes last week, but my customers said they arrived broken," Shelley said reluctantly. "So I did an experiment and sent cakes to Beverly in Augusta to see how they held up in different packaging. This is just the leftovers." She gestured to the cake on the table.

Frances peered into the box, her brow wrinkling. "It's broken."

"The packaging isn't quite strong enough."

Frances straightened and looked at her with a dispassionate gaze. "You know, Shelley, if you can't do a good job shipping your desserts, you shouldn't do it at all."

Shelley froze. Had Frances just said what she thought she said? Did she really think Shelley should just give up her business? She wasn't really doing too badly—she had a steady client in the Cove, and she had other clients for occasional work, and her Internet orders for extra income. Why did her mother-in-law feel the need to always criticize her and make her feel like a failure?

Wait a minute. Calm down, Shelley. She took a breath. She needed to stop jumping to conclusions. She needed to make sure she understood what Frances was saying.

"I'm sorry, Frances, I don't quite understand you. What exactly do you mean?" Her voice bordered on sugary, but it was polite, at least.

Frances blinked at her for a moment. "Oh. I mean that you shouldn't just be satisfied with substandard shipping. You put so much work into your desserts that the shipping should be top-notch too."

Shelley felt her shoulders relax, suddenly vastly relieved that she hadn't let her assumptions and her anger carry her away.

Frances continued, "You shouldn't just make the most of it. You should look into any solutions for doing the job right."

"I've been looking for packaging online, but haven't found any yet that I think will protect my pastries well enough."

"Then maybe you need to see if there are other outside-the-box ideas. Rather than looking at pastry boxes, how about looking at packaging normally used for other purposes?"

Now that was an interesting idea. It was true that Shelley had been focusing on packaging normally used for baked goods, not for other things. "Thank you, Frances. That's a good idea."

"I, uh...I didn't mean it to sound like a criticism," Frances said with a self-conscious look. "I'm really quite proud of you for all you've done with your business."

Shelley smiled at her mother-in-law. "Thanks. I couldn't have done it without support from Dan and from you and Ralph."

"You've maintained a very high standard for your business. So all aspects of it should be that same standard, including the shipping options. You might need to adjust your pricing, but don't stint on quality."

Frances had a good point. She did try her best with her baking. She had maintained a strict standard for the kitchen that Dan had built for her. She had asked Beverly to build a professional, easy-to-navigate Web site for her. So it didn't make sense for her to stint on other aspects of her business.

"I'll look into it, Frances," Shelley said. "Thank you. Want some cake?"

"I thought you'd never ask."

"Grandma, I found my rocket!" Aiden darted into the kitchen, holding his rocket aloft, but the sight of the cake made him detour to get a slice for himself.

"Aiden, where's Emma?"

"She's in the living room with my other rocket. I let her borrow it."

Shelley went to the living room to retrieve her daughter and rescue the rocket before it found its way into places like her mouth or stuck under the sofa.

Frances had cut slices of pound cake for all of them and poured milk for both Aiden and Emma. Shelley set Emma in her booster seat.

"Did you want tea with that?" she asked Frances.

"Oh yes, that would be nice."

While Shelley put the kettle on, Frances asked, "How's Diane doing?"

"Better today. Her daughter brought her laptop to her at the hospital so she got some work done, but she was complaining that the hospital wireless connection was slow."

"She'll get the history of Old First done for the commemoration booklet, won't she? It would be hard for me to find someone else to do it so last minute."

"Oh yes, she mentioned she hoped to interview you in a few days, when she's feeling better. She'll have it done before the end of the month." Shelley sat at the table and pulled her plate of cake toward her.

"Did she end up finding useful information in the rest of that box, then?"

"She did say that she found the names of Jeremiah Thorpe's children—Elisabeth and John." In contrast, that same day Shelley had looked through the main stacks for anything about Jeremiah Thorpe and hadn't found anything.

"Yes, that's right. I admit I was surprised because I had thought his daughter's name was something else, something shorter...but maybe I was thinking of Jeremiah's sister's name."

Shelley looked up from her plate. "Jeremiah's sister?"

At that moment, the kettle began to whistle so she had to get up and pour the hot water for tea. But she hurried back to the table and asked again, "Jeremiah's sister?"

"Yes, I think his sister came to Marble Cove after his wife died to help him take care of his children."

They hadn't come across anything about Jeremiah Thorpe's sister. "What was his sister's name?"

Frances thought a moment. "I don't remember. I should, because I think she wrote a hymn or something like that."

A hymn would be easy enough to find in a hymnal, right? Beverly had played for the church choir at Easter—perhaps she had a copy of the hymnal at her home, with the sheet music on her piano.

Shelley would have to try to talk to her tomorrow. Here was another possibility for the key to the cipher.

As soon as Dan walked through the door, Shelley knew something was wrong.

The skin around his temples was tight with pain and frustration, although he smiled at Aiden and Emma. But the smile didn't lift his cheeks or light up his blue eyes, and Shelley had to fight to appear normal so as not to alarm the kids.

But when he leaned over to kiss her, she grabbed his hand and squeezed. He hesitated, then squeezed back, but his face was still drawn and tense.

Shelley tried not to be worried as they had supper, and Dan did his best to entertain the kids, but he wasn't as cheerful as he usually was, and more than once, Aiden had to say "Daddy" a couple times before he got Dan's attention.

Dan lingered over tucking Aiden into bed, as if drinking in the peace of the room as his son drifted to sleep. Then he sighed and followed Shelley out to the living room.

They sat on the sofa and she took his hands in hers. "Are you all right? Is there anything I can do?"

He disentangled one hand from hers to reach out and briefly cup her cheek. "Oh, Shell. I just don't know if this is what I should be doing."

"What happened today?"

"Wayne seems to criticize everything I do. I don't know if I'm cut out for this job."

Shelley's temper flared in defense of her husband, but then she remembered what had happened that very afternoon with Frances. She had thought Frances was criticizing her, when actually she had meant something else. So Shelley took a deep breath and asked, "What did he criticize you about?"

He shook his head. "Stuff. Everything."

"But what exactly did he criticize?"

Dan thought a few seconds, then started describing a complicated circuit-something that Shelley didn't understand at all. But at the end, he said, "Wayne wanted me to do it exactly the way he does it, treating me almost like a child. I know I'm still learning, and I don't intend to be unteachable or anything like that, but the way he says things is pretty condescending." Dan's frustration rolled out of him in almost tangible waves.

Shelley mulled over what he'd said. "So Wayne wants you to do things exactly the way he does, right? Is he a micromanager?"

Dan hesitated before answering. "*N-nooo...*" he said slowly. "Not exactly a micromanager, not like that one boss I had at the docks, do you remember? Wayne's not overseeing absolutely every little thing I do. He doesn't come in and try to fix or tweak everything I do. Instead, he looks at what I've done and then tells me everything I did wrong, even stuff I thought I did correctly. It's like I can't do the job right."

"Doing the job right... You know, that reminds me of something your mom said to me this afternoon. You remember I told you about how the cakes are breaking in the containers I'm shipping them in because I bought the cheaper containers?"

Dan nodded.

"Frances saw one of the broken cakes and asked me about it, so I told her. At first, she said that if I couldn't do the job right, I shouldn't do it at all, and I thought she was criticizing my work. But when I asked her what she meant, she explained. She hadn't meant to criticize me at all. At least, not that way."

"So what did she mean?"

"When she talked about doing the job right, she meant maintaining a high standard for all aspects of my business, not just the baking, but the shipping and packaging too. And that I shouldn't be satisfied with just getting by with substandard packaging."

"But Shell, I'm not sure how this relates to my job."

"When Wayne criticizes what you've done, I'm wondering if this is what he means, too—not that he's saying you *can't* do the work, but that you aren't doing the work correctly."

Dan shook his head. "I'm still not quite following you."

"For all the other jobs you've been doing, you've had to get things done quickly, right? Working at the docks, painting and handyman jobs, even completing the frames you were making with Allan. There was a time factor involved."

Dan thought a moment, then nodded. "Yes, you're right."

"But Wayne says he wants you to do things exactly the way he does them. Yet he's not micromanaging you or trying to do things for you. Instead, he's trying to get you to do things a certain way."

"The way he does things."

"Yes. What if his criticism is him trying to tell you that you need to slow down and do things correctly and carefully? This job is slightly different from your other jobs—you can't hurry too much. Maybe he wants you to be more detail-oriented. It's the same thing about high standards that Frances was telling me about. Every small detail of my business needs to have the same high standard."

"And maybe Wayne is saying the same thing to me, that every small aspect of my job needs to have the same high standard, the same attention to detail." Dan sat and thought about this a moment, but Shelley could see some of the frustration and worry starting to ease from his face. "But how do I know that's what he means? If I take his words at face value, that might not be what he's getting at."

"He could be a little like...your mother," Shelley said delicately. "He might have a different communication style. It makes his words seem to mean one thing when he means something else."

"You think it's just a problem with communication?"

"I'm not sure, but think about it. I have always had a problem communicating with Frances. Just today I thought she was being critical, when actually it was constructive criticism and some very good advice. But if I had continued to misconstrue what she was saying, I would have been offended and hurt."

"It seems like such an easy solution," Dan said doubtfully.

"I don't think it is an easy solution," Shelley said. "I think it'll take time and effort to understand exactly what's going on. But you obviously really like the work, and I think if you can better understand what Wayne is getting at, then things will start to feel better when you're on the job."

Dan slowly nodded. "I really do like this job. And because of that, it's worth it to me to do all I can to make it work out."

"That's the spirit." Shelley smiled at him, and he returned a sheepish one of his own.

He leaned over to kiss her. "You're my own personal cheerleader."

"You've done the same for me."

Dan seemed less stressed now, and Shelley was glad for it.

She just wished the solution to her own dilemma was as clear.

CHAPTER TWENTY

Beverly had just walked in the door from her morning jog when her cell phone rang. It was Shelley.

"Hi, Shelley."

"Hi, Beverly. I knew you were awake because I saw you run past my house."

"One of these days, you should come join me."

"I do enough running after Aiden all day, thank you very much." Shelley laughed. "The reason I'm calling is because I heard something interesting yesterday. I tried calling you, but..."

"Yes, I was in Augusta all day yesterday. I finally finished packing up my house."

"Congratulations! Does it feel good?"

Beverly hesitated a moment, but then said decisively, "Yes, it does. Like a weight on my shoulders has been lifted, and I didn't even realize I had been carrying it."

"I can understand that. After all, your husband designed and built the house. It must have a lot of memories."

"Both good and bad."

"I think selling it will help you move on in your life." Shelley smiled and added, "And pursue new relationships."

Beverly thought about Jeff. "I think you're right. So what did you have to tell me?"

"Oh, that's right. Frances talked to me yesterday and mentioned that Jeremiah Thorpe had a sister."

"A sister? But we haven't heard or read anything about her."

"That's what I said. Frances couldn't remember her name, but mentioned that she wrote a hymn for Old First."

"I have one of the hymnals. Let me go check." Beverly felt a rising hum in her chest as she went to the piano and found a battered old hymnal. Estelle Baumgardner, the church organist, had said she could take the old book home with her since the spine was too fragile to use for Sunday service, but the music inside was still perfectly fine.

There was an index of composers at the back, and Beverly scanned the list. "No, I don't see any hymns written by a Thorpe."

"Oh." Shelley sighed. "I was really hoping her hymn might be in there."

"Wait a minute." Beverly turned to the front page. "This is a hymnal published by a national publisher, so any local music wouldn't be included in this book. But obviously the congregation sang the song, or at least knew about it, or Frances wouldn't have heard about it."

"So if Jeremiah's sister wrote a hymn, where would it be?"

"I'm not sure. There's a bunch of sheet music in the organ at Old First. Maybe it's in there?"

"Do you think we'd be able to go look?"

"You'd like to come?"

"Of course. I can ask Adelaide to watch the kids."

"Let me call the organist, Estelle."

"Okay, call me back."

Beverly hung up and looked for Estelle's telephone number. She spoke to Estelle at church often, but she hadn't had to call her many times. She finally found the number on a piece of paper left over from Easter, when she'd had to play the piano for the church choir and Maddie Bancroft had given her Estelle's contact information. She dialed.

"Hello?" Estelle's no-nonsense voice answered the phone.

"Hi, Estelle, it's Beverly Wheeland." She almost added the Parker at the end of her hyphenated name, but she'd come to realize that most Marble Cove residents associated her with her father and thought hyphenated names were newfangled or pretentious. *Maybe it's time to officially become Beverly Wheeland again,* she thought.

"Hello, Beverly. What can I do for you?"

"I have a favor to ask. I'm looking for an old hymn written by a church member, probably from the first congregation the church ever had. It's for the Founders Day celebration."

"Well, now. A hymn written by a church member?" Estelle paused. "It might be in the organ. There are lots of pages of sheet music stored in the bench."

"I thought maybe it was there. Do I need a key to get in?"

"Oh no. It has a lock, but I never lock it. Just head to the church and take a look."

Beverly thanked her, then called Shelley.

"I'll be over in a moment," Shelley said. "I already called Margaret and asked if Adelaide can watch the kids, and I walked them over a couple minutes ago."

Beverly and Shelley headed to Old First, the light summer breeze circling in the car as they drove, bringing with it the scent of wildflowers and the sea.

"I hope Jeremiah's sister didn't marry and change her last name." Beverly turned into the parking lot for Old First, its crenellated tower rising into the blue sky.

"I didn't think of that." Shelley gave Beverly a dismayed look as they parked and she got out of the car.

Beverly loved approaching the brick and brownstone exterior, interrupted by intricate stained-glass windows. They tried the heavy wooden front door, but it was locked.

"We'll have to go around to the offices in back." Beverly led the way around the side of the Gothic building.

The church looked like it had had various chambers added to it over the years, making the rooms outside the main sanctuary wander in broken lines, a bit of a maze. At the very back of the church and to one side stood the newer bell tower. The older one was at the very back of the building surrounded by an old storage room.

They followed the flagstone sidewalk around the side of the building and followed the small brass signs to the "office." They pushed open the heavy wooden door into the tiny reception area, dominated by the secretary's desk. There was no one in that position at the moment, and a door in the wall behind the desk stood ajar, with Reverend Locke's name on a plaque on the dark stained wood.

"Reverend Locke?" Beverly called into the empty reception room.

"Come in," he called from his office, and they crossed the small space to enter the open door.

He sat behind his large mahogany desk, papers all around him, but he gave them a polite smile and his full attention. "Beverly, Shelley. What can I do for you?"

"I came by to see if I could look at some music in the organ bench."

"Oh." His brow wrinkled. "Are you playing something for service?"

"No, but I was interested in some music Estelle mentioned might be in the organ bench. There are a few pieces written by church members, and we thought they might be nice to play for Founders Day."

Reverend Thorpe looked a little wary, but he said, "Well, if Estelle sent you ... "

"Thank you." Beverly and Shelley went to the reception area and pulled open another heavy wooden door that led to a short, dark hallway that eventually spilled them out into the main sanctuary.

Empty of people, the sanctuary was especially impressive with its high ceilings and stained-glass windows. The June sunlight cast brilliant color over the rows of pews, although the space smelled musty.

Beverly headed to the pipe organ that stood to the right of the front altar and lifted the seat of the organist's bench. Inside were sheets and booklets of music, in no particular order and scattered rather carelessly in the small drawer.

"Let's take these out to look through them, and then put them back in as we sort." Beverly grabbed a stack of papers, and Shelley followed suit.

They laid the papers down on the smooth, dark wooden floor, stacking them on top of each other until the organist's bench was empty of music. They started paging through them, looking at the song titles and whether or not there were any composers listed. Some pieces had the writers at the top or at the bottom, but some didn't have any identification at all, and several pages looked like they had fallen out from a larger booklet, but there was nothing to identify which booklet. Many of the booklets were old and had torn or separated covers, and Beverly and Shelley handled them carefully so that their pages didn't fall out. As they sorted, they put the music back into the bench, trying to stack them a bit more neatly than before.

They were almost through the entire stack of music when Beverly's cell phone rang. She didn't have the number programmed into her contacts list, but it looked familiar to her, and it was a local number. "Hello?"

"Hello, Beverly, this is Estelle. I hope you don't mind my calling you, but I called your home and your father told me your mobile number."

"Of course I don't mind, Estelle."

"I was cleaning my house when I remembered something. There were some old hymnbooks that Old First had printed locally, which we used to use until they got too shabby. Plus they didn't have all the hymns in there, only a few of the very old ones, and the congregation wanted to buy newer ones."

"Why did they have the hymnbooks printed locally? Wasn't that expensive?"

"That's what I remembered—they were printed locally because there were several hymns written by congregation members that were in the book. If Jeremiah Thorpe's sister did write a hymn, it might have been in that hymnbook, although I believe the book was printed in the thirties. I remember one of my great-aunt's hymns was in that book."

Beverly straightened. "Where are the old hymnbooks now?"

"Most of them were falling apart and they were thrown away or given to congregation members who wanted them. But I believe there are one or two that are in Reverend Locke's office."

"Wonderful. Thanks, Estelle."

"I hope you find them."

Beverly told Shelley about the hymnbook as they sorted through the last of the music from the bench.

"Well, it doesn't look like any of these are what we're looking for." Shelley put the last page into the bench.

Beverly rose to her feet. "Let's go back to Reverend Locke's office."

They navigated the dark hallway again and then knocked once more on the reverend's office door. "Reverend Locke?"

He looked up at them. "Yes? Did you not find the music?"

"Actually, I just got a call from Estelle." Beverly held up her cell phone. "She said that there might be one or two copies of an old hymnbook in your office. Apparently Old First had hymnbooks printed locally back in the thirties?"

He nodded, his glasses glinting in the light from his desk lamp. "I think I have one or two copies. But they're very old and fragile."

"May I borrow a copy? I promise to take good care of it."

Reverend Thorpe frowned. "No, I'm not comfortable with that. They're in very poor condition and they're the only copies we have."

"Estelle said that there are original hymns written by Old First members in that book," Beverly said.

His dark eyebrows rose toward the fringe of hair circling his head. "Oh yes, I had forgotten about that."

"While we could play generic hymns for the commemoration service, it would be nice to play songs written by our own local church members."

"I agree it would be nice, but is it really necessary?"

"It would be excellent publicity," Shelley said. "And the publicity would bring in more interest in the fund-raising efforts my mother-in-law is overseeing."

Beverly added, "If it makes you more comfortable, I could scan in the few hymns I think we should use and then return the book to you tomorrow. That way we can use the scanned copies instead of the original book."

He frowned, but couldn't think of anything to object to in that. "I suppose so." He got up and went to a bookshelf in one corner of the office, kneeling down and searching the older books neatly arranged on the bottom shelf. Beverly saw the titles of a few commentaries, but he eventually picked out a book with a cover so faded that the red had turned into a pinkish yellow color. He handed it to her.

There was only the faintest hint of gold in the lettering stamped on the front cover. Beverly just read "Hymns," and at the bottom, "Old First Church, Marble Cove, 1932."

"Thank you very much, Reverend Locke."

"Please take good care of that. We only have one other copy, and the other one is in worse shape."

Beverly could feel that the clothbound cover was loose over the pages, and she could already see a crack in the binding where the pages fell apart. "I'll be very careful with it. I'll be by tomorrow morning to return the book to you."

"Yes, thank you."

Beverly and Shelley headed out the office door and back toward the car, but Beverly couldn't resist peeking into the book. She sighed. "No index. We'll have to look through each song one by one."

"It's not a very big book." Shelley got into the car. "It's not as large as the hymnbooks in the pews right now."

They headed back to Beverly's house, and Beverly made coffee while Shelley hurried down the street to bring back some extra scones. When Beverly saw them, she smiled. "Reverend Locke once mentioned to me he likes your currant scones."

"I'll remember that if we ever need to sweeten him up." She winked.

They sat at the kitchen table and poured through the book together, page by page. The paper was badly yellowed and many pages had dark brown age spots from weather damage. Also, the binding was extremely fragile and Beverly had to be extracareful how she handled the pages lest the binding crack even more at certain places.

"How did they arrange this hymnal?" Shelley complained. "The hymns aren't in alphabetical order, and they're not in order by composer, either."

"I think they grouped them by topic, like 'worship' and 'Sabbath' and 'Easter.'"

Shelley bit into a scone. "I suppose that makes sense, but it makes it hard to find Jeremiah's sister's hymn."

They did find a hymn written by Theodora Baumgardner, whom they thought might be Estelle's great-aunt, titled "He Always Saves."

But they hit pay dirt about two-thirds of the way through the hymnal. "There!" Shelley pointed to the top of the page.

"Eliza Thorpe" was printed on the top right as the composer of the hymn, "Carried On the Waves."

"Hooray." Shelley and Beverly shared a high-five.

"And Eliza is five letters." Beverly couldn't stop the grin spreading across her face. "Let's try it." She went to get the sheet of paper she'd printed out a few days ago, which had a polyalphabetic graph so she could try to translate the cipher. She had already tried the names they'd discovered like Edith Mauer—she had tried *Edith*, *Mauer*, and *EdithMauer* with no luck—as well as *JohnThorpe*.

Beverly started decoding the message using the name Eliza.

"M...Y...D...E...A." Beverly's heart began to race with each letter.

"Keep going," Shelley said. "I'm going to guess the next letter is an R."

"You're right. 'My dear.'"

"This is it!" Shelley's voice rose to a squeal. "We did it!"

"We found the key word for the cipher."

Chapter Twenty-One

Diane was surprised to see all three of her friends invade her hospital room that afternoon, faces shining with some secret. She was eager to ask what it was, but Beverly's quick, significant look at Jessica and Martin quieted her tongue.

"Hi there," Margaret greeted her enthusiastically. "How are you feeling?"

"Ready to claw the walls." Diane grimaced. "But the doctors say I can leave tomorrow morning."

There was an awkward pause, and Diane could almost see Margaret's mind spinning, trying to figure out a polite way to ask Jessica and Martin to leave the room so that the four of them could talk privately. Diane was about to ask her daughter to do just that when Jessica said, "Mom, we'll step out to get some lunch. We'll be back in about an hour."

"Take as long as you like," Diane told her cheerfully, and the two young people left the room.

"Now tell me what's gotten you three so excited," Diane demanded.

"We cracked the cipher." Shelley beamed at her.

"What? You did? That's terrific!"

Shelley and Beverly told her about talking to Frances, and then Estelle Baumgardner, and then Reverend Locke. Diane was a little disappointed she hadn't been able to do any of that. Well, that taught her to land herself in the hospital just when there was something interesting going on. She was never going to forget to eat again, that's for sure.

"Beverly translated the entire message this morning," Shelley said.

Beverly pulled out a piece of paper and began to read.

My dearest sister,

I am hoping that our frequent puzzles together will enable you to translate this letter to you. This is the reason I have ensured that my prayer book is delivered to you should anything untoward befall me. I entrust to you my orphaned children and I know you will care for them as though they were your own. The bounty given to me by our mighty provider has been hidden away for you and for my children. I have secreted instructions for finding it in the church in the library under the bell. God bless you.

Your brother,
Jeremiah

Diane could hardly dare to breathe after Beverly finished reading it. "The bounty," she whispered. "Do you think that's the treasure?"

"This proves it exists," Shelley said. "And 'the library under the bell' has to mean the old bell tower."

"Well, that's what we think, anyway," Beverly said.

"This is amazing," Diane said. "We need to get back into that little room under the old bell tower."

"I think that'll be the difficult part," Margaret said. "Reverend Locke told us there was no such thing as the treasure and we were just being foolish in looking for it."

"But this proves it exists," Shelley said again.

"Does it? The message says 'bounty,' not 'treasure,'" Beverly said.

"Maybe we shouldn't tell Reverend Locke about this message just yet," Margaret said.

"But what excuse will we give for wanting to go up into the bell tower room?"

They all looked at each other in silence.

Then Beverly said, "Diane, didn't you say there were some old pieces of furniture up there?"

"Yes, a table, a chair, and that trunk where we found the letters."

"Was there anything else in the trunk?"

Diane paused. She remembered opening the trunk—the cover had stuck a little—and seeing the bundle of paper tied with a ribbon. "Yes, there were other papers in the trunk under the letters, but I couldn't see what they were. They could have been newspaper for all I know."

"Maybe we could ask Reverend Locke for permission to look in there for items that we can display for Founders Day."

"Beverly, you're brilliant," Shelley said.

Margaret frowned. "I don't know if he'd think that was a good enough excuse. He did block it off for some reason."

"We can ask him why he blocked it off when we talk to him," Shelley said.

"I think I should be the one to talk to him," Beverly said. "He was relatively friendly to me this morning because of my playing for the choir, and I'm also a member of Old First's congregation."

"And none of the rest of us are," Diane added. "Yes, I think that's a good idea. You don't mind?"

"Not at all. I don't want to bother him tomorrow since it's Saturday and he might be working on his sermon for Sunday, but I can speak to him after service on Sunday."

"I hope he says yes." Shelley's eyes gleamed. "Now I really want to get up there, no matter how dusty and dirty it is."

"I hope the treasure is really there," Margaret said.

"I hope the treasure really exists," Diane added. "For Old First's sake."

It was a slow Saturday, which was unusual since Margaret normally had a lot of traffic on weekends during the summer. She resolutely set up her easel to try to paint.

She hadn't picked up her paints in a week, and her brushes felt heavy in her hands. The loss of *Sea Breeze* still weighed heavily on her, but she was cheered because Diane had promised to go with her on Monday to talk to the Marble Cove shop owners again, but this time about the tall, thin woman with the wild gray hair.

She stared at the blank canvas and decided to try to paint another one in the same abstract style. After all, the buyer, John Wilson, had seemed interested in any other paintings she might do, so she might as well try something to take the place of the one she'd lost.

But not too much like *Sea Breeze*. The similarity might only make her feel more discouraged than she already did.

She stood in front of the canvas and closed her eyes, trying to clear her mind and dig deep for inspiration. All she felt was a slight swaying because her eyes were closed.

But that swaying motion could also be from someone onboard a ship. Maybe she could start with what someone at sea would be looking at as they gazed toward the shore. Try to capture the rocking motion of the boat with color and shapes.

She opened her eyes and started.

The painting came slower this time. She hesitated in her color choices in a way she hadn't before. She also second-guessed herself with each brush stroke. Should she twirl the color in that fashion? Or should she sweep it out in a different direction? Was she just slapping paint on the canvas or was she really creating art?

She tried to still the critical voices in her head, and every so often she could dull their whispers. But their insidious words crept into her ears and made her hand hesitate more than she liked.

Would she ever see *Sea Breeze* again? Or would this theft undermine her creativity for even longer than it already had?

CHAPTER TWENTY-TWO

I don't know how you got Martin to volunteer to babysit." Diane sat on the sofa and faced her daughter, who curled up on the other end of it. "You must have some sort of hold over him."

Jessica laughed. "He really does like kids. Kind of like how Dad would always light up when I brought home my friends from school when I was still in elementary."

"I remember that. I had forgotten." Eric hadn't often been exposed to young children after their kids grew up, although he loved teaching. He said that his literature students kept him young.

"I really like him, Mom." Jessica smiled, and something in that smile reminded Diane of a fond look in Eric's eyes when he looked at her.

"What about him do you like the best?"

"You know my life has been pretty stressful since I started working for the law firm. I like the work, but it's very demanding. Martin is…" Jessica gave a contented smile. "Martin is peaceful. Restful. Gentle. He reminds me a lot of what Dad was like."

And then Diane could see why she'd started dating Martin. Diane might think he was bland, but she realized that he fit into Jessica's busy life the way Eric had fit so snugly into her hectic life as a newspaper reporter. Eric had been her rock and supporter. It looked like Martin was that for Jessica too.

"He takes really good care of me," Jessica continued. "He's so considerate and kind. He's never demanding and he completely understands my crazy work schedule. He never minds if I end up with some last-minute work and have to arrive late for a date or postpone it. It's because he sometimes has crazy work hours too."

"He works in IT?"

"Yes, he's often on call. So if someone has a computer emergency, he's got to drop everything to help fix it. His company has some large businesses as clients, and they depend on their computers being up and running. Once a company's servers went down at two in the morning, and he had to go with his team to try to fix things before the business opened at 7:00 AM."

"Poor guy."

"I delivered breakfast for him and his team that time."

"That was nice of you."

"Well, there are times I'm stuck at the office and he's arrived with dinner for me. He's such a great guy."

"Your father did that for me a few times. I was at the paper and he surprised me by showing up with a home-cooked meal."

"Dad was great at taking care of you." Jessica hesitated, then said, "Mom, I'm worried about you."

"I know I scared you when you arrived, but normally I'm not that bad."

"But you yourself told me all the things you've been doing lately. I think you're taking on too many things at once."

"It's only because of this blog tour."

"No, it's everything else. I understand you have to get your blog tour work done, and you had your deadline for your manuscript. But Mom, you're always the one people go to when they need help with something or advice."

"Not always—"

"I'm not saying it's bad for your friends to depend on you, but when you're busy, you have to learn to say no, Mom."

"But they're my friends. I have to help them when they need me."

"You also need to know when they could get help from someone else."

Diane opened her mouth to protest, but then she thought about going around Marble Cove with Margaret and helping Shelley with her kids that one night, and of course all the time she'd spent researching ciphers and trying to crack the encoded message. Perhaps she hadn't needed to go with Margaret that particular day, and perhaps she could have asked Shelley to ask if Margaret or Adelaide could have watched the kids for her. She certainly didn't have to spend so much time working on the Jeremiah Thorpe mystery when she had a deadline coming up.

"Mom, you're great at helping everyone else keep things together, but it shouldn't be at the expense of your own health. Even before you stayed up to do the chapters, it sounded like you were pretty tired and stressed from all the things you were doing. Now, if I'm wrong, tell me, but I don't think I am."

Diane reluctantly nodded. "You're right. I was feeling run-down some days."

"You need to do a better job taking care of your health."

"You're right. Not eating was just plain stupid. It's because I was so disappointed in myself and so stressed about the chapters, but that's no excuse. I guess I'm still used to your dad taking care of me."

Jessica smiled. "He was great at nagging you. You'd listen to him when you wouldn't listen to me or Justin."

"That's not true! I listen to you two."

Jessica gave her a look.

"Okay, well, most of the time." Diane grinned sheepishly.

Jessica reached over to touch Diane's hand. "Just don't forget about yourself, okay, Mom?"

"All right, I will. I mean, I won't forget about myself."

Jessica laughed.

Diane nestled back into the cushions of the sofa, content with the world. She still had work to do, but she'd do it tomorrow. Today was for herself and her daughter, and she felt very blessed to be loved by so many people.

Beverly thought she might be in luck, because Reverend Thorpe seemed to be in a cheerful mood at church today.

His sermon had been about being thankful and how we often forget to thank God for His blessings. He had gone on to challenge people to think about the things in their lives that were blessings from God. Perhaps that had helped to put him in an uplifted frame of mind.

After the service ended, Beverly made her way to the front. She was stopped a few times by church members who greeted her and asked about her father, and she couldn't help but feel the warmth of their concern for her. Since she'd started slowly growing in her faith and attending Old First, she'd felt welcomed by the congregation and embraced as part of their church family.

Reverend Locke was listening to an elderly woman who seemed to be speaking very earnestly to him about something, so Beverly stood to one side, patiently waiting for their conversation to finish. She couldn't help overhearing a few phrases here and there and it sounded like the woman was complaining about another parishioner.

Reverend Locke seemed to be getting distressed over the woman's complaints because his mouth formed a deeper and deeper frown the longer he listened. He tried to interrupt her a few times and placate her, but the woman wasn't about to be calmed down.

"And she took my parking space, Reverend Locke." The woman's querulous voice rose.

"Now, Mrs. Hartley, you know that we don't have assigned parking spaces."

"But everyone knows that the one nearest to the door is mine because of my bad hip. And Mrs. Bentley won't listen when I tell her again and again that it's my parking space!"

Finally Reverend Locke sighed and said, "All right, Mrs. Hartley, I'll speak to Mrs. Bentley." He ran a hand over his balding pate and scratched at the fringe around the edges.

"And make sure you mention about the flower arrangement she donated last week..." Mrs. Hartley went off on another tangent of complaints for another few minutes.

Finally another elderly woman approached them, moving around the few groups of people congregated in the aisles of the emptying sanctuary. "Edna, are you still here bothering the reverend? It's time to go to lunch."

"I'm not bothering the reverend! I have legitimate concerns—"

"Oh, you're just a windbag with nothing better to do."

Beverly blinked at the woman's words, but they were spoken without rancor, and the two women were apparently good friends used to speaking bluntly to each other, because Edna just frowned at her, sighed, and said, "Fine, fine. Let's go. Good day to you, Reverend Locke."

"Good day, Reverend Locke," the other woman said, and the two of them headed down the aisle toward the doors of the church.

Reverend Locke sighed before turning to Beverly. "Yes, Beverly, is there something I can help you with?"

"I had a favor to ask you. When Diane looked in the old bell tower room before—"

"The what?"

"The old bell tower at the back of the church. You know, in the crawl space above a small storage room."

Strangely, the reverend's face seemed to close up. "Oh. Yes. You and Diane were up there before when you found the letters."

"Diane noticed some very old furniture and some papers in the trunk in there. I wondered if perhaps you'd give us permission to go up there again to look for things we can display for Founders Day."

His dark brows contracted. "What would be up there?"

"We're not sure, but we thought—"

He shook his head emphatically. "It's too dangerous up there. That's the reason I had it sealed off."

"We'd be very careful, and we wouldn't be up there more than a few minutes—"

"No, absolutely not. The floor is too unstable and I don't think there's anything up there you could use for Founders Day."

His belligerent tone surprised Beverly. "But, Reverend Locke—"

"No, I can't let you up there. It's just not possible. Now, you'll have to excuse me. I'm very busy today." And he abruptly turned and headed toward the heavy door beside the choir loft, which would lead to the dark hallway back to his office.

Beverly stared at his disappearing back. He'd been almost rude in trying to get away from her. Why had he done that? Was there something in the bell tower room that he was trying to hide? But what in the world would that be?

She couldn't think of anything but Reverend Locke's strange behavior as she headed home. She'd never known Reverend Locke to be secretive or elusive about anything, except when it came to the idea of the treasure.

She was making a salad for lunch for herself and her father when the doorbell rang. Her breath caught in her throat when she opened the front door and saw Jeff standing there.

"Jeff! Hi." Her immediate reaction upon seeing him was pure delight. She also felt a little guilty for not keeping in touch with him as much lately because she'd been so busy.

"Hi. I hope it's all right I came by? I just got back from a photo shoot."

"Of course. Come on in." She held the door open for him.

"Hi, Jeff." Her father walked into the living room and promptly knocked a box askew. "You'll need to navigate through this maze, I'm afraid."

"Sorry about that. These are things I still need to take up to the attic."

"Did you need help?" Jeff turned his warm eyes to hers, and she felt a little blossom of warmth in her chest at his thoughtfulness.

"Thanks, that would be great. Why don't you have lunch with us first? If you'd like salad?"

"Salad would be perfect. It's gotten pretty hot outside."

During lunch, she listened as Jeff chatted with her father. They were so easy together, making jokes with one another, talking about "men" things that she never talked about with her father.

And she found that the slightly uncomfortable feeling she'd had with Jeff was gone now. She was able to relax with him, to enjoy the deep sound of his voice, to smile back when he turned his handsome smile on her.

Was all this because of the house she was selling? It seemed overly dramatic. But then again, here she was, happy to be in Jeff's company. Yes, happy. Without the crippling guilt that used to accompany it.

After lunch, her father headed back to his library where he was working on a little writing, inspired by Diane's success and prodded by Beverly. Jeff followed Beverly into the living room, where she double-checked the contents of a box before letting him carry it upstairs to the attic. She followed with a second box.

The attic smelled like hot metal and dusty papers, and it was sweltering under the eaves.

"Where do you want this?" Jeff asked.

She laid her box down and looked around, then pointed. "Just put it in that corner. I'll stack this one on top."

They escaped the attic oven in a few minutes, but sweat beaded her brow by the time they reached the cooler living room again.

"Here's an idea," Jeff said. "Let's take all these boxes to the hallway outside the attic door. When they're all up there, we'll open the attic door and move them inside all at once."

"That's a brilliant idea." Beverly dabbed at the sweat on her face.

"Are you heading back to your grandfather's in Augusta tonight?" she continued.

Jeff turned to look at her, and his intense gaze made her feel both uncomfortable and safe at the same time. "I came to spend some time with you, Beverly."

Of course he did. Why did she seem to always assume he had other, better things to do? Maybe because being with him made her a little afraid of herself.

Except that wasn't the case today. Things might change tomorrow, but today, she felt different in his company.

"I'm glad you came today," she said.

"Not just because I'm helping you move boxes?" He smiled.

"It's been a little overwhelming packing up the house. A part of me says it's wrong to sell it. That it's like getting rid of Will in my memories. And then another part of me can't wait to have it out of my hands. And I feel guilty for feeling that way."

He didn't answer right away, weighing his words first. "I can understand how you feel—both the guilt and the relief. I would have expected it."

"I feel fickle. Or undecided. I don't know my own mind and feelings."

"I think you do know your own mind and feelings. I think you feel both the guilt and the relief, and I think it's fine to feel both. I think it would be odd if you didn't.

"At some point," Jeff said, "you need to decide if you want to break with the past or not. Sometimes you don't want to. Sometimes you shouldn't. But if the past is only weighing you down, maybe it's time to let it go."

"Is the past weighing you down?" she asked him.

"I try not to let it. I try to walk forward, to live in the present. I respect the past if it teaches me something, but not if it holds me back."

She thought about what Mr. Maker had said about Jeff's one year in medical school. It had taught him that there was a different direction he wanted to go, and he had gone for it.

"I just don't want to have these mixed feelings about selling the house," she said. "I want to be confident in my decisions."

"You can be confident in your decisions and still have mixed feelings. This is Will's house. You were married to him for several years. You can't expect to simply sell it like you'd sell a used car or an old television set."

She thought about the last time she'd been in Augusta, and the feeling she'd had when driving up to the house and then when leaving it. The feelings of relief as she put her gowns in the box for the consignment store. "Yes, I'm actually feeling mostly relief."

"I'm not saying that's a sign, but maybe it'll help you as you pack up the house."

"I'm already done." She gestured to the boxes. "This is the last of it."

"When's the closing date?"

"June twenty-ninth."

He nodded. "Are you feeling antsy? Do you want to back out of the sale?"

She grew very still. She took a moment to look deep inside herself, to assess what she felt at the thought of backing out of the sale. "No, I don't think so. I don't want to stop the sale."

"Then I think you should just allow yourself to feel what you're feeling, mixed and all."

She gave him a small smile. "I feel like a box of Lucky Charms."

He laughed. "I like Lucky Charms."

They continued moving boxes and finally got them all put away in the attic. Afterward they sat out on the porch with glasses of ice-cold lemonade. They didn't talk much, and when they did speak it was about safe topics, like Margaret's painting theft, Diane's recent trip to the hospital, Shelley's problem with shipping her desserts.

And then other times they didn't say anything at all. And Beverly began to appreciate how Jeff didn't push her to feel a certain way about the house, just as he had promised not to push their relationship forward at a pace she wasn't comfortable with.

And his question about how she felt about canceling the sale had been significant for her. Maybe she really could feel this was the right decision. Maybe she could stop feeling so guilty.

Maybe she could finally let part of the past go.

CHAPTER TWENTY-THREE

"A re you sure you're feeling fine?" Margaret asked Diane as they walked down Main Street.

"For the third time, yes." Diane laughed. "If you hadn't called and wanted to talk to shop owners today, I'd have been puttering around my house with nothing to do, because Jessica took my laptop power cord with her so I wouldn't do any work."

"That's rather extreme."

"I hope she doesn't lose it."

"Where is she?"

"She and Martin are taking a drive up and down the coast today."

They headed toward the Cove. "I'm glad you're able to come with me again. I hope we can find out more about that tall, thin woman who looked at my painting."

"And gave her very decided opinions on it to two different people."

They caught sight of Brenna, who was making a latte for a customer. "Be right with you ladies."

After she rang the customer up, she turned to them. "What can I get ya?"

"I hope you don't mind if we ask you more questions today."

"Oh, sure. This is about Mrs. Hoskins's painting?"

Diane nodded. "There was a woman who was looking at the painting the day before it was stolen. Shelley talked to her just before delivering an extra tray of blueberry muffins that morning."

"That's right. I remember that day." Brenna grimaced. "I didn't know I'd dripped coffee on the floor and I slipped on it when I was taking out the tray of muffins. Splat! They went all over the floor. Shelley really came through for me."

"Just before Shelley delivered the muffins," Diane said, "or maybe right afterward, did you happen to see a tall, thin woman? She was dressed in, uh . . ." Diane looked to Margaret.

She thought back to what Shelley had said. "Magenta blouse, and lime-green or yellow-green pants with pink flowers. And gray hair, kind of long and wild."

Brenna's eyes widened. "I remember her. She comes in once or twice a week. I think she's here in Marble Cove for the summer because I've seen her at least a few weeks already. Hair looks like she got hit by lightning?" Brenna shook her straight raven tresses to try to mess it up a bit.

"I think so," Margaret said. "It was Shelley who saw her."

"She hasn't come in this week, though. Well, I remember her coming in with that magenta blouse, but she hasn't been here since then."

Margaret bit her lip. What if the woman had skipped town with her painting?

"But I'll keep an eye out for her," Brenna said. "She came in regulah enough the past few weeks. She's bound to come in soon-ah or lat-ah."

If she hasn't already left town, Margaret reflected.

"Thanks, Brenna." Diane gave her a smile and they left the coffee shop.

"Another useless interview," Margaret said.

"What do you mean? It was very helpful. If that thin woman has been here for a few weeks, then she's either renting a cottage—which we might be able to ask the Realtor about—or she's been renting a room in a hotel for a long enough time that the hotel might be willing to tell us her name. We can give the information to Detective Little if the Realtor or the hotel won't tell us. It'll help him find her, at least."

"I guess that's true."

They spent a couple hours interviewing more shop owners, who all confirmed what Brenna had said, that they'd seen the woman occasionally for most of the summer, but not in the last week or two.

Diane checked her watch. "We had good luck at Captain Calhoun's and it should be open by now. Let's see if Kirsten's there again."

The young woman was standing by the reception desk speaking to someone on the phone when they walked into the restaurant, which was nearly empty at this time of day. Kirsten saw them and held up a finger to ask them to wait while she finished the call. "Yes, Mrs. Pruitt, I have you down for a reservation for tonight for twelve people. All right, thanks. See you tonight." Kirsten hung up the phone. "Hi, Mrs. Hoskins, Mrs. Spencer."

"I hope you don't mind, but we have another question to ask you. There's another woman we want to find in connection with the missing painting."

"Oh, sure."

"A tall, thin woman with a magenta blouse and a yellow-green skirt with pink flowers talked to Shelley Bauer outside Margaret's gallery about the painting the day before it was stolen," Diane said. "She has long, rather wild gray hair. We wondered if you might have seen her around town."

"Oh yes. But I'm afraid I don't know her name. She always pays in cash."

"How often do you see her? And have you seen her lately?"

Kirsten frowned as she thought back. "She used to come in once a week or so, but she hasn't come by in a little over a week. She was here the first day I started working."

"So she might have been in town before then," Margaret said.

"Or she might have arrived just when Kirsten did," Diane pointed out. "But at least we know she's been in Marble Cove for at least six weeks."

"I'll keep an eye out for her." Kirsten's eyes twinkled. "I might even try to chat her up and get her name if I'm lucky."

Margaret smiled. "Maybe you should be a spy instead of a psychologist."

They left the restaurant, and Margaret asked, "Where to next?"

"You know, I keep hearing that she's been seen for most of the summer so far, so maybe we should go speak to Patricia Finley. This woman might have rented a cottage through her."

"That's a good idea."

They opted to walk to Patricia Finley's office, which was a few blocks away from Main Street, tucked in between a clothing boutique and a gift shop. Once through the plate-glass door, the scent of hazelnut coffee greeted them as they entered the room, which had red brick walls on two sides and white plaster walls on the others.

Patricia rose from behind her wide white desk and greeted Diane warmly, since she'd helped her buy her own cottage only a year ago. "Patricia, do you know Margaret Hoskins?"

"We've seen each other around town." Patricia held out her hand to Margaret. "I love the mural you did at the Cannery with that other local artist."

"Why, thank you."

Patricia leaned back against the edge of her desk. "So what can I help you ladies with?"

"We think one of your renters might know something about the painting that was stolen from Margaret's gallery a couple weeks ago," Diane said.

Patricia's pretty face paled. "How terrible. Who are you looking for?"

"We don't know her name, but she's been described as having long, wild gray hair, and she probably dresses in very bright colors." Diane hesitated. "I'm not sure if you can give out information about your renters."

Patricia shook her head. "I'm afraid you're right. I can't give out information about my renters." She hesitated, then added, "But I can tell you that I've seen someone with that description around town."

"Where? When?"

"For the past few weeks, both this summer and perhaps last summer. And the summer before that." Patricia looked sweetly innocent as she said this, but her eyes gleamed with hidden meaning.

So this woman was a regular summer renter, Margaret surmised.

"Where did you happen to see this woman?" Diane asked.

"I often see her hanging out with a group of amateur artists who meet down by the beach area once a week to paint together." Patricia turned to Margaret. "I don't remember her name, but that artist who painted the Cannery mural with you? I've seen her with her a few times."

"Bernadette Lassiter." Margaret perked up.

"I'm sorry I couldn't help you ladies, but my client list is confidential." Patricia gave them a bland look that didn't fool them for a second.

"Thanks, Patricia." Diane and Margaret hurried out of the office, and Margaret had her cell phone out and was dialing Bernadette in seconds.

"Hi, Margaret," Bernadette answered the phone.

"Bernadette, I wondered if you might be able to help me. It has to do with the painting that was stolen."

"Of course. Anything."

"The day before the painting was taken, a woman was seen outside the gallery looking at it. Normally that wouldn't be anything unusual, but she was seen outside the gallery at two different times that day, and she talked to two different people about my painting."

"*Hmm.*" Bernadette sounded stern. "That's suspicious."

"That's what I thought. I don't have a name for the woman, but I have a description—magenta blouse, a yellow-green skirt with pink flowers printed on it, and long, wild gray hair."

"Very curly gray hair? And you're sure it was a magenta blouse?"

Margaret's heart beat faster. "Yes."

"That's Gloria Peterson. I know her."

Bingo! "Who is she?"

"She's involved with an artist's coffee group that meets once a week down at the beach. I'm not that close to her—I don't go to the group regularly—but I have to say, it doesn't seem like her to steal a painting."

"We don't mean to accuse her of stealing the painting, but we would like to talk to her to ask why she went to go look at the painting twice on the same day."

"Yes, that does seem odd, even for Gloria."

"What do you mean, 'even for Gloria'?"

"Well, she's rather opinionated about art. I'm sure that's not a surprise to you—most of us artists are opinionated about art. But Gloria has forceful ideas about it. She only started painting two or three years ago, so she still considers herself an amateur, but she's not afraid to give her decided opinion on something to anyone who asks."

That sounded similar to what Shelley had told Margaret about her conversation with the woman. "Do you have Gloria's phone number or address?"

"I don't know her exact address number, but she's renting that bright yellow cottage on Elm Street—you can't miss it. And here's her phone number, although I think it's the cottage landline, not her cell phone." Bernadette rattled it off for Margaret.

"Thank you so much, Bernadette."

"No problem." Bernadette hesitated. "I kind of hope it isn't Gloria who stole the painting, but I do hope she can help you find who did."

After hanging up with Bernadette, Margaret told Diane what she'd learned.

"Let's go." Diane headed to her car. "You can call her while we drive."

But no one answered the phone and no answering machine picked up, although Margaret let it ring ten times. "No one answers," she told Diane.

"That's okay, we're almost there." Diane turned the car into Elm Street, a small, shady lane that loosely paralleled the beach, with houses on either side of the road and nary an elm tree in sight. The street was short, with only perhaps a dozen houses total, and there was only one yellow one, a tiny cottage halfway down the road on the right.

Diane parked the car outside the cottage and they approached the front door, passing past pretty rows of bougainvillea bushes in flower. They knocked on the lime-green painted door once. Twice. Three times.

"No one's home." Diane went to the front window to peer inside, then shook her head.

As they walked back toward the car, an elderly woman from the neighboring house exited her front door and saw them. "Looking for Gloria?" Her voice was reed-thin and wavering.

Margaret nodded. "Have you seen her?"

The woman proceeded to uncoil the water hose from the front corner of her house. "She's on a trip down the coast. She should be back in a week or so."

Margaret groaned. "How long has she been gone?"

The woman turned on the water faucet and began watering her rosebushes. "Oh, a couple weeks. So she probably won't be gone for much longer."

"Thanks." Margaret and Diane headed to the car.

"I know that's disappointing, but we can come back in a week." Diane started the car.

"I thought I was learning patience in my old age, but I guess not. I wish she'd been home."

"Don't worry, Margaret, we'll find her. And find out what she knows about your painting."

CHAPTER TWENTY-FOUR

O
n Tuesday morning, Diane was out walking with Rocky on the beach when she saw Beverly on her way home on her morning jog.

"Hi there. Did Jessica already leave?"

"Yes." Diane sighed. "She left this morning."

"Did you enjoy her visit?"

"Oh, so much. I wish she could have stayed longer." Diane turned around and walked with Beverly on their way back to their homes.

"What did you think of her boyfriend? I didn't get to see him much."

"At first I thought Martin was too bland for Jessica, but then we had a good talk together on Saturday night and I began to see how Martin's personality is actually a lot like my husband's. Martin is a very restful sort."

Beverly cocked her head and thought about it a moment. "I can understand how that would appeal to someone like Jessica, who's in a high-stress job."

"Speaking of stress, how's everything going with the house sale? Is it progressing smoothly?"

"Yes. My closing date is June twenty-ninth, and I've pretty much got the house cleared out except for the furniture that's being sold with it."

Diane hesitated before asking, "How are you holding up? I can imagine it must be a little hard, selling your old home."

"Earlier this month, it was a lot harder. But as I've cleared my things out of the house, I've had to decide what I'm going to give away, what I'm going to throw away, what I'm going to keep. And there was a lot in my old life that I've found doesn't fit in my life now. So I've started to feel better about selling the house. But we'll see. I might be an emotional wreck on the closing date."

Diane put an arm around her in a brief hug. "Let me know if you need me."

"I will. Thanks. How are things going with you? You look a lot better."

"Oh, I've felt back to normal for a couple days now. And I've caught up on my blog tour work. Now I'm working on the rest of the manuscript. And this time, I made sure I put the due date in my calendar."

"Another thing you might think about is figuring out how many words you'll need to write each day as a minigoal."

"Yup, I figured that out last night. I think it'll make it easier for me to stay on track. You must be busy with your work too."

"Things recently picked up. This afternoon I have two meetings. One is with a woman who owns a house along the beach who wants to convert it into a small B and B. The other is a woman with an open property that has a view of the lighthouse. It used to be a working farm, and she has some empty cottages that used to house the farmhands. She wants to convert them into rental cottages."

"I think those are both great ideas. Marble Cove is a terrific place for summer vacationers and they'll be sure to get business."

"But this morning I'm going to visit Reverend Locke again. I tried to speak to him on Sunday about going up into the old bell tower, but he acted very strangely."

"What did he do?"

"He seemed almost furtive. When I asked about the bell tower, he very brusquely said it was too dangerous and he practically ran away from me."

"Maybe he was having a bad day."

"That might have been it—he had been talking to a church member who had a lot of complaints. That's why I'm going this morning to talk to him."

"Did you want some company? After all, Frances asked me to help with the commemoration booklet, so I can express interest in any papers that might help me write the piece."

"That's a good idea, if you're sure you have time. I don't want your daughter coming down on my head for overworking you." Beverly's eyes danced as she glanced sideways at Diane.

Diane gave a rueful smile. "I promise I'm not too busy today. And this mystery with the encoded message is interesting to me. I'm itching to get back up in that bell tower room."

"You can go. I used up my dust quota for the week when I put boxes in my attic on Sunday."

Diane hurried home and then headed to Beverly's house, where she found Mr. Wheeland in his library. He was typing away at a manual typewriter that had been set on a small folding table in front of his leather chair.

"Hello, Harold."

He turned toward her with a smile. "Diane, how are you?"

"I'm fine. What are you working on?" She glanced at the typewriter.

"I'm still working on a few short stories that've been rattling around in my head for a while."

"I hope you'll let me read them when you're done."

"Of course. Although they probably won't be as good as your novels."

"Oh, you've given me so much good advice on my writing that I'm sure you're ten times as talented as I am."

His ears colored a little at her praise, but he only answered gruffly, "Nonsense, nonsense. How's your second book coming along?"

"I've gotten to a crossroads, and I'm not quite sure where I want to go from here."

They discussed her plot for a few minutes until Beverly arrived, her hair still damp from her shower. "Sorry to keep you waiting."

"Not at all. Your father was just helping me with my novel." Diane turned to him. "Thanks again."

"Anytime."

Beverly kissed his cheek. "We'll leave you to your own work, Father."

"Yes, my Pulitzer-Prize winner."

Diane and Beverly grinned at each other as they headed out of the house toward her car.

The drive to Old First was short, and the day was again growing hot. They entered the coolness of the reception area and knocked on Reverend Locke's open office door.

He glanced up at them from some papers he was poring over. "Hello, Beverly." He gave Diane a guarded look. "Hello, Diane." He hadn't forgotten that she'd invaded a hidden room in the bowels of his church and absconded with ancient letters she'd found there, even though she'd returned them recently.

"Hello, Reverend Locke."

He shook her hand. "How can I help you?"

He looked busy, so she figured it wouldn't be good to beat around the bush. "Frances Bauer asked me to write a historical piece for the commemoration booklet for Founders Day," Diane said. "When I was, er, in the room where I found those letters of Jeremiah Thorpe, I noticed some other old documents in the trunk with the letters."

Reverend Locke's face closed down like a pair of shutters over a window and his eyes grew very stern.

Diane faltered, but went on, "I was hoping to go up there again to retrieve those documents. I'd like to see if there's anything I can use for the historical piece or for the commemoration booklet."

"Ladies, it is out of the question," Reverend Locke said curtly. "It is very dangerous."

"When I was up there before, the floor was extremely solid," Diane said. "And if you look at the beams crossing the ceiling in the storage room beneath, they're very large and stable. We could get a contractor in to examine them before we go up, if you'd like."

Mention of the contractor seemed to confuse him. "Examine?"

"Or did you already hire a building inspector to examine the room?" Diane asked. She was fairly certain he hadn't, and she didn't think Reverend Locke was the sort of person who would lie just to insist on his own way in something.

"N-no." He frowned at the papers in front of him, then closed his eyes and sighed. "Why does this room hold such fascination for you?"

"It's not fascination," Diane said. "We'd just like to examine the documents and see if there's anything we can use for Founders Day. If there's something very old and valuable up there, it might help fund some badly needed renovations, wouldn't you agree?" Diane knew her logic was sound. The question was, would Reverend Locke see that?

He looked at them both, his eyes behind his glasses searching and questioning, not cold or closed or resistant.

Finally he said, "That area above the storage room has been largely undisturbed because…well, that room is special."

"What do you mean?" Beverly asked.

"It's… There's something unexplainable about it that people have always respected. And so we've left it alone."

Except when Diane, with Beverly's help, had climbed up inside it.

"Unexplainable?" Beverly asked slowly.

Diane glanced at her and knew what she was thinking of—the few times that the old bell had been ringing. An old bell that had no way of being rung as far as they could tell, and which had once saved Maddie Bancroft's life.

"You've…" Reverend Locke paused and wiped his forehead. "You've seen it. You've heard it." Locke turned and peered at Beverly over his glasses. "The bell rang and drew you away from underneath the light fixture when it nearly fell on Madeline Bancroft."

Diane could only stare at him. While she and her friends believed that the bell had saved Maddie, to have Reverend Locke willingly admit that he did too was another thing entirely.

"There have been other occurrences," he went on. "Times when the bell has rung and warned of danger."

"Maybe it's just someone ringing the bell and they happen to have good timing," Beverly said.

"But there's no way to ring the bell. Not the old one," Reverend Locke said.

Diane inhaled quickly. She hadn't been sure before, because she'd only had that quick glimpse up into the tower with her flashlight, but she had no reason not to believe the reverend.

"Have you heard the bell yourself, then?" Diane asked.

"Once, many years ago, I heard the bell ring just as I was about to get into my car to go home one night. There had been high winds all day. I went to investigate the sound and a moment later, a tree fell onto my car."

Diane gaped at him.

"And it's not just that one time. Other people have mentioned to me about hearing the bell ringing at strange times, warning them of danger. So you see, I can't let you up there. It's simply not right. We shouldn't tamper with it."

Diane was about to say that they weren't going to tamper with anything, but then his telephone rang.

"I'm sorry," he said, although he didn't look all that sorry to Diane. "I have to take this. I have a conference call with another pastor."

"Of course." Beverly led the way out, so Diane followed. She glanced at her watch and saw that it was the top of the hour on the dot, so she doubted Reverend Locke had been only making an excuse to get them to leave.

They walked to the car. "I can't believe he knows about the bell," Beverly said.

"I know. I wouldn't have expected him to."

"I understand why he doesn't want us up there, but now it only means it's going to be doubly hard to convince him."

"Let's talk this over with everyone," Diane said as they got into Beverly's car. "If we can all meet tonight, maybe we can come up with ideas about how to get him to let us up there."

"Do you really think we can?"

"I'm determined to do it. Reverend Locke may not think so, but I just know there's something important up there that will point us to the treasure that can save Old First."

Chapter Twenty-Five

Shelley read the e-mail with nausea gnawing at her stomach.

Hey,

I got your cookies but they were broken! How terrible is that? I paid so much for them and for shipping, I expect them to at least arrive in pristine condition. This is such a ripoff. I'm going to tell ALL MY FRIENDS what a scam artist you are. Also, none of them had enough chocolate chips. We ate all of them just to be sure, and they all had way too few chips. How can anyone be so cheap as to not put enough chips in a cookie? I want my money back!

Have a blessed day,
Carla Amsden

The harsh words felt like knives stabbing at her. She couldn't stop reading. And then she despised herself because she read the e-mail all over again.

"Mama, what's wrong?" Aiden's wide blue eyes stared at her from over the edge of the kitchen table. He stood watching her, the spaceship in his hands forgotten.

Shelley dashed the tears away quickly and sniffled. "Nothing, honey. I just have something in my eye." She slammed the laptop closed with a little more force than was necessary. "Did you want to show me something?"

He nodded, but the wary look didn't leave his eyes.

"Well, what is it?" Shelley tried to infuse as much cheerfulness into her tone as she could.

He proceeded to demonstrate how his spaceship escaped the evil plant monster by some clever moves by its crew and intrepid captain.

A knock at the door interrupted him. "Hold on, Aiden. Let me answer the door." Shelley scrubbed at her face and hoped her eyes weren't red as she opened the front door.

Beverly smiled when she saw her, then frowned. "What happened? What's wrong?"

Shelley sighed. Her eyes must be redder than Aiden's plant monster. "I got an e-mail today."

"From who?"

"I don't even remember." She led the way inside and opened the laptop, but simply pushed it toward Beverly. She finished listening to Aiden's spaceship adventures while Beverly read the e-mail. Beverly's cheeks began to glow as she read.

"Why don't you head outside and take Prize out for a little while?" Shelley said to Aiden.

"Okay, Mama. Can Emma come too?"

"She's still napping. You can play with her later."

"Okay!" His shout might have woken the toddler up anyway as he raced to the back door calling, "Prize!" The puppy scrambled to the door and the two of them disappeared outside.

"I can't believe this woman!"

Shelley had never heard Beverly raise her voice that way.

"I understand she'd be upset if the cookies arrived damaged, but her language is so rude," Beverly continued. "And she has the nerve to say she ate them all just to see if there were enough chips in the cookies. They obviously weren't so damaged she couldn't eat them."

"But the point is—"

"For her to call you a scam artist is just horrendous," Beverly said, obviously not done. "She's the scam artist, because she ate them all. And then to sign it 'have a blessed day' after all that? It just turns my stomach." Beverly scowled at Shelley.

"You're not mad at me, are you? Because you look awfully fierce."

Beverly blinked, then laughed. "Oh, sorry. I'm just appalled at this woman."

"The point is that the cookies still arrived damaged even though I used the more expensive packaging and I put extra bubble wrap in there too." Shelley sighed, but it sounded like a sob. "With the cost of the ingredients and the price of the packaging, I actually ended up losing money from this Internet order."

"Oh, Shelley." Beverly reached across the table and touched her hand. "I'm so sorry."

"I did try to research other packaging options. I spoke to Margaret about what she uses for the sculptures in her gallery, and while the boxes are really sturdy and would probably be great for my pastries, they're very expensive and I'd have to increase my shipping and handling charges. I just can't win." She shook her head. "Could you please do me a favor? Could you take down my orders from my Web site? I can't afford to do more Internet orders if I have to refund them all."

"Of course."

Shelley stared at the surface of the table. "I don't know how I'm going to tell Dan about this."

"I think he'll be supportive, the way he always is."

"I know he will, it's just that..." She bit her lip. "I so want this business to do well. I want to fulfill his faith in me."

"Your business isn't exactly failing, Shelley. You've got local standing orders, right?"

"There's the Cove. That upscale restaurant in the next town, Alexander's, canceled their standing order, although they do ask for special orders once in a while. I have a caterer in town who does occasional orders too."

"See? You do have some business."

"But not enough. I really needed those Internet orders."

"But not if they're making you lose money."

Shelley sighed. "That's true. And I do want to avoid dealing with people like that." She nodded at the laptop, which was still open in front of Beverly.

"Tell you what: I'm going to refund her order for you and reply to her so you don't have to." Beverly began typing.

"You don't have to do that," Shelley protested.

"Yes, I do. Why should you have to deal with such an unpleasant person when I can do it just as easily, and it doesn't upset me as much as it upsets you?"

Beverly's reaction to the woman's e-mail had sounded intense but she was right in that she could respond without dissolving into tears, like Shelley would.

Beverly spoke as she typed. "Dear Ms. Amsden, I apologize that the cookies arrived damaged and I'm sorry you didn't enjoy them."

Shelley couldn't help giggling at how Beverly's ireful tone contrasted with the polite words she was typing.

"I am sending you a full refund. Have a nice day, Shelley Bauer." Beverly finished typing, and with a few clicks on the laptop, she'd sent the e-mail and the refund. "And give me a minute..." Beverly clicked the mouse button and then did some more typing. "There. I just disabled your ordering system. Instead, people get a note saying, 'Lighthouse Sweet Shoppe is not accepting Internet orders at this time.'"

"Thanks, Beverly."

"What are friends for, if not to shield each other from vicious people?"

"Did you want some of my cookies-without-enough-chocolate-chips?" Shelley stood and brought a plate back to the table to set in front of them.

"I honestly don't know how you can get more chips in these." Beverly took a bite. "*Mmm.* If there was any more chocolate, there wouldn't be any cookie."

"I hope you won't be ruining your dinner."

"Oh, that reminds me why I came over. Can we have a meeting, all four of us, tonight after supper? Will Dan mind watching the kids for half an hour or so?"

Shelley was about to say yes, but the memory of Dan's tired face from the night before made her hesitate.

Beverly saw her hesitation. "I don't want to cause problems for you and Dan."

"No, it's not that." Shelley took another cookie. "Dan's still stressed at work."

"Still having problems with his boss?"

"He says he's trying, but Wayne's still pretty critical of him."

"Sometimes it takes time."

"That's what I said, but last night he was cranky about it. He said Wayne nitpicked on all kinds of things Dan forgot to do."

"Well, but didn't you say that it might be because Dan tends to be more concerned with quick work than details? Maybe he still needs to work on that."

"That's true." Shelley chewed thoughtfully. "Maybe I can give him a gentle hint tonight."

"If Dan's too tired to watch the kids for you, we can meet tomorrow."

"That might be better. I can ask Margaret if Adelaide can watch the kids for me tomorrow morning."

"That sounds good. We can see if we can meet before she has to open the gallery."

Beverly was about to close the laptop when she said, "Shelley, you just got another e-mail from that lady."

"Oh no. Will you read it for me?"

"Sure." Beverly scanned it, and her eyebrows rose toward her hairline. "I don't believe this."

"Is it bad?" Shelley held her breath.

"I'm not sure whether to laugh or cry. Carla Amsden e-mailed to complain that your Internet orders aren't working."

"What? That means she tried to order something."

"Exactly. She says, 'Honestly, I don't know how you expect to make money when you aren't accepting any orders on your Web site. My husband specifically wanted more of your cookies and now what am I going to tell him? I demand you put your Internet orders up again right now.'"

Beverly and Shelley looked at each other, and they both began to laugh.

CHAPTER TWENTY-SIX

Margaret opened the door to Shelley, Aiden, and Emma. "Hi, come on in."

"Hi, Aiden." Adelaide gave Aiden a wide smile. "Let's go out into the backyard, okay?"

"Okay!" Aiden zoomed toward the backdoor.

"Aiden, don't run," Shelley called after him.

He slowed for a half step right at the back door before darting outside.

"I'll take Emma, Miss Shelley." Adelaide held out her arms, and Emma was only too happy to go.

"Good, we're all here now. I'm dying to find out what happened." Margaret went to sit in Allan's dark green recliner.

Diane and Beverly were chatting on the worn leather couch, and Shelley plopped down in a chair with a rust-colored pillow.

"So what happened at Old First?" Margaret asked Diane and Beverly.

"Reverend Locke knows about the way the bell mysteriously rings." Diane's eyes were shining. "And he even mentioned it."

"He did?" Margaret sat up in her chair.

"He said that the bell rang once, saving him from being hit by a falling tree," Beverly said. "And the bell has rung at other times, for other people, warning them of danger."

"I think that since the bell has done this, he views that room as something...sacred," Diane said. "He doesn't want us up there messing with things."

"But you were up there before, and the bell still warned Maddie," Shelley said.

"I think the only way he'll let us up there is if he's under pressure from other church members," Beverly said. "We presented a very logical argument that there might be stuff up there that we can display for Founders Day. It's an important event for the church, so he's got to give in if enough people ask him to."

"But who else can ask him? Beverly's the only one of us who goes to Old First," Margaret said.

"Well, Dan's family goes to Old First," Shelley said. "And Frances is a very important, prominent church member."

"Yes, I remember how Reverend Locke seemed respectful of her when I went to see him about the fund-raiser," Beverly said. "She's on the building committee."

Shelley said tentatively, "I could speak to her, I suppose..."

"Why don't I speak to her?" Margaret offered. "She and I get along rather well, so she might be more open to the idea if I talk to her about it."

Shelley looked relieved at Margaret's suggestion.

"I'll come with you," Beverly said. "Frances and I got along well when we planned the fund-raiser together and when I helped her and Maddie last month in going through the donations and finding the prayer book."

"I'll give her a call and ask when we can come over to her house."

"I think she'll be home this afternoon," Shelley said. "She called this morning and said that since it's supposed to be so hot today, she wants Dan's dad to fire up the barbecue, and she invited us over for dinner."

"How's Dan doing, Shelley?" Diane asked.

Shelley hesitated before answering, but it was more a thoughtful look on her face than a sorrowful one. "He might be doing better at his job. Maybe."

"That's great," Margaret said.

"He's still having a hard time with Wayne's communication style," Shelley said. "So I told him to remember to ask him exactly what he means rather than assuming he's denigrating his skills."

"I know Dan will eventually figure out how to make it all work," Margaret said. "He's a smart guy, and he's very dedicated. Once he's committed to something, he sticks with it."

Shelley nodded. "I was afraid, at first, that he'd be too discouraged to want to continue, but last night made me feel more hopeful about it all."

"Margaret, any news on your painting?" Beverly asked.

Margaret shook her head. "I talked to Fred Little yesterday, and he said he's been trying to track down some of the people from the art fair who asked about the painting, but he's had very little luck."

"But we found the woman Shelley saw outside the gallery the day before the robbery," Diane said. "She's out of town for a week, but we'll be sure to talk to her when she gets back."

"Bernadette Lassiter helped us find her," Margaret said. "Bernadette doesn't think Gloria had anything to do with a theft, but Gloria might still be able to tell us something. She might have been the last person to see the painting."

"And it was pretty strange that she went to look at it twice," Shelley said. "She seemed disgruntled with it when I spoke to her, so why go back to look at it again?"

"Well, sometimes paintings make me feel uncomfortable for some reason, but I can't help wanting to look at them again," Margaret said. "I've felt that way about some modern art pieces."

"But I never feel that way about your paintings," Shelley said. "At least, your regular ones. *Sea Breeze* was interesting, but your other seascapes are so restful."

"That's because you're nuts over lighthouses." Beverly grinned at her.

"No, I feel that way even about the ones that don't have lighthouses." But Shelley was smiling too.

Margaret smiled also, but inside, she was torn. Her new painting, in the same style as *Sea Breeze,* was going well, but so many people had mentioned they preferred her old style better. And many of them were people who had actually bought her paintings.

However, there were a few like Harriet Malcolm, the art critic from the *Courier,* and John Wilson, who bought *Sea Breeze,* who seemed to prefer her new style better.

She had been intending to continue in her new style, but now she wasn't so sure. Maybe she'd finish this new painting first and then decide what to do about her style.

After the ladies had left, Margaret gave Frances Bauer a call.

"Hello?"

"Hi, Frances, this is Margaret Hoskins."

"Hello, Margaret." Frances' voice took on a warmer tone.

"I have something to ask you and wondered if I could come over this afternoon with Beverly."

"Of course. I even have a plate of whoopie pies that I just made this morning."

"Much as I love whoopie pies, I don't want to take any if you need them for certain grandchildren of yours."

Frances tittered. "They won't eat that many, and if there's too many left over, I'll end up eating them all myself. Besides, Beverly needs more meat on her bones. Come on over around two o'clock."

"Thanks."

Margaret drove herself and Beverly to the Bauers' home and they arrived at the house outside of town a few minutes before two. The barn on the property stood out against the blue, blue sky as they got out of the car in the sweltering heat and walked quickly toward the house.

The whitewashed farmhouse looked pretty with its newly touched-up green trim, and they escaped onto the slightly cooler front porch to ring the brass doorbell shaped like a rooster.

Frances answered the door immediately. "Come in! It's terribly hot out there, isn't it?"

"I can't believe you were baking whoopie pies in this heat," Margaret said as they entered the air-conditioned house.

"I made them yesterday, thank goodness." She led the way into the living room, where she swept a stack of women's magazines off the sofa. "Forgive me, I was collecting these to give to Shelley. There are some really good tips on how to keep young children occupied without resorting to television."

Margaret and Beverly exchanged a quick, silent look. Yes, the two of them got along with Frances almost better than Shelley did, but they didn't deny that Frances was a mite overbearing, especially when it came to Shelley.

"Coffee? It's decaf," Frances said.

They nodded, and in a minute Frances had set a carafe, cups, and the coffee tray on the table in front of the sofa, along with a plate of chocolate whoopie pies.

"So, what did you need to ask me?" Frances stirred cream into her coffee.

"Do you know about the old bell tower? Not the one that rings for service, but the one at the back of the church?"

"Oh yes. It's part of the original structure that was salvaged after the fire in 1789. When the sanctuary was rebuilt, they built around the old bell tower." Frances sipped her coffee. "They installed the new bell tower in the mid-1800s, I believe, and so they boarded up the old one so kids couldn't find their way inside."

"Diane and I went inside a few months ago," Beverly said. "We thought we heard the bell ringing, so we went to investigate."

Frances frowned as she nibbled on a whoopie pie. "I can't imagine how the bell would be ringing now. I believe they dismantled the pull handle, and it's too heavy to be stirred by wind."

"When Diane was up there," Beverly went on, "she saw some old furniture and a trunk full of very old papers."

"Probably newspaper and rubbish," Frances said.

"No, she found some old letters from Jeremiah Thorpe," Margaret said.

Frances' eyebrows rose. "Are you sure?"

"They were difficult to read, but they were signed by him, addressed to his wife."

"Were they ever authenticated?"

"Uh, no." Margaret wasn't sure if they should mention about the map on the letters, but a quick glance at Beverly convinced her to not say anything about it. "We were thinking that there might be something else up in the old bell tower, perhaps in the trunk, that we could display for Founders Day. We might find more information about Jeremiah Thorpe."

But Frances was shaking her head. "I know that would be interesting, but as children we were always told never to go up into the old bell tower because it was unsafe. It can't have become safer over the years. You were probably very lucky not to have been hurt when you went up there." Her look was clearly concerned.

"Maybe if we only had one person go up at a time?" Margaret suggested.

But Frances still looked troubled. "We don't want anyone getting hurt just before Founders Day. That would put a damper on everything."

Margaret wanted to continue to argue, but Frances didn't look like she would be convinced to allow people to do anything risky, and arguing wouldn't accomplish their goals. "You're right, I suppose."

"I know it would be wonderful if you found something related to Jeremiah Thorpe, but while Thorpe built the church, we also want the commemoration service to highlight how we've grown and contributed to Marble Cove," Frances said. "Old First has always worked to show compassion while maintaining a stellar reputation in the community. We want to showcase our contributions and our dignity. If we focus too much on historical artifacts, we might look like we're still mired in the past."

Margaret could understand Frances' focus for the commemoration service, but she was still disappointed that Frances couldn't see the value of what they might find in the old bell tower.

They chatted for a few minutes longer, and then Margaret and Beverly took their leave.

"That's just too bad," Margaret said as they drove away. "I was counting on Frances to help us convince Reverend Locke."

"I admit, Reverend Locke would be more likely to capitulate if Frances Bauer were to ask him to let us into the bell tower room, but there is someone else we can talk to."

"Who?"

"Maddie Bancroft."

"Oh. You got to know her at Easter while accompanying the church choir, right?"

Beverly nodded. "She and I became closer. And she might see the logic of looking in that trunk for old documents. I know Frances wanted to highlight the congregation and the impact on the community, but some historical documents might get us more media coverage. I wouldn't have been able to explain that to Frances, but Maddie would definitely understand that."

"Plus Frances might be held back by the fact that growing up, she was forbidden to go up into the old bell tower. It must seem wrong to her to want to go up there now."

"True. Sometimes we don't realize we're being held back by things that no longer matter." Beverly's voice grew distant as she spoke.

"Are you thinking about your house?" Margaret asked gently.

"Among other things. Sometimes it's hard to let go of the past."

"It's not a bad thing to let go reluctantly, you know. Our memories shape who we are."

Beverly smiled. "That's true. I just wish it made things easier rather than harder."

"Don't we all."

"So I'll go talk to Maddie tomorrow. Did you want to join me?"

"No, I have to be at the gallery tomorrow. I have a delivery coming—sometime between eight and five, they said, can you believe it? I need to be there to sign for it."

"I hope it's worth it," Beverly joked.

"It will be. It's a shipment of new paintings from Luellen Lumadue. They've been selling like hotcakes."

Margaret was genuinely happy for Luellen's paintings' popularity, though a part of her wondered if her own paintings would ever gain both the critical acclaim and hot sales that the experienced artist did. It seemed with *Sea Breeze* and her seascapes, it was one or the other.

But wasn't there a way she could have both?

CHAPTER TWENTY-SEVEN

Beverly drove up to Maddie Bancroft's enormous two-story home, marveling at how tidy it looked even though she knew Maddie had four kids. She parked in the driveway and headed up the paved walkway to the front double doors.

She hadn't even knocked when the door opened to Maddie's cheerful face. "Come on in. I put the kids in the playroom so we'll have a little peace and quiet."

"Will they stay there long?" Beverly asked with a smile.

"They will if they want to make cookies this afternoon," Maddie said. "They usually listen to me when it comes to cookies."

Beverly had to admit she was impressed, but then again, she'd seen how efficient Maddie was when directing the choir. She could imagine her being efficient and a firm disciplinarian with her children too.

They sat in Maddie's living room, which was completely clear of any toys. In fact, it could have been out of a Martha Stewart magazine except for the small stack of papers on a corner of the coffee table.

"Excuse the mess." Maddie grabbed the papers. "I'm still grading the kids' homework."

"You homeschool, right?"

"Yup. I love it." Maddie's green eyes were bright. "Plus we get classwork done before noon every day. It leaves me so much time to do other fun things with the children."

Beverly knew Maddie was very organized, but her packed schedule and boundless energy did make Beverly feel tired just thinking about it.

She sat and Maddie brought some glasses of fresh-squeezed limeade and some mini strawberry tarts. "Not homemade, I'm afraid." Maddie grinned. "I 'contract out' for my pastries, except for the one day each week I bake with the kids."

Contract out her pastries. That gave Beverly a germ of an idea, but she filed it away to look into later.

"How's your mom doing?" Beverly asked.

"Really great. The cancer treatments seem to be working, thank goodness."

"That's terrific."

"At the last doctor's appointment, the oncologist said that the cancer looks like it's shrinking."

"How does your mom feel?"

"Great. She hates being a burden on people, you know, so she really didn't like that we all had to take care of her. Now that she's got more energy, she's able to do more things for herself, which is what she prefers."

Beverly nodded. "My father is like that. He likes doing things for himself, in his own way."

They chatted about Beverly's father. Beverly also asked Maddie about her husband Roger, who was a lawyer with his office in downtown Marble Cove.

"He just got called a week ago by a headhunter who wanted him to interview for a firm in Boston, but he said absolutely not." Maddie sighed in relief. "I would hate to move. Both our families have been here in Marble Cover forever. I wouldn't want to move the kids away from their grandparents."

Maddie nabbed another strawberry tart. "So what did you need to talk to me about? It sounded so mysterious over the phone." She grinned at Beverly.

"Do you remember when I thought I heard the bells ringing and we went to investigate and moved away from under that light fixture—"

"Well, I remember that chandelier, just as we were heading out of the sanctuary. Your curiosity saved my life."

"Well, Diane and I were up in that old bell tower a few months ago and saw some old furniture and an old trunk with antique documents."

"Like what?" Unlike Frances, Maddie sounded intrigued.

"We found some letters from Jeremiah Thorpe to his wife. At least, that's what we think they are."

"How neat! What else?"

"That's where I need to ask a favor from you. Diane said that she saw more documents in the trunk, but she didn't take any of them with her when she climbed out of the room. Reverend Locke has sealed the room up, saying it's dangerous. But we think that some of those old documents might be interesting to display for Founders Day."

"Oh, definitely. Especially if some of them can be authenticated. You could even make a big to-do over them for the paper. And not just the local paper, but all up and down the Maine coast."

Beverly smiled. Maddie's thoughts were exactly in line with hers. "Diane also wants to look at them because they might have information she can use for the historical piece she's writing for the commemoration booklet."

"That would be a nice touch, maybe a quote from one of Jeremiah Thorpe's letters."

"We approached Reverend Locke about letting us go back into the old bell tower room, but he's against it because it's dangerous. Also, people have just always avoided going in there in the past, apparently."

"It's a little creepy," Maddie said. "I can see how they wouldn't want to go up there."

"We thought that since you're a prominent member of the church, and since you've been a member for longer than I have, you might be able to persuade Reverend Locke to let us up there."

"I think that's a great idea. We might even find some antiques that don't have historical value to the church, but which could be sold to help repair the building."

"I'm not sure if there are antiques up there, but we can definitely look."

"Why don't you and I go and talk to Reverend Locke?" Maddie went to grab the cordless phone. "I'll call and arrange a time with him for tomorrow. Can you make it?"

"I'm sure I can," Beverly said fervently as Maddie dialed the church phone number. She would overhaul her schedule in order to be there.

Beverly couldn't help squeezing her hands together as she and Maddie walked down the pathway toward the church offices.

"I'm sure it'll turn out fine," Maddie said.

"I've been praying. Is that silly, to pray that we'll be allowed into an old room?" In saying it, Beverly felt a little foolish already.

Maddie laughed. "Not at all."

Beverly hoped that there was a treasure in that old room, one that would save Old First's historical building and its community. It had to be there. Jeremiah Thorpe's letters and that encoded message all said it existed.

They entered the church office and entered Reverend Locke's office.

"What can I do for you ladies?" he asked.

"Nothing terribly serious, Reverend Locke," Maddie said. "We have a favor to ask."

Reverend Locke eyed Beverly and muttered, "I think I already know what this is about."

Beverly's heart sank, but Maddie answered cheerfully, "Good. Then we won't have to explain everything."

"I already told Beverly that the old room is too dangerous for anyone to go up there."

"We naturally wouldn't want anyone else to go up there without asking for an inspector to come check the safety of the beams," Maddie said. "I've already spoken to Randy McDonald, and he's more than happy to check the floor of the room sometime this week."

Beverly glanced at Maddie. She had certainly come to this meeting prepared.

"Uh..." Reverend Locke had been rendered speechless by Maddie's efficiency.

"Beverly said that there's something we didn't think about when she first came to you," Maddie said. "There's the potential for an incredible amount of media buzz if we do find anything historically significant in the room. And it could garner us even more attention for Founders Day."

"Diane can use some of the antique documents in the historical piece she's writing," Beverly said. "We can use that as a sound bite for radio spots or in any newspaper articles."

"And not just the *Marble Cove Courier*," Maddie said. "Other newspapers in Boston and across Maine might pick up the story because of the hook of 'previously lost historical documents' found in a two-hundred-and-fifty-year-old church."

"Frances Bauer said that the whole point of Founders Day is to build up attention for Old First and its place in the community," Beverly said, "but wouldn't it also be helpful if Founders Day helped raise funds for renovations too?"

"Wouldn't you want to know that you had done all you could to help Old First?" Maddie added.

Under the barrage of their arguments, Reverend Locke bowed his head, his bald top shiny in the overhead light. "All right," he finally said in a resigned voice. "Yes, you can go up there. But *not* until Randy McDonald has inspected the beams to make sure they're sound."

"Of course," Maddie said. "I'll talk to Randy and see when he has time to come out to look at it. When that's arranged, I'll call everyone about when we'll be able to go up into the room."

"And I insist on being with you when you go into that room," Reverend Locke said sternly.

"Naturally," Maddie said.

He sighed and looked at them all. "I hope you ladies know what you're doing."

Beverly hoped so too.

CHAPTER TWENTY-EIGHT

M argaret had just finished wrapping a painting for a customer when the gallery phone rang. The customer thanked her and headed out the door with the painting as she answered the phone. "Shearwater Gallery, Margaret speaking. How can I help you?"

"Hi, Margaret! It's Bernadette Lassiter."

"Hi, Bernadette."

"Do you remember you talked to me a week ago about Gloria Peterson?"

Margaret suddenly felt as if the walls of the gallery had expanded around her. "Yes?"

"I just saw her coming out of the Cove."

"When?"

"A few minutes ago. I was all the way down the street at the post office, and I called her name but she didn't hear me before she got in her car and drove off. She might be heading back to her cottage right now—she didn't have her painting things with her."

"Thank you so much, Bernadette."

"Sure. Will you let me know what you find out? I'd really hate to think Gloria had anything to do with the theft."

"Of course."

Margaret hung up with Bernadette and immediately called Allan. "I need you to come and take over the gallery for me. I think I might be able to talk to that woman I've been trying to find."

"Sure thing. Oh, there's Diane. Should I ask her if she wants to go with you?"

"You're an absolute doll."

"That's why you married me." There was a smile in his voice, and he hung up the phone.

Margaret called Gloria's number at the cottage, but again got no answer. Was she not there? But Bernadette had seemed to think she had been heading back there.

It seemed to take forever, but then Allan was walking in the gallery door, gesturing with his thumb behind him. "Diane's pulling up right now in her car. She said she'd drive."

"I hadn't even thought about that, but thank goodness she's so practical." Margaret gave Allan a peck on the cheek. "Thanks!" She rushed out the door.

As she climbed into Diane's car, her friend asked, "Is she finally back? Did you talk to her?"

"No. Bernadette saw her in town a few minutes ago. I tried calling the cottage but she hasn't answered."

"She might not be home yet." Diane pulled away from the curb into the flow of traffic down Main Street. "Let's head there and see if we can catch her."

"What if she stole the painting and sold it?" Margaret's hands kneaded the seat belt. "What if that's why she left Marble Cove for the past few weeks?"

"Bernadette didn't think it was like Gloria to steal anything. Let's trust in that for now." Diane gave Margaret a sidelong look. "But keep your eyes open and watch her reactions when we talk to her."

This time, when they pulled up in front of the yellow cottage, there was a beat-up Volkswagen Beetle also parked along the street, so faded that the original blue was more like a misty color.

Margaret almost ran up to the front door and knocked loudly. Immediately she heard footsteps inside, and she raised a hand to her chest, where her heart seemed to be thundering.

The woman who opened the door had long, thick, curly hair in streaks of silver, white, black, gray, and steel, and it waved over her shoulders like a mantle. It contrasted with the brilliant carnelian blouse she wore over peach and red striped capris.

She saw Margaret and her dark eyes widened. "You're Margaret Hoskins." Her voice lilted with surprise—not guilt.

"Yes, how do you do?"

"I'm Diane Spencer." Diane held out her hand, which Gloria limply shook. "Are you Gloria Peterson?"

"Yes."

"Would you mind if we came in? We wanted to ask you something."

"Of course." She held the door open and they entered the tiny cottage.

The front door opened into the living room, which was wide and not very deep, but with large French doors leading to a terrace that fronted the ocean. Though the ceiling was low, the sea breeze blowing through the open doors gave the space a pleasant airiness. There was a single door against the far wall through which Margaret saw the foot of a wrought iron bedstead, whereas on the other side of the living room was a tiny kitchen.

"Sit down." Gloria gestured to the futon. Margaret and Diane settled on the sofa while Gloria perched on a wicker chair. "How can I help you?"

"We heard that you had been looking at Margaret's painting a few weeks ago," Diane said.

"Oh yes. The day before I left on my trip."

"We think you were the last person to see it before it was stolen."

Gloria did a double-take. "Stolen? What do you mean?"

"I went to the gallery in the morning and it was gone from the window," Margaret said.

"What was even stranger was that there was another painting in its place," Diane said.

But Gloria was nodding. "Yes, that *Orlean Point Summer* painting."

Margaret blinked at her, but then realized she'd probably seen it in her gallery window once she got back to town.

But Gloria continued, "I put it there."

"What?" Margaret and Diane said at the same time.

Gloria looked at Margaret for a moment, searching her face. "You mean...you didn't find it?"

"Find what?"

"*Sea Breeze.* I put it in the back of the gallery so it wouldn't be stolen."

Margaret literally couldn't speak. She stared at Gloria in disbelief.

"I think you need to explain it all from the beginning," Diane said in a calm voice.

"I went to your gallery twice that day," Gloria said. "I just couldn't stop looking at *Sea Breeze.* It was so strange. I really don't like it at all but I couldn't stop myself from going to see it. I know you won the award and all, but your other paintings are really much better."

"So you went back twice?" Diane prompted.

"Oh yes. I decided just to go in and see you that evening and tell you how much I disliked your deviation from your usual style. So I went back to the gallery and I entered it, but there wasn't anyone there. Then I noticed that all the lights were off."

"The door was open?" Diane asked.

Gloria nodded. "I realized that you had probably left the door unlocked by accident. I knew that the abstract was the most valuable painting in the gallery, and to be honest, I didn't like it hanging in the window. I also think it wasn't getting you more sales because people would assume all your paintings are like that, when your other seascapes are so much better. You really shouldn't listen to all those art critics who say your style is too commercial—"

"So what did you do with *Sea Breeze*?" Diane asked.

"Oh. I took it and put it in back behind some other paintings. I figured you'd probably hang those other paintings in the morning and find it there. I'm terribly sorry." Gloria's face crumpled. "I didn't mean for you to think it was stolen. I thought you'd find it soon enough that you wouldn't be too upset."

Margaret finally found her voice. "Where exactly did you put it? I don't have any finished paintings in my back room." She had done an inventory the next day, and she hadn't found *Sea Breeze*.

"Those paintings covered with drop cloths."

"Drop cloths? I don't..." Suddenly Margaret realized what Gloria was talking about. She had blank canvases in her back room, covered with drop cloths to protect them. She hadn't bothered to go through those when she did the inventory because, well, they weren't part of the inventory she was selling. "You put them behind those canvases?"

"Yes. I thought about just leaning it against them in front, but then realized that any thief coming in the open gallery would see it, so I hid it behind the other paintings."

Margaret could have kicked herself. Why hadn't she thought to look behind her blank canvases? She'd been so focused on the inventory that she hadn't even been looking for the missing painting.

"Why did you hang the other painting in the window?" Diane asked.

"Well, I thought it looked obvious the painting had been moved, since the window was empty. And it looked pretty bare. I thought, why not put a different painting there to show you that if you hung that instead of *Sea Breeze,* you'd get tons more tourists coming into the gallery? And you did, didn't you? Well, I'm assuming you did, anyway, since I've been gone for a few weeks."

"Uh...I really couldn't say."

"I'm so very sorry." Gloria's knuckles were white as she kneaded her hands together. "I didn't think I would cause all this trouble. You didn't call the police, did you?"

"Well, yes, I had to. I thought it was stolen."

"Oh no." Tears glazed over Gloria's eyes. "Oh no. I'm sorry."

"It's okay." Margaret reached out and touched the woman's tense hands. "You thought you were protecting my painting from real thieves. I appreciate that." She stood. "I hope you don't mind if we head out now." She needed to get back to the gallery. She'd thought that painting was missing for the past three weeks, and she wasn't going to waste another minute before going to make sure it was really there.

"Of course. I'm so sorry. I really do love your work. I've only been painting for a little while, and I still have so much to learn, but I love the atmosphere here in Marble Cove, and the beach is so inspiring," Gloria rambled as they headed to the door.

At the front door, Margaret impulsively reached out to give Gloria a hug. "Thank you for trying to protect my painting, even though you don't even like it that much. I am very grateful that you were so thoughtful."

"Will you tell the police about the mistake?"

"Oh, of course."

They said good-bye and Diane headed back toward the gallery.

"That was not what I expected to hear," Diane said.

"Me neither."

They arrived at the gallery and Margaret ran inside. Allan looked up from where he stood behind the desk. "Honey?" he said in confusion as Margaret hurried to the back room.

She found the blank canvases, covered with the drop cloths, and hastily grabbed them, moving them aside. The drop cloths had rumpled on the top edges, obscuring the canvas closest to the wall.

There it was—*Sea Breeze,* the colors melting and drifting like ocean foam, with the starfish in the foreground.

"It's been here all along?" Allan's astonished voice sounded over her shoulder.

"I guess so." Margaret sighed and reached out to lift the painting up. "I feel so stupid."

"Don't be." Diane squeezed her shoulder. "You certainly weren't expecting it to be here. Plus the drop cloths hid it from sight."

"I'll call Detective Little to let him know." Allan headed to the desk to pick up the phone.

Margaret stood and drank in the sight of her precious painting. "I've never been so happy to see this in my life. I can't wait to call John Wilson and tell him the good news."

Diane gave a soft chuckle. "You know, there's a common theme among the people we've been talking to about this."

"You mean the fact that more people like my old style better than my new one?" Margaret nodded toward the abstract.

"Except for that one art critic and, of course, the person who bought the painting."

"But *Sea Breeze* won that award," Margaret protested.

"I'm not saying you shouldn't do more in your new style, but it's obvious you shouldn't abandon your old one, either."

"I've been trying so hard to please both the critics and my fans, and I thought I had done that with this painting."

"You definitely pleased the critics, but perhaps not your fans."

"I suppose it is possible to paint to my peers in the art world, and it's also possible to paint what my customers want to buy..." Margaret sighed. "But perhaps not at the same time."

CHAPTER TWENTY-NINE

Shelley had just slid a tuna casserole in the oven when she heard the doorbell. She opened it to see Beverly's excited face. "Come on in."

"I have some great news."

They sat at her kitchen table and she set out two of the currant scones she'd just made. "What's up?"

"I just signed two new B and Bs as clients," Beverly said.

"That's wonderful!"

"That's not the great news. What's so exciting is that it occurred to me that I'm in a perfect position to help you with your business so that you won't need your Internet sales."

"What do you mean?"

"One B and B client is a woman who owns a house by the beach. Prime property, but she's retired and her income can't support both her and the house, so she decided to hire me. The house is perfect for a bed-and-breakfast, because she can rent out the bedrooms upstairs and move into the bedroom on the first floor. I suggested she also offer continental breakfast to her guests, but she doesn't want to do the cooking. And then I thought of her 'contracting out' for her baking."

A smile began to spread across Shelley's face. "You mean me as her contract baker?"

"Exactly. You can deliver a basket of pastries to her each morning and all she has to do is make coffee for her guests."

"Did she say she was interested?"

"Oh, definitely."

Shelley couldn't quell the rising excitement in her chest. "Is it the same setup for the other B and B?"

"It's even better. The property used to be a working farm, and the owner lives in the main farmhouse. There are eight small cottages on the grounds that used to house the farmhands, with the Orlean Point lighthouse as the view."

"Pretty."

"She's going to rent out each of the cottages and renovate the barn, since it's empty. She'll have breakfast delivered to her guests and she wants you to deliver an assortment of pastries every morning."

"Where are these two places? They sound close."

"They're a lot closer than Alexander's in the next town that you used to bake for."

"That's fantastic, Beverly. With these two extra B and Bs, my income will be the same as it was before they canceled their standing order."

"If I start to get more clients in the area, I can continue to scout for businesses that might need your pastries. Even hotels nowadays will often give cookies as welcoming gifts for guests, and they might not want to have to bake their own cookies every day."

"Oh, Beverly." Shelley leaped up and ran around the table to give her a hug. "Thank you so much for helping me."

"No problem."

Shelley sat down again, and Beverly said, "I was also thinking that if you wanted to, you could still do your Internet sales."

"How?"

"You could offer only cookies online, and you could try mailing them with those special boxes Margaret told you about. You'd have to increase your shipping and handling prices to cover the costs, but people who taste your pastries at these B and Bs might be willing to pay to ship your cookies once they go home."

"I didn't think of that."

"I'd suggest limiting your online offerings to cookies because cakes just don't seem to hold up to all the wear and tear of shipping."

"Plus cookies are really fast to make, as opposed to cakes and things."

"If your Internet business starts to pick up, we can look into cheaper postage costs by going with a shipper like UPS or FedEx." Beverly glanced at the wrapped plate of scones on her kitchen counter. "I also think you should stop doing free little pastries for your friends and family."

"What? Why?"

"Because if you get too busy doing those, you won't be able to squeeze in the B and Bs. And I'd rather you send your friends—like us—to the Cove to buy your pastries than for you to turn down a B and B simply because you don't have time."

Shelley glanced guiltily at the scones. "Well, I heard Reverend Locke likes my currant scones, so I made a batch to give to him as thanks for letting us into the bell tower room. It's all set, right?"

"June twenty-ninth at six o'clock in the evening."

"I wish we could have gotten into the room earlier. That's Friday, and the commemoration service is Saturday."

"I wanted it earlier, but Randy McDonald couldn't come out to inspect the beams for safety until the twenty-eighth, so Reverend Locke set it for the twenty-ninth."

"Wait, isn't the twenty-ninth the closing date for your house?"

"Yes, but that all happens in the morning. It'll be done by the time we go into the bell tower."

"Are you okay with it? With selling the house?" Shelley asked gently.

Beverly sighed and looked down at her hands for a moment. "Yes and no. It seems like my feelings go from one end to the other in a matter of hours."

"Is there anything I can do to help?"

Beverly gave her a quick smile. "No, but just the fact you offered makes me feel better."

"Did you want me to go with you for the closing? I could get Adelaide to watch the kids."

"N-no," Beverly said slowly.

"Are you sure?"

"I'm sure," she said more firmly. "I think I'll be okay."

After Beverly had left, Shelley said a quick prayer for her friend, for wisdom and guidance about the entire situation. It must be so hard for her to sell her husband's house, especially in light of all it meant to him, and yet Shelley thought it would be a good thing for Beverly to let the house pass to people who would appreciate it fully, without the bad memories to mar their enjoyment of the house.

She steeled herself as it drew closer to the time for Dan to get home from work. While he'd been a little more upbeat a few days ago, on the evenings since then, he'd come home feeling disgruntled and uncommunicative. She'd done her best to be supportive, but she worried about him, and the fact he knew she was worried seemed to annoy him even more. She wanted to talk to him about it, but he didn't want to discuss it, and she couldn't force him to share his feelings and thoughts with her.

But as she set the table, she also reflected that God had come through for her with her baking business. The two B and Bs as new clients had come from out of the blue. She had to believe it was God taking care of her.

So maybe she also needed to trust God with the situation with Dan. Her worrying wasn't doing him or her any good.

Lord, please help everything turn out okay. Please help me to just trust You.

The sound of the front door drew Aiden and Emma, and she heard shouts of "Daddy!"

But Dan's responses sounded more chipper than they had been for the past several weeks. Shelley paused in laying out the silverware. Was she hearing him right?

Then Dan came into the kitchen and wrapped her in a gigantic hug. "Hey there, Shell."

Yes, he definitely sounded happier. She found herself smiling into his shoulder. "How are you doing?"

"Really great." He released her, but kept a hand on her waist as he turned to Aiden and Emma. "Okay, guys, go wash up for dinner."

Aiden ran off, Emma following.

Dan gave Shelley a kiss on the cheek. "You were right."

"About what?"

"All of it."

She laughed. "That's very specific."

He looked deep into her eyes, his blue ones tired but satisfied. "I concentrated really hard today on being more detail oriented. I wasn't perfect, but I was better than I have been."

"And how did Wayne treat you?"

"The same. But this time, I remembered about how you asked my mom what she meant rather than getting bent out of shape, and so I asked for clarification. I didn't quite understand his answer, so I asked more questions and finally figured out what I haven't been doing right."

"That's wonderful, Dan."

"Don't get me wrong, I know it's only today, and tomorrow will be just as tough, but I guess I'm learning not to be as offended by what Wayne says to me, or the way he says it."

"You seem less stressed tonight."

"I'm bone-tired, but I do feel better."

"Daddy!" Aiden yelled from the bathroom. "Emma dropped the soap!"

He gave Shelley a rueful look and then went to rescue the soap.

Shelley hummed as she got dinner ready, but inside she wanted to sing at the top of her lungs. God was so good to her family. Why did she ever doubt Him?

Chapter Thirty

Beverly fingered the sapphire bracelet, then decisively clasped it around her wrist. It seemed fitting to wear it today, when she finished the sale of Will's house.

She was grabbing cereal in the kitchen when the doorbell rang.

"I'll get it," her father said. She heard him shuffling to the door, then a surprised, "Hello, Jeff."

Warmth flooded through her. She swallowed her cereal and wiped her mouth just before he entered the kitchen.

"Hi, Beverly." He looked especially handsome today in a suit with a dark blue tie.

"Why are you dressed up?" she blurted.

He smiled. "The same reason you're dressed up." He nodded at her business suit. "For the house closing."

"You're coming with me?" As soon as the words left her, the thought of him being with her made her shoulders and neck relax.

"You don't mind, do you?"

"I'm...I'm really glad you're here."

He hesitated, then walked forward to reach out and take her hand. It felt a little strange to feel his warm fingers against hers, and yet it felt nice too.

"I thought you could use the support today. How do you feel?"

"Better than I did yesterday."

"What happened yesterday?"

"I had a box of things from the house. Some of it was stuff I took to the consignment store but was rejected. Other stuff was just junk that I didn't need and couldn't sell. I threw it all away, and for some reason I started to cry."

He didn't answer, simply looked at her with concern in his eyes.

Beverly continued, "I didn't cry for very long, and after I was done, I suddenly felt better than I had in a long time. Is that weird of me?"

"Not at all."

"It's just that I saw all that stuff in the trash can, and I realized it was all my old life. And it was okay that I was throwing it away, because it's a part of my life that I don't want anymore."

"And the house?"

"I'm okay with selling it today, really okay. I feel better than I have since the day I decided to put it on the market."

"I'm glad. Not because I wanted to push you into getting rid of all the memories, but because I just want to support you in whatever you do."

Beverly smiled at him, then drew closer and gave him a hug. His arms wrapped around her, comforting and supportive.

She realized how lucky she was to have Jeff with her, because he didn't question her or judge her—he just wanted what was best for her. He was patience itself with the slow pace they were progressing in their relationship, and she was grateful to have him here with her today.

Despite the emotionally turbulent month she'd had with cleaning out the house, she saw that it had been a good thing. Maybe even a God thing.

She would never forget Will. But she also didn't want to regret him.

And this month had helped her say good-bye to him.

The sudden crack of thunder made Diane start and peer up at the ceiling, but all she could see was the square hole of the crawl space, not the mutinous sky high above them.

"The weather report wasn't kidding when it said there was a storm blowing in," Margaret said to her.

"I'm glad we're in this nice safe church," Shelley said.

Beverly looked dubious at that statement but said nothing.

"Okay, I think we're ready." Maddie stood at the base of a ladder set up under the hole in the ceiling. Randy McDonald, who had examined the ceiling the day before, hadn't gone into the room, but he'd said the beams of the storage room were sound, so the small room above should be fine too.

Reverend Locke stood to one side, looking like a stern schoolmaster with his dark beard and dark tweed jacket. However, he didn't object when Maddie gestured to the four women.

"Okay, who's going up first?"

Diane looked around, but they looked at her, so she said, "I'll go."

She climbed the ladder up to the crawl space hole, then grasped the edges and hoisted herself up.

She pulled her flashlight out of her pocket and looked around. As before, the small room was almost claustrophobic with its barely six-foot ceiling. The dust seemed heavier than the last time she'd been here, but in the same places were the chair and the table missing one leg and the trunk.

She started toward the trunk, but something compelled her to look at the second crawl space hole in the ceiling that led to the actual bell tower.

No, she should look in the trunk. Reverend Locke wasn't going to allow them to stay up here long and look around, and Diane knew for certain there were old papers still in that trunk.

But her eye again fell on the square in the ceiling.

"Coming up." Margaret's voice preceded her head by only a second, and soon she was standing with Diane, fishing her own flashlight out of her pocket. "Ugh, it's so cramped up here."

She ran her flashlight around the room. "What's what?" The beam centered on a stack of something in the corner that looked like someone had thrown a bunch of old coats in a heap.

"I don't know. I didn't see that the last time I was here."

Margaret went to investigate and began pulling clothes out of the pile.

Diane again turned toward the trunk...and again looked up at the ceiling, centering the beam of her flashlight on the square that led to the bell tower.

She hesitated another second before going to the square of wood and giving it a push.

"What are you doing?" Margaret said.

"I don't know," Diane muttered. The board over the hole was stuck this time, perhaps from the wood warping in the change in the weather. She shoved harder, managing to push the board to one side of the hole. She then grabbed the rickety chair and dragged it underneath.

"Wow, it's really small in here." Shelley's head appeared from the entrance hole. "What's that?" she asked Diane.

"It's the entrance to the bell tower." Diane climbed on top of the chair and poked her head through.

She shone the light around the tall, narrow space, the beam glinting off of the old bronze bell high above. The air was strangely cool and yet seemed charged as she looked around. She peered high above at the bell, which was made of thick bronze in a dusty grayish brown color. It looked smaller than she had remembered it being, but then again she'd only had a brief glimpse of it before. It stood motionless. In fact, it looked like it might even be rusted in place. How had it rung?

She shone her flashlight at the top of the narrow tower, trying to peer into the gloom and see if there was a bell pull still attached to the top of the bell. Cobwebs strung across the vertical wooden beams of the tower, which looked roughly hewn, and of much older wood than even the ceiling of the storage room. The wood must be over two hundred years old, and yet it was still standing strong, supporting the bronze bell.

Her light flashed over something slimmer than the wooden beams, and she squinted at the narrow circle of light from her flashlight. Was that—? *There,* she saw a rope, twisted and grayish colored... and frayed at the end. It swung at least five feet above her. There was no way anyone could have rung the bell with that bell pull unless they'd climbed all the way into the tower itself and reached up to grasp the frayed end of the old rope.

A sudden *bong! bong!* startled her so much that she dropped the flashlight back down into the room below, where it bounced off the edge of the chair she stood on. The sound clanged in her ears, deafening her. She clapped her hands over her ears, but the sound continued.

It was the bronze bell overhead. Ringing. But how?

"Diane! Get down!"

She dimly heard Margaret shouting to her and jumped off the chair.

Without her hand over her ear, the sound rang through her skull as if the bell were right on top of her head. Shelley was gone, probably already down the ladder. There was only Margaret in the small room, clutching a small envelope and pulling her toward the hole in the floor and the ladder.

She forced Margaret through first, and when she was clear, Diane lowered herself until her feet touched the top rung. She scrambled down as fast as she could.

As soon as her head cleared the crawl space hole, the sound didn't reverberate as painfully in her eardrum, but sounds were still muffled. Margaret said something to her, and Diane yelled, "What?"

Margaret gestured, and Diane saw that everyone was running out of the storage room. Diane and Margaret followed.

They followed everyone out of the church through a side door into the whistling wind, but no rain yet. Diane saw a flash of lightning, then seconds later felt rather than heard a crack of thunder that drummed through the air.

Then she realized that the sky was lighter than it should have been. She looked up.

The roof of the church was on fire.

Orange flames licked the night sky, fed by the wind. It glowed an angry red and gold, as if a dragon were trying to destroy Old First with its malevolent breath. The fire raged higher and higher even as they watched.

But then it started to rain. The fire was already too large for the rain to have an immediate effect, but Diane hoped it would stop it from spreading farther.

"I called the fire department," Maddie said, although to Diane, deafened by the bell, her voice was soft and tinny.

Reverend Locke's face was ghostly, his eyes large and sunken. His lips moved, but Diane couldn't figure out what he was saying. He shook his head, over and over.

She could guess his thoughts. With the fire damage, Old First as they knew and loved it would have to close. What hope did it have now of staying open?

If only we could find the treasure! Diane stared at the fire, helpless, devastated.

Suddenly she remembered seeing something in Margaret's hand when they'd left the bell tower room. She moved closer to her friend, who held a folded piece of very thick, old-fashioned paper.

"Margaret, what do you have there?" she asked. Shelley and Beverly stepped closer.

"I haven't had a chance to take a look yet," Margaret responded slowly. Sheltering it from the rain, she slowly unfolded the paper and pulled out a small, dusty bronze key.

"A key!" Diane exclaimed.

"It looks ancient," Beverly said.

"What do you think it unlocked, Margaret?" Shelley asked.

"I don't know," Margaret replied. "I can't imagine why it would have been in the bell tower room. Do you think this was what Jeremiah Thorpe wanted his sister to find?"

Diane stared at the small key in Margaret's hand, stunned at the possibility. She looked back to her friends, huddled around her against the pouring rain, and grinned. "You know what I think? This could this be the key to saving Old First!"

About the Author

Camy Tang grew up in Hawaii and now lives in San Jose, California, with her engineer husband and rambunctious dog Snickers. Camy graduated from Stanford University and worked as a biologist researcher for nine years, but now she writes full-time. She is a staff worker for her church youth group, and she leads one of the worship teams for Sunday service. On her blog, she ponders knitting, spinning wool, dogs, running, the Never Ending Diet and other "frivolous" things.

A CONVERSATION WITH CAMY TANG

Q. This is your first book in the Miracles of Marble Cove *series. Which of the characters are you most like, and why?*

A. I'm actually a great deal like Beverly, not only because she and I are the same age, but also because I worked for several years in corporate jobs and can relate to her work stresses as well as her desire for her own business. I don't think I'm as smart as she is [*grin!*], but I love her devotion to her father and her determined sense of purpose when she's got something she needs to do.

Q. What was the most challenging/rewarding/enjoyable scene in the book to write?

A. The scene that was most challenging *and* rewarding *and* enjoyable to write was the one where Beverly is in her house in Augusta and packing up her things. I have never lived in a big, fancy house, so I did Internet research to look at the outsides and insides of homes, the types of furnishings and appliances and knick-knacks that people have. That was a lot of fun.

Q. You have written a number of mystery books. How do you think that affected the approach you took to writing Pressing On?

A. It made the mystery thread absolutely fun to write! I am very bad with word games and ciphers of any sort—my friends trounce me in Scrabble and Words with Friends—so I had to do a lot of research for the cipher that the friends found in the Prayer Book. Doling out the clues one by one always feels like I'm leaving breadcrumbs for the reader, and I hope readers like the climactic ending to the cipher mystery.

Q. When did you know you wanted to be a writer? How did you get started?

A. I have always loved writing, and I was in high school when I wrote my first novel, a fantasy-genre monstrosity that took two reams of paper to print out and still resides under my bed. But I felt like God was telling me to lay down my writing because I was more interested in my name on a book than in writing for His glory. So I didn't seriously start pursuing writing as a career until I was laid off from one of my biology jobs, and I felt God telling me now that it was okay for me to start writing again. I got another biology job but wrote during my lunch hours and at night when I got home, and eventually got my first book contract. Now I'm blessed to be able to write full-time rather than working in biology research anymore.

Q. When you're not writing, what other activities do you enjoy?

A. I love knitting! My Ravelry username is camytang if anyone wants to Friend me. I love knitting gifts for people, but I'm especially fond of knitting lace. My favorite knitting book is *Victorian Lace Today*—I am working on knitting every project in that book.

Baking with Shelley

Sand Tarts

2 sticks butter
1 teaspoon vanilla
2¼ cups flour (sifted)
5 tablespoons powdered sugar
1 cup chopped pecans

Cream butter, add vanilla and stir. Sift flour and powdered sugar together, and add to mixture. Then add pecans. After mixing all ingredients together, form into long rolls, wrap in plastic and refrigerate for at least thirty minutes. Slice into thin cookies and place on cookie sheet. Preheat oven to three hundred degrees. Bake for ten to fifteen minutes. Roll the baked cookies in additional powdered sugar and cool. Makes about five dozen cookies.

From the
Guideposts Archives

This story, by Carolinda Jankel of
Tujunga, California, originally appeared in
the October 2009 issue of *Guideposts*.

My husband Bob had health problems, and it had gotten so bad he worried he might have to give up the job he loved, teaching art at a middle school. His longtime doctor had urged him to see a specialist, but Bob was really worried about finding the right person. "I don't know this new doc," he complained. "How do I know if he's right for me?"

I thought back to the beginning of our marriage, when we traveled to galleries and art fairs throughout California, selling Bob's work. We'd pack the car before dawn with his abstract paintings, along with a metal cash box for the money we hoped to make. Those were such carefree days. It was exciting to show his work and meet other artists even if we didn't make many sales. What mattered was finding people who liked his work.

One time, at a street fair in Westwood, near UCLA, we'd sold nothing all day. We were packing up our car to leave when a young boy and his father came up to us. "How much is that one?" the man asked, pointing to the last painting we left out. We told him, and he asked if we had time to show them more. Did we ever! Our two patrons walked away with eight paintings! What a great feeling. "That," said Bob, during the drive home, "was a real godsend."

So my heart ached for my husband when he finally went off to see the specialist. Bob looked so miserable that I said a prayer for him.

But he was different when he returned. Smiling, bright-eyed, a bounce in his step. "What happened to you?" I asked.

Bob told me that he had been reluctant to enter that specialist's office. He sat in the waiting room and flipped through some magazines for something to distract him. He glanced around the room at the other patients, at the receptionist, but he couldn't stop mulling over the difficult decisions he had to make about this specialist, his health, his job.

Then he looked up. And immediately he felt reassured. He knew he was in just the right place. There, hanging on the office walls, beautifully displayed, were eight paintings. Those same eight paintings we'd sold on that day so many years ago.

Read on for a sneak peek of the next exciting book in
Miracles of Marble Cove!

Family Heirlooms
by Pam Hanson & Barbara Andrews

I can't stop shivering," Shelley said, sinking down on
a leather couch covered with pillows in her friend
Margaret's house. "It's the middle of summer, and chills are
running through me. When I smelled that awful smoke, I
was terrified we wouldn't get out of the church alive. My life
flashed before me, and all I could think about was leaving
my children motherless."

"You're probably suffering from shock," Margaret said.
"Here, wrap this throw around you."

"Who wouldn't be in shock?" Beverly asked. "No one
would expect a fire at a church like Old First. Those walls
were meant to last for centuries."

"The walls, yes," Diane said, "but the flames were coming
from the roof. I give our fire department lots of credit. They
certainly got there quickly. Maybe the damage won't be as
bad as Reverend Locke thinks."

"He thinks the smoke damage alone will be enough to
force the church to close indefinitely," Beverly said.

Of the four friends, she was the only member of Old First, and Shelley's heart went out to her. Any fire in the small town of Marble Cove was a blow to everyone who lived there, but it had to be especially heart-wrenching for a person who attended services at the beautiful old church.

"Here you are, ladies," Margaret's husband Allan said as he carried a tray into their cluttered but homey living room. "Tea to calm you down, and banana bread just because it tastes good."

"He made it this afternoon," Margaret said, attempting a smile as her good-natured husband did his best to take care of her friends.

Still feeling shaky, Shelley took a cup of tea but refused the banana bread. She was far too upset to swallow anything solid, but the tea felt soothing on her dry throat.

"We never should've been in the church at night," she said.

Margaret nodded in agreement, but Beverly shook her head vehemently.

"It was our only chance to investigate the tower. Reverend Locke was adamant about the timing," Beverly said. "He was only willing to let us inside at a time when he could be there with us. And he specifically wanted the church to be empty of other people."

"It was just bad luck. No one can predict a lighting strike," Diane said, clutching her cup with both hands.

"True. My father was stunned to hear about the fire."

"Oh dear." Shelley put her empty cup on the coffee table and stood up, letting the knitted throw fall behind her. "That reminds me. I'd better call Dan. He wasn't keen on having me go. If he's heard about the fire, he'll really be worried. And I didn't bring my cell phone."

"Use the phone in our bedroom," Margaret offered.

Grateful for the privacy, Shelly hurried to the couple's room, turning on the overhead light but not really noticing her surroundings. Somewhat to her surprise, Dan didn't answer right away. He finally picked up on the fourth ring.

"Yeah," he said in a sleepy voice.

"Don't tell me you slept through the sirens," Shelley said, not sure whether to be relieved or annoyed.

"I heard them, but I fell back asleep. Where are you?"

"At Margaret's. The fire was on the roof of Old First."

"No kidding! Are you okay? Were you in the building when it started? I had a feeling you shouldn't poke around there at night. Do you need me to come over?"

"No, but thanks. I'm fine," Shelley said, although this wasn't strictly true. She still felt shaky and disoriented. "I'll be home in a little while. Get some rest. Diane has her car, so she'll drop me off when she goes home."

"Okay, Shell," he said, sounding unconvinced. "I'm just glad you're all right."

After her brief conversation, she rejoined the others just as Allan was clearing away the others' cups. Everyone knew Margaret's husband was more at home in the kitchen than she was, but Shelley especially appreciated him this evening. He'd refilled her cup on the table, and she gratefully drank more tea. Distress combined with smoke from the fire had parched her throat, but she wasn't going to feel comforted until she was home in Dan's arms.

"Are you feeling a little better?" Beverly asked.

"Yes, I'll be fine." Shelley tried to sound normal, but she couldn't get the image of the fiery roof out of her mind. What if they'd been trapped in the tower and the flames had spread? Or if they'd been overcome by smoke? Her eyes welled just thinking of the danger they had faced.

"At least we came away with something from the tower room," Margaret said. "Maybe this key is the answer to finding the treasure and saving Old First."

Shelley leaned forward to see the small, dusty bronze key Margaret had grabbed on her way out of the tower. Everyone's attention turned to the unexpected find.

"It's so tiny. What could it possibly open?" Shelley asked.

"A small box," Beverly suggested, passing the key to Diane.

"Like a jewelry box." Diane examined both sides, but there was nothing to support either guess.

"I suppose it could even unlock a diary. When I was a girl, I had one with a lock and key," Margaret said, taking her turn to study it.

"Do you think they had locks on diaries back then?" Shelley asked, reaching out to examine it. The key weighed surprisingly little in her palm.

"I imagine they could design locks for almost anything that needed protecting," Beverly said.

"The question is, is this what Jeremiah Thorpe put in the tower room for his sister to find?"

"And if so, how will it help us find the treasure?" Diane added.

"In spite of the fire, we were lucky Reverend Locke let us into the tower tonight. I doubt anyone will be allowed inside the church for quite a while, at least not until the roof is repaired." Margaret took back the key and started to rewrap it in the aged piece of paper.

"Is there any writing on the paper?" Diane asked.

"Or any hint of a secret message?" Beverly reached for the paper and held it up to a table lamp. "No, it appears to be a plain sheet of rag paper, undoubtedly old but only a wrapping for the key."

"So we have another mystery," Shelley said, feeling weary in every bone of her body now that the crisis had passed.

"Or possibly a clue to the whereabouts of Jeremiah Thorpe's treasure," Diane said. "Wouldn't it be wonderful if we could discover it?"

"This would certainly be an opportune time to find it—if it exists. I imagine the church has some insurance," Beverly said, "but the building is going to need more than a new roof. Everything from carpets to furniture could have smoke damage, and there might even be structural problems as a result of the fire." She shook her head. "There wasn't enough money for all the needed repairs to Old First even before this disaster."

"Unless we really do find a treasure," Diane reminded her. "Anything from the time of the early settlers would no doubt be quite valuable. I can't even imagine what a dealer would pay for coins from that period."

"Yes, even if they weren't gold. Age alone would make them valuable," Beverly speculated.

Now that her chills had passed, Shelley felt drained. Old First wasn't her first fire, and it brought back bad memories of the blocked flue that had started a blaze in their own chimney at home. She still had nightmares about their home catching on fire. There had only been minor smoke damage that time, but it horrified her to think of what could have happened. First thing tomorrow she was going to check the smoke alarms to be sure they had fresh batteries. She and Dan had been entirely too casual about fire—and fire protection—before their own experience with it.

"Do you want me to keep the key?" Margaret asked.

"Yes, that's only fair since you found it," Diane said. "Of course, someday we'll have to give it back to Old First."

"I don't think Reverend Locke wants anything to do with treasure hunting—or with us right now," Beverly said. "He'll probably be totally occupied with all the problems the fire has created."

"Maybe another church will share space so the Old First congregation can continue having worship services," Shelley said. "Not much happens at our church on Sunday afternoon, if Reverend Locke is flexible enough to hold services then."

"That could be a good solution, but I'm not sure how Reverend Locke would feel about that," Beverly said. "Anyway, the local ministers have some kind of alliance where they get together and discuss mutual concerns. I'm sure they will address the problem."

"I can talk to my pastor about it," Diane offered.

"They'll work something out," Margaret said in a pragmatic tone. "I have my hands full now with the Fourth of July coming up in a few days. All the merchants in town have high hopes for the tourist season this year. Already I'm hard-pressed to keep my gallery walls covered with art to sell, but that's a good kind of problem to have."

"It's wonderful how well your gallery is doing this summer," Diane said. "But right now, I'm exhausted. Ready to go home, Shelley?"

"Yes, please. Dan will be waiting up for me."

Any other time she would've walked the short distance, but Marble Cove didn't seem like the cozy, safe place it had been only hours ago. If she'd learned one thing from the fire, it was that even a building with thick stone walls and a long history could have bad things happen to it. She felt very small and vulnerable.

Outside the bad weather had passed, but the end of June had brought unseasonably hot temperatures. The air was cloyingly humid, but she took deep breaths, still able to detect the rancid smell of smoke that clung to her clothing and hair.

Diane seemed to take forever putting on her seat belt and starting the car, perhaps a sign that she was more rattled than she let on. Shelley wanted to tell her to hurry, but, of course, she would never be rude to her neighbor and friend.

Instead of parking by her own cottage and letting Shelley walk from there, Diane pulled into the Bauers' drive and waited until Shelley waved good-bye to her from the front door.

"You're finally here," Dan said as soon as she stepped inside. He was barefoot in sweats and a T-shirt, his hair still unruly from the pillow.

"We had tea and talked a little," Shelley said, then she was in his arms, feeling safe for the first time since she'd been in the church with the others.

"I like your friends, but I hope this is the last time you poke around dangerous places with them," he said, releasing her and speaking only half-jokingly. "I don't know how I went back to sleep after I heard the sirens. I should've known the four of you were in some kind of mess." He smiled, but concern shone in his eyes.

"It's not like we planned to get caught in a fire." She was comforted by his protectiveness, but also a bit irritated. Didn't he think she could look after herself?

"I know you care about that old church, but can't you find another way to help them out? I'm not sure this treasure hunting is really worth it. I mean, what could you possibly find? It's not as if Marble Cove was the Port Royal of the north. If any pirates really did come here with gold, they certainly didn't leave pots of it buried here and there for you to find."

"You make it sound like we're doing something silly. We all read the letters written by Jeremiah Thorpe. He mentioned a hidden treasure. If we can find it, we'll give it to Old First. That church will need it more than ever after the fire."

"Shell, I'm sorry. I know you think there's a treasure, but it's been hundreds of years. I just don't want to see you be disappointed spending time looking for something you'll never find."

"You don't know that."

He walked into the living room, flopped down on the couch, and crossed his arms. "At least try to be realistic."

"You think this is some game we made up!"

"No, I don't, really. I just worry when you're out doing who knows what. What if you'd been trapped in the church when the fire started?"

"It was on the roof. We got out."

Shelley realized it was true. They hadn't been in mortal danger, and she'd overreacted. The shock was wearing off, and all she felt now was a deep weariness—and annoyance at Dan's attitude.

He stood and came to her. "Shell, I was scared silly when you called about the fire. What if it had spread while you were inside the church? What would I do without you?"

His tender words touched her heart, and she understood why he didn't want her in dangerous situations.

"We won't be going back inside the church. Reverend Locke won't allow it while there's any risk from fire damage. Anyway, it's my friendship with Diane, Margaret, and Beverly that's important to me, not just the treasure. But you and the kids come first. You always will."

"I know," he whispered, drawing her close and kissing her.

Dan was able to accomplish what a warm wrap, tea, and friendship hadn't. He made her forget her fear and focus on what was really important in her life.

Still, part of her *knew* there was more to discover about Jeremiah Thorpe's treasure, and she very much wanted to help her friends find it.

A NOTE FROM THE EDITORS

We hope you enjoy Miracles of Marble Cove, created by the Books and Inspirational Media Division of Guideposts, a nonprofit organization that touches millions of lives every day through products and services that inspire, encourage, help you grow in your faith, and celebrate God's love in every aspect of your daily life.

Thank you for making a difference with your purchase of this book, which helps fund our many outreach programs to military personnel, prisons, hospitals, nursing homes, and educational institutions. To learn more, visit GuidepostsFoundation.org.

We also maintain many useful and uplifting online resources. Visit Guideposts.org to read true stories of hope and inspiration, access OurPrayer network, sign up for free newsletters, download free e-books, join our Facebook community, and follow our stimulating blogs.

To learn about other Guideposts publications, including the best-selling devotional *Daily Guideposts*, go to ShopGuideposts .org, call (800) 932-2145, or write to Guideposts, PO Box 5815, Harlan, Iowa 51593.

Sign up for the
Guideposts Fiction Newsletter
and stay up-to-date on the fiction you love!

You'll get sneak peeks of new releases, recommendations from other Guideposts readers, and special offers just for you . . .

And it's FREE!

**Just go to Guideposts.org/newsletters
today to sign up.**

**Visit ShopGuideposts.org
or call (800) 932-2145**